A
NOVEL

D R I F T L E S S

QUINTET

JOE SACKSTEDER

schaffner
press

Tucson, Arizona

First edition
Trade Paperback Original

Cover design: Evan Johnston
Interior design: Darci Slaten
Author photo: BJ Enright

The author acknowledges the generous support of Jackie Osherow and the
Taft-Nicholson Center at the University of Utah for generous support in
working on this project, and Craig Cutting of the Winneshiek County Protectors
for an enlightening lecture at Taft-Nicholson on hydraulic fracturing.

The Freshmen
Words and Music by Brian Vander Ark, Bradley Vander Ark,
Donald Brown, Douglas Corella and Jeffrey Dunning
Copyright ©1996 LMNO POP MUSIC
All rights Administered by Sony/ATV Music Publishing LLC,
414 Church Street, Suite 1200, Nashville, TN 37219
International Copyright Secured All Rights Reserved
Reprinted by Permission of Hal Leonard LLC

Brick
Words and Music by Ben Folds and Darren Jessee
Copyright © 1996 Sony/ATV Music Publishing LLC and hair sucker songs
All Rights Administered by Sony/ATV Music Publishing LLC,
424 Church Street, Suite 1200, Nashville, TN 37219
International Copyright Secured All Rights Reserved
Reprinted by Permission of Hal Leonard LLC

ISBN: 9781943156863 (Paperback)
ISBN: 9781943156870 (PDF)
ISBN: 9781943156870 (Epub)
ISBN: 9781943156870 (Mobipocket)

For Library of Congress Cataloguing-in-Publication
Information, Contact the Publisher

Printed in the United States

To my teammates

Can you blame me? Or maybe sports are the problem, huh? Look, all I did was fall in love.

–Ovid, *Metamorphoses*
Book X

DRIFTLESS QUINTET

A NOVEL

JOE SACKSTEDER

1

There is a man in the stands who is cheering for no one.

Colton fumbles the puck as he tries to hand it to the ref. "Sorry."

The ref does his rendition of the SportsCenter theme as he picks the puck up off the ice. "Better wash my hands—you pulled that one outta your ass."

The man in the stands is interested in the game, but not in the score. Cheering for no one, but focused.

Alone, his seeming lack of affiliation wouldn't be enough. But the man, he's holding a clipboard.

Even the most stat-obsessed parents don't bring clipboards to games. Especially not to the Metro Northwest summer hockey league, championship game or not. The league doesn't even bother putting the stats online in the summer.

A couple teammates tap him on the pads with their sticks. "Nice save, Crouton." "Quit showing off, Vogler." Chatter he ignores so as not to get distracted.

Too late.

The man with the clipboard who is cheering for no one is sitting apart from the Rockford fans, the Fremd fans. There's a little landing wedged into one corner of the Bensenville Edge Ice Arena that the upstairs viewing area opens onto. He's this perch's only occupant—above and to Colton's left, a perfect view of that glove save. Colton tries to remember if, when teams switched sides the second period, this man followed him from one side of the rink to the other. Like goalie dads do.

Focus. It's obvious from the way Fremd's center is positioned that he'll try to shoot it off the draw.

But Colton knows that telling yourself to focus is proof that you aren't. When a goalie is focused, the last thing on his mind is focusing. For example thirty seconds ago, back when the stands might as well have been totally empty.

Spezak keeps the center from putting a shot on net, but the puck gets kicked back to the blue line where the D's stick is already raised. Crouching to peer through a tangle of shin guards, Colton hears but doesn't see the slapper that glances off the center and sails an inch high.

"Careful, that one almost hit me," he says to Lalande as Krpata picks it up and clears the zone.

Who uses clipboards?

Other than his jackass friend Rudy when he wants to make restaurant employees think he's there for a surprise health inspection.

Scouts. Scouts use clipboards.

Or he's just some emotionless parent who appreciates having a flat, hard surface to write on.

But there's a third thing. He's wearing a track jacket, and that track jacket is not Rockford Glaciers blue and green, nor Fremd green and gold. The guy's track jacket is maroon and white.

Who's maroon?

Golden Gophers? Boston? Denver? Duluth?

Four teams that won't be interested in you if you don't get your head back in the game stat—because dude has a breakaway and you might as well impress everyone no matter who's watching.

Colton c-cuts to the hashmarks, beckons with his glove, and starts back when the forward hits the blue line. DeStefanis giving chase but not gonna catch him. This is the guy with the ripped pants who blocker-side deked Colton last season then tried to tuck it in behind him glove side.

Colton leans left, shows him daylight right.

Guy fakes glove side this time then goes blocker, takes the bait.

Colton knows it's a save before he's made it, but pop goes his leg as he extends nearly into the splits, skate blade clanking the goal post.

Groin.

DeStefanis is all over the rebound.

The pain in Colton's crotch transforms the fans' cheering into screams of agony. He gasps as he pulls himself back to standing position, trying to hide what happened from the man with the clipboard.

He spots his friends through the glass—Rudy, Nate, Paige. Paige is waving her sign, having outdone herself in a one-sided joke to embarrass her boyfriend as much as possible. COLTON SAVES MY HEART FROM LONELINESS.

There's a whistle—somewhere, for something—and team-mates again skate by to pay him homage. But Colton's head is dizzy with vague calculus. The Glaciers are up two to zero with eleven minutes left in the third. Scant breathing room. It's the most important game of a very unimportant summer league, the trophy a t-shirt. His backup Routhier is capable but cold from two plus periods with his ass parked.

Colton should give himself the hook. Not worth worsening a fresh injury of unclear severity.

But he won't.

Not because he cares about the team or the t-shirt or his groin.

But because a stranger in a maroon track jacket with a clipboard, now making a phone call, has driven a long way to see him play.

2

Driftless.

Colton's a little disappointed it's not a junior or college team, but with the school's reputation, he'll hear what the man across the table has to say.

Embroidered on the breast of his jacket: Coach Riessen. Don, he'd introduced himself in the lobby as Colton ignored the cheers of Rudy and Nate and Paige.

Driftless. No nickname, the Eagles or Tigers or whatever. No mascot, other than the team they're trouncing at the time. Maroon and white. No third color, other than their opponents' blood. A school across the border northwest of Madison, Colton thinks. They win states most every year.

"I already spoke a bit with your parents in the lobby."

This rink room had hosted a birthday party not many minutes ago. A cake box is smushed into a garbage can smaller than the cake. Pizza boxes continue to waft their cheesy reek. Colton can still hear an untuned children's choir torturing the birthday song to death. Though he's starting to feel dangerously celebratory, the confetti and orphaned balloons are at odds with the gravity of the conference.

It's life decision time.

"I didn't give them any information, just asked if they'd let me speak with you for a few minutes. I'm sorry to pull you away from a well-deserved party."

Colton shrugs. "It's summer league." Was that too cavalier, like he doesn't take some games seriously? He just meant no problem.

"You're big, but you play even bigger. How tall are you?"

"Six-three."

"The highlight reel saves were fine, but what got my attention were the ones you made look routine, the pucks that hit you square in the chest. You're always in the right position."

Anything he'd reply would sound cocky, so he averts his eyes, gives a faint nod. Whatever's transpiring seems more fragile than it probably is.

"I find myself down a goalie for next year," Coach Riessen outs-with-it. "I don't need you to give me a decision tonight, but the reality of the situation is that it's August and I need to find a keeper ASAP."

Until they moved into the MB Arena downtown last year, the Bensenville Edge was the Blackhawks' practice rink. Once, Colton was lugging his bag to the locker room and Corey Crawford clomped right by in full gear.

"Would I—" Colton starts. "When are tryouts?"

Coach Riessen pretends to consult his watch. "About forty-five minutes ago."

"And I'd have to go to school in Driftless?" Of course you would, shitbrains. "Would there be, like—"

"You'd be staying with a host family. Flynn Rentschler and his wife, Alma."

"You mean… it's not… *the* Flynn Rentschler?" NHL enforcer and journeyman, played for six or seven different teams between 2000 and 2010.

"The same. One of our many proud alums now dedicated to helping continue a mining town's tradition."

An image flashes through Colton's mind of Flynn Rentschler kicking the shit out of him for violating curfew.

Coach Riessen smiles. "Actually, he's a nice guy."

"I'd resigned myself to finishing out my high school career in Rockford."

"Resigned—there's an appropriate word. Colton, I get it. You're a hometown guy. You've got friends here, a girlfriend too, if I read the signs right."

Oh God…

"Rockford's done well for itself in recent years, and I know you're keen on that fourth state championship ring. But you know and I know there's a big difference between a high school state championship, and a *combined* high school state championship. In Wisconsin we call it the Independent League, as if it's liberating—not having enough studs at one school to fill a bench. Let me know if I'm pressing too hard. Every Driftless varsity player with hockey dreams will end up at a Division Three college, at least. A lot of them go D One, and I could start listing the guys who've gone pro. What's the farthest any player from Rockford has gone?"

"D Three, maybe."

"D Three JV. And Tyler Bianchi was for sure good enough to play varsity. But he never got a shot. Problem was, he came from a town with no connections. You know what scouts hear when you say Rockford?"

"Rock bottom."

"You said it, brother. Moving at a glacial pace. What NCAA colors do you dream of wearing?"

"Red and white."

"Wisconsin's head scout is Will Tremblay. He comes up twice a year to play poker and see what we've got. Great eye for talent, terrible poker face."

Colton shifts in his seat, and his groin sings out further

complications. He wonders if his friends are getting impatient, if his parents will let him ride home in Nate's Jeep.

Coach Riessen misreads his grimace. "We have a rink on campus, a personal trainer, a full gym. We'll get you suited up with new gear. Full set, customized."

Happy birthday.

"What's your goalie situation at Driftless?"

"There we go. If you talked like you play goalie, those are the kinds of questions you'd ask. I don't make promises I can't keep, and I don't want you getting complacent over what little's left of the offseason, but I'm scouting for the number one. We've got a great sophomore goalie, Max, but he doesn't have the mental toughness for state playoffs yet."

"What happened to your starting goalie?"

For the first time during their talk, Coach Riessen is taken aback. Like Colton had asked a little too good of a question.

He leans back in his chair, looks older. "Bad story. Wrapped his car around a tree. No parties that night, but he was pretty drunk. He'd signed a letter of intent to Merrimack."

The drywall swallows the last echo of "Happy Birthday."

"What was his name?"

"He survived, or his brain did at least. Name's still Shane."

3

Another table, this one with food. The festive air plus the smell of the birthday pizza plus the couple thousand calories he'd burned during the game had given Colton a bottomless hunger.

The weed, no doubt, had been a contributing factor.

In addition to a whole pot of coffee, he'd polished off something called the Big Biscuit Breakfast: two fried chicken filet sandwiches smothered in gravy and cheese, plus hash browns, scrambled eggs, and bacon. Now he's eying the dessert menu for anything with cake frosting.

Probably good, soak up the bourbon they'd slugged in the parking lot.

"I don't see it on the menu," Rudy is saying to the waitress, and Colton's been on enough late-night Perkins runs with this friend to know what's coming next, "but do you have the lemon cream pie by chance?"

"We have lemon meringue."

Rudy leans back, a cat distancing itself from an evil smell.

"They never have lemon cream pie," Paige says. "They phased it out like five years ago."

"They had it one time when I asked."

"When none of us were there to witness the event."

"It has this little gummy lemon wedge on top," he informs the waitress, who is trying her best to care at one a.m. "Alright,

I'll have boring ol' peanut butter silk."

"Make that two."

"Three," Paige says. "Nate, should we get a whole pie?"

"Nothing for me, thanks." Nate flicks a sugar packet over his coffee like he thinks it's holding out on him.

"Nate!" Colton collapses on the table. "Cavort with us! It's on me." Colton is high.

"I'm fine," Nate snaps.

"Three slices," Paige tells the escaping waitress.

"No food, no booze, no–" Colton holds two fingers up to his lips. "What's up, Termi*nate*r?"

"Why do I only get nicknames when you're high?"

Colton has foggy recollections of the bygone era an hour ago when he too had been thinking very seriously about forgoing all the joys in life. "Nick*nates*." The idea of Driftless, of Badger scouts' poker faces, had messed with his head enough that he'd considered a different type of celebration: starting this new life by regimenting his diet pronto. "*The Nate Natsby*." What if, instead of eating a piece of pie that contained an entire stick of butter, he drank three glasses of water and went jogging through the night streets like a maniac? "*Late Night with Seth Meyers*."

"You forgot to change that one. I think you meant *Nate Light*."

"Boylan's gonna suck without you next year," Rudy says.

Colton feels a flash of paranoia that, in his highness, he'd spoken aloud the words that were running through his head— but, no, Rudy is talking to Nate, who's a year ahead of them at Boylan.

"You guys'll have to get another fool to find you booze."

Colton spots a fugitive fry trying to make its escape. In sixth grade he'd started to get chunky, and he'd responded by going borderline eating disorder, counting every calorie and charting his weight and exercises. Once a growth spurt stretched him out and he discovered fun in high school, he relaxed. Now he hits the weight room once in a while to pretend he has a future in athletics that requires a hard body, but he knows that a lot of his success in hockey has been coasting off that early drive.

An hour ago, as Colton pondered going to bed with a very empty stomach, that junior high taskmaster version of himself said hello, whispered *I never left*. And, though his appetites won the night, Colton felt again the grim satisfaction of treating his body like a precision instrument.

The pie arrives.

Fuck it. He might have to reevaluate shit now that NHL dreams are a reality again after years of slow, steady evaporation—but tonight is for reveling.

"How can we outdo your senior prank without you here to help us?"

One spring morning, soon after news of Vice Principal Klonski's DUI appeared in the Rockford Register Star, Nate had removed choice letters of BOYLAN CENTRAL CATHOLIC above the student entrance so that it read

BOYLAN   AL CA HOLIC

"I'll stay on as a consultant"—Nate's hands are trembling from the coffee—"for a small fee."

More difficult to banish is the image of the Driftless goalie—Colton has forgotten his name—pulled from a mess of metal that no longer resembles an automobile. It's a daunting enough cautionary tale that he'd thought about volunteering to sober cab Nate's Jeep home from the rink. But abstinence has been Nate's moody m.o. the whole night.

Nate, who's the wildest of them all! Nate, anti-everything except drugs, booze, and screwing. *The Dark Nate Rises. The*

Nateful Neight. Nick at Nate. The Hunchback of Dotre Nate.

"You'll have to grow out that hair," Nate tells Rudy. "Give Klonski a new adversary to chase around with his clippers."

"Do your imitation of the Klown when you got your letter from Columbia."

Despite horrendous grades, Nate received scholarships to several top schools based on his ACT scores and his writing samples alone.

"*Well, young man*"—Nate hunches one shoulder and reels around—"*I knew we'd make something of you. I always had faith. Never doubted it.*"

The pie is so rich it seltzers Colton's nervy stomach, and he has to set down his fork and Zen himself away from the brink of puking. His new groin injury is stiff from the ride back from Bensenville. Paige is threading one prong of her fork through the curlicue chocolate shaving atop her slice of pie, and she gives him this little mischievous smile, and he's not sure he can do it. Senior year is the best social year of your entire life. Nonstop parties. Teachers don't give a shit—if Nate is a reliable source. He can always take a year off if he wants, go play juniors before heading to college if there's still any fire inside him. Wisconsin? You sure about that?

"I can't imagine you in a dorm. Colt, can you imagine rooming with this hooligan?"

Colton disguises nausea as laughter.

"Guys, I'm not going to Columbia," Nate tells his coffee mug.

Everyone stops eating their pie. Everyone in the restaurant, it seems.

"What? Where else–"

"You know that girl I've been hanging out with?"

"Really can't call her a girl, buddy. You should have brought her—we'd get the senior discount–"

"Rudy," Paige says. "Shut up."

"She's pregnant." Nate's eyes are red for a different reason than his friends'. "I'm going to hang around and see if I can get a job. If not, at least I can help out with her other kid while she's at work."

They're all afraid to talk.

"Have you…" Rudy stops himself.

"It wasn't that much of an accident. I'm going to marry her, I think."

"You'll be a great dad," Paige knows the right lie. "And at least we'll have another year of hanging out before–"

"Before you guys say goodbye," Nate finishes her sentence. "Yeah, this is how people stay in their hometowns their whole lives."

Maybe it's not a lie, Colton thinks. After all, Nate's controlled himself tonight. Just twenty thousand or so more nights to go, if he's lucky.

Colton realizes he has a lazy erection, and he assures himself that sometime when he's not high he'll interrogate what aspect of Nate becoming a dad gives him a boner. Hopefully it's the weed. File that one away.

"Sorry, buddy," Nate says to Colton. "I was going to wait till the second trimester, but I guess I wanted to steal your spotlight."

Suddenly Driftless—missing senior year here in Rockford—is the littlest thing in the world.

Money. Nate hadn't ordered food because he was already thinking about money.

Still, the nerves in Colton's stomach are volcanic, and he's only eaten the one bite of pie. Across the table, Paige is kind and pretty, and Colton hallucinates marrying her and working long hours and pinching pennies to afford a house and food to feed the small, screaming facsimiles of themselves. He thinks about how they save each other's hearts from loneliness.

"Don't worry about it," Colton tells the table. "I've got newer news."

4

It's less of an adventure having to follow the HAM RADIO license plate of his slow-ass dad, who's drifting back and forth in the lane, exploring every inch of its lateral space—but each time Colton's VW Golf climbs the slightest Wisconsin hill or sinks into a curve, he's at the helm of a mighty vessel indeed–

Going sixty-five miles per hour, cruise control set.

In the left lane.

His father is only stubborn about stupid things.

The Rockford Roadrunners play in a Dane County league, so as a kid he'd made the trip north on 94 several times a week, the Hormel factory with its chili can water tower always signaling that he'd crossed into an even Midwesterner state. The Glaciers, on the other hand, play most all their games in the Chicago area, so it's been a while since he'd been up this way. He'd made a playlist called *Driftless!* for the trip, mixing recent favorites that signify triumphant new beginnings with back-in-the-day nostalgia tunes that trigger a checklist of memories. One hockey tournament a year, and always in some Wisconsin town that likewise started with a W—Waupaca, Waukesha, Winnetka, Wausau, Waubonsie Valley. His mom would pack the Caravan with a Longaberger basket full of oatmeal cookies and peanut butter crackers, a thermos of "gourmet" hot chocolate. Snowfall masqueraded Wisconsin hillsides Nordic in miniature, white slopes veining thorny brown; his body's memory of the dizzy buoyancy dismounting a ski lift causes him to press the gas pedal, zooming him close to the bumper of his parents' van.

His dad responds by tapping the breaks.

… .–.. – – – .– – / –. .– – – .– – –.

And suddenly they're going forty miles per hour. The thing about using a break pedal to spell out *slow down*, is that it forces compliance.

"Speed up, old man. I've got a team to impress."

Each green EXIT sign resuscitates a rink from oblivion. Beloit with its tarp walls, subzero games during which the players could return to the benches' heat lamps but the two goalies had to stand there freezing, hand warmers shoved into gloves. Janesville, where Colton attended his first goalie camp, Vic's. He still has his "report card," including a photo taken of his stance after coming up from his tenth butterfly. Terrible form. He remembers the St. Norbert's goalie giving an equipment talk, waxing poetic about a goalie's intimate relationship with his glove, blocker, pads, remembers dryland training on a scratchy slope, Colton's arms trembling from holding a bucket of pucks out to either side. The Oscar Meyer factory on the road to Hartmeyer, the Wienermobile often parked out front. At "The Hart" you had to walk behind the bleachers' skeletal scaffolding to reach the dinky locker rooms on the far side of the ice. Now, McFarland—those were *giant* locker rooms. The first place Colton heard the urban legend about the kid whose ballsack was split open via towel whip.

And "The Dump." Could never forget The Dump. It probably has a more municipal name, but none of his teammates bothered to learn it since the nickname was so apt. The worst of the rinks, but all Colton can remember are walls the color of pit stains. It didn't help that it was right next door to the shiny Kohl Center, the first big stadium Colton had ever played at, a real scheduling treat from back in his peewee days. They couldn't get into the locker rooms—he can't remember why—and they'd had to dress out in the concession area. Once on the ice, they kept forgetting to play hockey, too busy ooh-ing and ahhing the Badger banners and retired numbers, and dark seats stretching up to dizzying heights. And "The Shell," a practice rink on UW's campus, where the blank white ceiling made a goalie feel dangerously small trying to fill out the four-by-six goal frame. He felt even littler at the Pettit Center, with the speed skating oval enclosing double ice surfaces, Olympic history causing a kid to hear the *Miracle* soundtrack and all sorts of lofty talk about representing one's country.

Colton's dad, in his ongoing war against smartphones and their newfangled navigation apps, had printed up MapQuest directions for both of them. Colton looks for the twentieth time down at the pushpin indicating his home for the next nine months. He's read the short Wikipedia page on Driftless, browsed photos online, but even as his car eats up the distance between here and there, it doesn't seem real to him yet. Flynn Rentschler and his wife are real enough, though—he's spoken to them on the phone. It sounds like they have a big place, and he'll have his own bedroom. There are two sons—Ben, who's also a senior, and Leo, who's younger. When Colton asked if Ben was on the hockey team, there was a pause before Mrs. Rentschler replied that he was not—Ben was more into *theater*—and Colton was left wondering if he'd offended them by bringing up a sore subject. Then Flynn joined the conversation, and Colton was actually speaking to the guy who knocked out Dale Venner in the '07 quarterfinals, one of the only real primo player/goalie fights in the history of the NHL. On the phone, Flynn spoke slowly, like he needed to think up each word by itself—too many shots to the head, no doubt. Or too many shots.

He does another mental inventory of all his possessions, worried he left something behind. No big deal—Rockford's not that far away, and he's sure his parents will make the drive for games. Some of them at least. Because of his Golf's compactness, the ends of his Sher-Wood goalie sticks are jutting between the front seats, blocking the cup holders, and he squeezes his hand around the taped knob of the one that will break the soonest, sniffing the rubbery smell of rink and leather and sweat stamped onto his palm. His pads and bag are in the trunk, his mom having joked that she didn't want to be cooped up with the reek for two hours. In truth it's not that hazardous at this point in the offseason, Colton not having skated since the summer league championship. He could have gone to Sunday night drop-in games, but he's hoping time away from hockey will be good for his groin. He'd located a scary document on his computer detailing his junior high "WORKOUT ROUTINE for Getting and Staying in Shape," and he'd started back on a regimen of what plyometrics his injury would permit. There's always this group at the park doing slow-motion karate moves, and Colton enjoys showing them what real exercise looks like. He'd started jogging again on the horse trails of Rock Cut to the point of dehydration, then more. Started weightlifting some at Boylan's gym, but goalies aren't supposed to get huge. And back to not shoving whatever in his mouth food-wise. Fish and eggs and smoothies had replaced Uncle Nick's gyros and Panino's panizzas. No more weed, and less booze than before. His abs are starting to surface for the first time in a while.

A twangy, tropical melody. Colton grins. Despite being raised on classic rock by his dad, Colton didn't know any songs by the Eagles other than "Hotel California" until a Google search while compiling *Driftless!* had introduced him to "New Kid in Town." New kid... it's not the terrifying prospect it would be if he was younger, or if he wasn't entering his new school at the top of the athletic food chain.

Colton is so lost in time that he almost misses it. A landmark over which it's impossible to sentimentally linger. A barn reborn a billboard, branded with words white on red.

I-94 MANGLED ACRES

Heartland heartburn. A punk barn, role model, an advocate for arguments against—

How could Colton have forgotten this barn?

As a kid, he'd had no idea what it meant, that this patch of America's Dairyland had been bisected against its owner's will to save a turn of the steering wheel, a half-mile circumlocution multiplied every year by millions. Back then he'd thought that the farm *was* the acre mangling. That the barn was boasting about what its plows had wrought.

But today: whatever gets him to Driftless sooner. Northwestward ho!

5

Maroon balloons tied to the mailbox of 5293 Osprey Lane. He checks his directions one last time, but the very long driveway gives him a minute to worry that this might not be the place. GPS had led them around Driftless itself to the wooded outskirts, houses set far apart and far off the road, custom architecture only visible in glimpses through the trees. Not mansions per se—flaunting acreage more than square footage, private access to Four Turm's Golf Course and bike paths that boardwalk over wetlands.

He shouldn't be surprised though; Flynn Rentschler might have been a goon, but he was still a pro athlete. And his career was longer than most enforcers'.

Globe lamps are spaced the length of the winding driveway, little moons dulled by daylight. He tells himself it's stupid to be anxious, but of course that never works. His stomach feels pre-game. (A big game.)

The VW crests a hill and the Rentschlers' house comes into view. It's a one-story ranch with a flat roof—the word "compound" enters Colton's mind despite the house's big windows. It's a sprawling structure, like several houses sutured together.

As they pull up to the three-car garage, Colton sees a man off to the side of the house, splitting wood with an ax. He straightens up—way up—when he hears them, plunges the ax into the chopping block. All six-foot-four, about two hundred thirty pounds of Flynn Rentschler. He smiles, yanking off his work gloves finger by finger.

Getting out of their car, Colton's parents hang back a little, and he knows that they're making their son be the one to lead the greeting.

"Mr. Rentschler."

"Call me Flynn. Sorry I'm filthy." He wipes his hand on jeans that are in no condition to do any cleaning.

Bracing himself to have his hand crushed in the enforcer's fist, Colton is surprised to find Flynn's handshake on the gentle side.

"I don't often get the chance to look people in the eyes. How tall are you?"

"Six-three."

Flynn whistles. "Do they let goalies be that tall?" As on the phone, he chews his words like he's tired or he isn't one hundred percent fluent. His hair is longer than it ever was in his playing days, and his nose has obviously been rearranged a few times. "And you must be the *parentis* we're *in loco* for." Flynn shakes hands with Colton's father, then mother.

"It's a pleasure to meet you," Colton's dad says, and Colton can tell the dork is trying to decide whether or not to add some flattery about Flynn's career.

"It's so good of you to take Colton in," is his mom's hello. Her son, the stray dog.

"That document they made us sign said *in loco parentis*, and I thought that meant *loco*"—Flynn spirals a finger around his ear—"like crazy."

Colton's mom gives a nervous laugh. "Well, parenting can make you a little crazy."

God, c'mon *Mom*...

Flynn leads them through the open garage doors, between

a Land Rover and a pegboard of Festools. "I'm afraid all the garage space is taken. After you're unloaded, there's a spot off to the side you can pull in." Next to the Land Rover is a Jetta, in the far spot a BMW M6.

The mudroom is bigger than Colton's bedroom back home.

"Should we take our shoes off?" Colton's mom asks.

"I don't care. It's not China."

The kitchen looks like it's never been used: Viking appliances, poured concrete countertops, a rainbow of those cast-iron pots and pans that are impossible to clean but which his mom covets anyway. Colton can see her trying not to gawk.

"Alma!" Flynn calls out, opening the fridge. "The Voglers are here." He cracks a Spotted Cow, letting the cap fall on the floor. "Am I pronouncing that right?"

Yes and no.

"How we pronounce it, the V's a V, not an F."

"Got it." Flynn takes a swig. "I guess you don't wanna sound like Nazis. We've got that same problem around here."

Mrs. Rentschler appears in the doorway to disrupt the flustered silence. "Honey, I told you to change into decent clothes. They'll think we're a bunch of backwoods hillfolk." She turns to the guests. "Welcome."

Colton's mind blares a warning, *do not* get caught checking out your host mother. That's the worst first impression you could make. But, as he keeps his eyes locked on her maybe-Botoxed face, his peripheral vision is hard at work. She's tall and thin, a natural blonde, big tits, big hips too. How many leering dudes has Flynn kicked the shit out of for this woman?

She's been talking this whole time, his parents too. Saying… something. In lieu of verbal response, Colton has so far only managed to assemble his face into a dopey grin.

"Oh, you have such nice teeth," she says, stepping closer to him. Her distressed jeans and loose button-down shirt are hot housework cosplay.

"How tall are you?"

"Six-three," Flynn answers for him. "Or so he claims."

"It's nice to meet you, Mrs. Rentschler." Colton blushes, having delivered this line too late in the conversation.

"Please," she says, "Alma. Let's give you the tour! This, of course, is the kitchen. *Your* kitchen. I know how teenage boys eat, and we need you strong for games, so help yourself to *anything*. That pad of paper on the fridge is my grocery list; add whatever you want to it."

She leads them out of the kitchen into the dining room. "Most nights we eat family dinner at about six o'clock, so of course we'd love to have you at the table."

Potted plants harvested from an alien planet are taking over the house. "Flynn grows orchids. I know that might be hard to believe–"

"Because I'm a dumb jock."

She ignores her husband. "He has one hundred and fifteen varieties of them. When they're in bloom, they come upstairs to visit me. This one smells the best."

She bends over to give it a sniff but comes up disappointed. "I think only at certain times of the day."

The house opens into a wide family room with skylights and sliding glass doors that lead onto the deck. Black leather chairs and a matching sectional face the giant flatscreen on the wall.

"You have a piano." Colton can't stop himself from heading in that direction.

"A Bösendorfer. And we had it tuned in anticipation of your arrival."

"You hear that, Mom? They get their piano tuned once in a while."

"Oh, shush."

"You'll have to serenade us. I know you're here to play hockey, but I think you'll be impressed with the music scene in Driftless. Ben plays too, or used to. Speaking of which…"

She crosses the flagstone front entryway into a hall and knocks on the first door on the right. Colton's mind hadn't registered the loud pop music, but there's no ignoring it once the door opens. Colton can't make out what Alma says through the door, but a second later the music dies. Out steps Ben, annoyed at the interruption. He's as tall as Colton, his faux-hawk tipped in blue and green. As soon as he sees Colton, a sly smile appears on his face, and he fails to police his eyes—they move down Colton's body then back up.

Are you serious?

"Ben, this is Colton." Alma's noticed too, and she sounds frustrated. "Colton, Ben."

"Nice to meet you." Ben extends a hand. "I like your name."

Explains why he's not on the team. Again, Colton struggles to force his face nonchalant, forces himself to not look at Flynn or Alma or his parents, as a sidewise glance could be read as alarm.

"Nice to meet you too."

Gay is fine, sure—that's Colton's opinion—but shouldn't the kid at least get that this isn't the time or place? Or person? That host siblings are off limits? So maybe not by law... but...

"Leo's room is in the basement—you'll meet him later. He has learning disorders."

Ben doesn't care for this spiel, rolls his eyes.

"It's not like we *lock* him down there," Alma continues.

"I'm a special ed teacher in fact. He's just a little shy."

"Show him his room." Colton hadn't seen Flynn exit, but now it's PBR time.

"You'll be right across from Ben here." Alma keeps looking back at Colton, afraid he'll stop following or vanish.

Colton's parents excuse themselves to begin bringing stuff in from the car.

Colton glances into Ben's room, and it checks off all the stereotypes, right down to the Keith Haring wall stickers.

His own room is much sparer. It has a bed, a chest-of-drawers, and a desk with a lamp.

"We would have decorated it a little more, but we figured we'd leave that up to you. There's an IKEA-type place in town we can go this week."

"It's great." Colton wanders over to the window, which looks out on what would be the front yard if it wasn't all forest.

In the driveway, his mother is making animated gestures while his father's expression conveys that he's *suffering through* whatever it is his wife feels she needs to communicate. A martyr of domesticity. He can read his parents well enough to know that his dad is more excited about this opportunity than his mom. Also, he'd eavesdropped on them.

"We'll need to take you by Dr. Bielenberg's, too, for a sports physical."

"I already had one back in Rockford."

"Dr. B's the team doctor. I'm sure they'll want you to see him."

But his mom is downright pissed. What could it be? Not the gay kid across the hall—his mom isn't that conservative. Maybe cuz the Rentschlers are rich? Like her son will come back home next summer expecting foie gras and chocolate fondue. Maybe she's just sad, the whole empty-nest drama having sneak attacked her a year earlier than planned.

But he also knows: the decision's been made.

6

"There's the rink." Ben points as he pulls the Jetta into the parking lot of Driftless High.

Most rinks are no-frills from street view, but Colton can't tell if this one is frills or not. A collision of concrete blocks and arches, it matches the rest of the school's war bunker aesthetic. The backdrop of towering pines into which the campus is nestled accentuates its unnatural appearance, an alien influence emerging from the ancient forest.

"I've never seen a high school with its own rink. Lake Forest, I guess, but that was pretty much a barn."

"Don't let it fool you. The whole school was designed by this famous mid-century architect, Klement Brauer, and they're very proud of how ugly it is. 'Brutalist,' they call it. They're always talking about Klement Brauer. The rink has a gym nobody but hockey players can use."

There aren't many cars in the student lot, and they get a spot close to the entrance. Alma had insisted they leave extra early so that Colton would have time to get acclimated and "find his locker." They step out of the car and shoulder their backpacks.

"Ready?"

"Let's hope so." Colton wouldn't admit what he's most nervous about, his first impression as the new kid in town being lockstep with Ben's flamboyancy.

Colton's previous high school didn't have a real lobby, just an empty linoleum rectangle where you chose one of three hallways. Driftless High, on the other hand, resembles a shopping mall, with a food court, an atrium that lets in enough sunlight to sustain a jungle of tropical-looking plants, a wall of windows into the second-floor library, and plenty of seating. Some of the tables are for eating and studying, but there are also couches and womb chairs already occupied by coffee-drinking loungers.

"Check out *A Beautiful Mind* over there." Ben nods toward a student writing math equations on a pane of glass situated in the lounge for just that purpose. "Maybe school started last week and we missed it."

"How come the school doesn't offer Spanish? That's super weird."

Ben rolls his eyes, his default reaction to any situation. "Welcome to the whitest city in America."

"I had to register for German. I'm gonna be surrounded by freshmen."

"I'm in German, too."

"Good, you can help me with my homework."

"Wish I could, but it's all Greek to me. Show me your schedule."

"And I hoped I was done with math. My last school only required three years."

"We're in AP History together. That's it. Good thing we have"—Ben checks the watch he's not wearing—"twenty minutes to find your locker. It's not like they number them here." Colton looks at his phone. "It says I'm 302."

Ben touches Colton's shoulder, laughs. "I'm *joking*. 302's right near mine–"

"Hey Ben." A jock brushes past. "You and your new boyfriend are cute all tall together."

Colton opens his mouth, closes it. Maybe he's being a coward, but it turns out his worries weren't baseless.

"Careful, Karl." The sound of Ben's voice makes the situation worse. "This one's the new goalie."

Oops. Everything macho about Karl goes flaccid.

"We're his host family."

Karl makes brief, astonished eye contact with the new goalie, but then flinches away. "I'm so sorry," he apologizes for the first time in his life. "Can we not mention this to anyone?"

"Sure," Ben says, "we'll put it in the closet."

Karl's not down with that, and Colton can tell he wants to say more, to introduce himself to the new hockey player and clarify that he's only an asshole to legit fags. But instead he cuts his losses and lumbers off.

They start walking again. "Sorry," they apologize at the same time.

"Hockey squad has a lot of currency here."

"I feel bad cashing in on it, since I haven't stepped on the ice yet."

"That phrase 'host family' is so awful. Makes us sound like a disease."

"If your family is the host, I think that makes me the disease." Colton doesn't love this topic of conversation either. The lockers have a little digital keypad. "How does this thing work?"

"Punch the key button, then any four-digit combination. To unlock it, do the reverse. And don't leave anything expensive in there, because you can open it with a screwdriver."

"Would anybody dare steal from the new goalie?"

"*Touché.*"

Colton starts unloading his backpack, but it's difficult to

know what he needs, when he'll be able to swing back by the locker, since he doesn't know where any of the classrooms are. Is it better to risk not having a book he needs, or go all pack animal?

"Listen," Ben says, lowering his voice. "We have to get along because we're living in the same house for nine months—but I get it that we're not going to be BFFs. It doesn't make sense not to carpool, but we can separate in the parking lot from now on. Believe me, you're not gonna have any trouble making friends."

In a way, this is exactly what Colton wanted to hear. But now that he's heard it, nodding his head would seem like a hate crime.

"I guess–"

"Ben!" a voice interrupts him.

The girl wraps his host brother in a big hug.

"Charlie! I haven't seen you since *yesterday*. I almost died!"

The girl's name is Charlie. Buzzed black hair, but for sure a female.

"We secured another donor," she says, "enough to complete the falsework."

The what?

"Great!" Ben doesn't seem so confused by the reference. "Our dreams of terrorism live on."

Charlie registers Colton's presence for the first time, shuts up about the terrorist funding. "Charlie." She holds out her hand.

"Colton." Colton shakes, minor panicking over clamminess, sweatiness, pressure, terrorism, etc. Her hand is bird-boned, but her grip is firm.

"I have a host brother," Ben says. "Surprise!"

Colton didn't know he was into short hair on girls—

or black boots or ghostly hues or amulet necklaces. He has known, however, since he was about twelve, of his fascination with plaid skirts and white blouses—he checks the hall to confirm that Driftless High does not in fact require a Catholic school uniform.

"I'm the starting goalie on the hockey team." Where'd he get *starting*?

"Congratulations," she says, monotone.

Not the reaction he'd been hoping for, the girl version of Karl's swooning.

"Ben," Colton says, "real quick. About what you were saying before, I don't want us to have to treat each other like strangers because the Karls of the world are assholes. As long as it doesn't make you uncomfortable."

Colton's relieved to find that the speech *is* how he feels, that the words came to him so quickly because it's what the better part of him had wanted to say.

"Wait," Ben sounds suspicious, "are you hitting on me?"

"Never mind," Colton sighs. "I'll go back to being a phobe."

"I'm *joking*. Wanna come get coffee with us before class starts?"

Coffee was the most difficult thing Colton had given up during his recent relapse of health. He can already feel his hands start to tremble.

"Great, yeah."

7

Everyone is tall. So is Colton, so that's not what intimidates him. He'd said hi to Coach Riessen outside the D-Club Room and received a slight nod in return—as if the coach didn't remember having shown up at his game that summer to recruit him. Colton hopes he remembers what he said about how tryouts were a thing of the past.

There's always this electricity at camps and showcases and tryouts, guys sizing one another up and forming impromptu alliances, searching for secret signs that they are among the chosen. He figured he'd be able to spot the new guys by how quiet they were, but everyone is chatty, leaving Colton worried he's the only one who's worried—despite what he'd been led to believe. Lots of them are wearing maroon and white DRIFT-LESS HOCKEY athletic gear, and it's a good guess that these are guys who played last year. There are way more hopefuls here than would fill a varsity and JV squad to capacity. They've already overcrowded the tables and are moving chairs off stacks around the room's periphery. If one in ten guys plays the same position as Colton, there have to be at least five or six other tendies in the room. How many of them are upperclassmen, thinking they'd get a shot after Shane got injured? Sure they feel bad about his accident, but they're not gonna let this opportunity pass them by. Colton's an idiot for thinking he'd walk straight into the locker room on game day and find the one single backup goalie taping his stick for him. What if Riessen had given the same recruitment talk to a dozen other goalies to make sure at least one of them would be stupid enough to up and transplant his whole life for a JV job?

Colton is punched in the shoulder. He looks up and can tell that it appears to have been a friendly punch at least.

"You look nervous," the guy says, taking the seat next to him. Big forehead, sharp jaw, deep-set eyes, this dude's face looks like a skull. He has a bulge of chew under his lip, carries a Vitamin Water spitter.

"Lots of guys here…"

"My name's Spencer Trautsch, but everyone calls me Protein."

"Trautsch? Any relation to…"

"My brother." Protein points to a series of jerseys on one wall. Framed and signed. Must be current or former NHL players who passed through Driftless. Including RENTSCHLER—they had plenty of Rentschler jerseys to choose from, and they went with his rookie squad, the Islanders. And there's TRAUTSCH. Hugo Trautsch, Stanley Cup MVP and captain of the US Olympic Team. A Stanley Cup or several adorn the frames of the guys who've hoisted it. Nil for Flynn.

Protein waves away the wows. "I'm supposed to show you the ropes."

"Should I be? Nervous, I mean."

"You're the varsity starter. Your face should say *Don't fucking look at me.* No, it shouldn't even notice there are other people in the room."

"Okay."

Protein watches him try. "No, you're not doing it. That's worse than before. You look like you've got something stuck in your ass and you're in the waiting room at the ass doctor's to get it pulled out."

Colton takes off his hat and pushes it back on. "Speaking of doctors, do they make you do those weird therapy sessions with Bielenberg?"

"Dude, that's the least casual banter I've ever heard. Gumby!" Protein calls across the room.

A kid at another table turns back and stands and walks over. This kid is not so intimidating—won't have to start shaving for another decade or two.

"Gumby, do you know who this is?"

"Yeah, I've seen you in the weight room. Vogler, right?"

"See, Birdy, everyone knows you."

All of a sudden, Colton is Birdy.

"Gumby, if you saw him why didn't you say hello?"

Gumby shrugs.

"Birdy, this is Gumby, your backup."

Colton has to fight off modesty along the lines of *We'll see what we'll see.*

"Why do they call you Gumby?"

"Cuz I'm a goalie and I'm–"

"He can suck his own dick," Protein cuts him off. "He bragged, and we made him prove it."

Might be true, Gumby's face says, might not.

"And he doesn't even have a long schlong."

True, Gumby's face says. Too bad.

"Birdy's wondering why we'd fill a room with doomed fuckers."

Gumby hadn't noticed the room was crowded. "Trying out for the EG, I guess."

"What's the–"

"The EG is the JV, and JV is the EG. Elephant graveyard. You're dismissed, Gambino."

"See you out there," Gumby says to Colton before going back to his seat.

Protein: "You know those religions that think heaven can only fit a certain number of people?"

"The Elect?"

"The number is twenty, Birdy, and you're one of them, and most of these guys"—he gestures with his hand across the room—"aren't."

The wall opposite the framed jerseys offers a view of the stands and the ice surface, where a Zamboni is on its last lazy pass.

Every day when Colton comes to the rink he walks by other photos, a display case commemorating Driftless players who died young. Shane is there even though he isn't dead, but there were three others since 1990. Trent Ahlgren, Chris Abendroth, Jurgen Holz. He doesn't want to, but he finds himself stopping and staring at their young, smiling, dead faces every time.

"So, you were asking about *Herr Doktor*–" Protein starts, but everyone falls silent.

Coach Riessen, wearing maroon and white workout clothes, tennis shoes, and white socks pulled halfway up his calves, walks to the front of the room. That clipboard... He was coach enough before, but in gym clothes he's a reminder that most decent coaches were pretty damn good players back in the day. The Big Show—that's what he's heard the guys call Riessen.

"Alright, welcome to Driftless Dynasty Hockey. If you don't know me, you might as well leave."

Uneasy laughter.

"This is Chuck Lehmann, the assistant coach, and that's Slava, the goalie coach. Slava Cvikota."

Slava might have been cast in a crime show's non-speaking

role, EASTERN EUROPEAN THUG #2. He's not in peak physical condition—more of a valley, a chasm of physical condition, his gut hanging out there where he could set a beer on it. Colton didn't know he'd be working with a goalie coach.

"I'm passing around a stack of papers with all the important dates," Riessen continues. "We don't start official practice until October, but I want you guys on the ice before that. Most of you enjoyed the offseason a little too much. Dustin, where the hell were you all summer?"

"Moose Jaw," a guy Colton can't see replies.

Riessen does a double take. "Well you look like shit."

The room eats it up, but it feels rehearsed to Colton. Like maybe it's not Dustin every year, but it's someone.

"Captain's Practice is every Tuesday and Thursday. Chance to get back in shape before tryouts. You're organizing that, right Spencer?"

"Yeah," Protein mumbles. "Hit me up for info."

"What's your email?"

Protein doesn't want to say, but Riessen uncaps a marker, steps up to a white board, and looks back over his shoulder. Protein surrenders the info and Colton hears him swear under his breath at all the kids writing his email address down or snapping it with their phones. Riessen adds Protein's name, his real name, on the board and gives him a little smirk.

"Bell and Bucket is the week of September twenty-fouth. Other places call it tryouts—we just take whoever's left alive."

Still in a whisper, Protein tells him, "There's another reason we don't call them tryouts…"

"Everyone on the team will get a track suit, gym clothes, and a duffel bag. Cost is thirty-five dollars—that's way less than we're paying for them. We'll get your sizes once we know if you're joining us for the year. Varsity guys will receive a hockey bag, gloves, pants, and a helmet if you need one. Let your parents and boyfriends know, we've got hoodie sweatshirts for twenty dollars, hats for five, coats for forty. As far as twigs go, we pay for the first six, half for JV guys—sorry. Equipment reps will be here next week from Bauer, CCM, Warrior, and Graf, so make sure you know what patterns you want. Other equipment is available at a significant discount. Prices are on the sheet if you don't have one yet. Words of wisdom at the bottom of the page there: get sleep and manage your time. Sit in the front row of your classes. That's where the smart people sit. Not smart?—well, you might fool the teacher into thinking you are. Grades come first, hockey comes second… or so they tell me."

The room likes that one too.

"This'll be a tough year for us. I'd use the word 'transitional,' but that's the word teams use when they know they're shot. And that's not the case. True, we'll have to work a little harder and dig a little deeper. Losing Shane is tough, both roster-wise and emotionally. He wasn't just one of the best goalies this program has ever seen; he was smart and brave in a way most of us can only dream of, and losing him"—for a second Coach Riessen might cry—"is a fucking punch to the stomach."

Colton misses his cue to nod with the rest of the room.

"But we've got each other for emotional support, and we won the recruiting lottery. I don't know how many of you've had a chance to meet our new goalie yet, Colton Vogler"—he motions toward Colton with an open palm, and Colton starts to stand, then doesn't—"but we're damn lucky we got to him first."

Someone claps, and the room joins in. Most of it.

"Aw shut up," Riessen says. "The kid hasn't made one save yet."

8

"Nope," is Protein's hello when Colton opens the door. "Huh?"

"It's sweatpants night, not... skinny chinos night."

"You're not wearing sweatpants. You're wearing skinny chinos."

"That's cuz I've already done sweatpants night, Birdy. C'mon, there's important people waiting."

Colton doesn't know if he should invite Protein inside, so he leaves him standing there as he goes back to the room he just left. Does he have clean sweatpants? He sniffs his one pair of Lulus out of the hamper, the same pair Rudy used to call his "formal sweatpants," and changes into a t-shirt that matches better.

"Hi, Mrs. Rentschler," Protein calls into the kitchen when Colton reappears.

"Hello, Spencer."

Colton hopes he doesn't–

Protein points at Colton. "Sweatpants night."

"Oh, fun!"

Car in the driveway is an Audi, Cammo wedged behind the wheel. Protein gets in the passenger seat, and Colton finds himself sitting in the back with Mark, a junior D-man everyone calls CC because his last name is Sielaff. CC's wearing sweatpants too, and they both want to know what the other one knows. CC: lots. Colton: nada. Colton tries to think of a way to interrogate him without looking uptight. If he had CC's phone number he could text him—then hope he wouldn't announce it to the car.

The car fills with angry bass, and Cammo peels out in reverse. Instead of informing Cammo there's space up by the garage to turn around, Colton just prays, stomach down in his bowels. CC sees he's tense. CC's amused. Colton chills out about their imminent deaths, watches globes of light going the wrong direction. The dark forest spits them out onto Osprey Avenue, and Cammo swings the car around, heading south.

"You dip?" Protein offers, spitting brown juice into a Gatorade bottle.

"Sure."

"Don't lie to me. Have you dipped much?"

"Not much, but–"

"Great," says Cammo.

"If you don't want him to spew, stop drifting your turns."

"*Fast and the Furious, Driftless Drift.*"

"Why would I spew?"

"You won't."

Cammo does seem to adjust to the nation's driving laws as Colton inserts a pinch and offers the tin to CC, who smiles and waves it off. There are empty bottles aplenty on the floor of the car.

The buzz hits Colton with more of a wallop than he would have expected from a product that is ubiquitous and legal. He'll be fine. No information forthcoming as to their ten-four–

"It's ten-twenty," Protein says.

What is?

"Ten-four is message received. Ten-twenty is location."

Colton doesn't care. Colton is along for the ride! If you

think about it, Colton's body is zooming at the exact same speed as the car, but the car is to gasoline as dip is to drunk, turns out. Cammo and Protein—*Proteeeen*—are bitching about this year's "yield" of freshmen and Boots sure did get fat this summer and do you think Middleton's got any new studs this year? Talk moves to Protein's all-star brother, as Colton is noticing it tends to when Protein is around. Now watch Protein pretend to resist the topic, brush off his brother's stats, and watch now he'll give up. Protein has opinions on the Blackhawks' chances this year, and there are *a lot* of variables.

But this car is no longer moving, and Colton's door swings open by itself. Cammo's standing there with a car door in his hand. Colton is floated toward the shine of beaten gold. No, neon. (What he *thought* was beating gold is neon.) Off-limits shrine lights.

"Why do I need sweatpants for this? It's not going on my ass cheek, is it?"

Sweatpants are for later.

They enter the tattoo parlor, and Colton's eyes flit around the walls of possibilities like a bird trapped in the room. He tries to recall every tattoo flirtation he's vetoed in the past. *Any* tattoo idea—

Mega Man! Mega Man? No, not Mega Man.

"What are you guys getting?"

Cammo laughs.

Protein: "We're not drunk bitches out for an affirming night on the town."

Hot in here— No, it's Colton's body's radiating heat, neon *heeeat.*

Tattoos hurt. There will be pain soon.

"Two more for branding?" A tattoo artist with no visible tattoos has materialized. Guy probably does *expe*riments in back, sews people together.

Tattoos are forever. Let's think about that some more.

Cammo hands the mad scientist cash, and there's an open beer in Colton's hand.

"Spudnutt here's gonna need to throw up every so often."

"Great, nothing makes my job easier than the shakes."

"This tat should be second nature by now."

A garbage can leaps into Colton's path, so he bends over and pukes onto—*into*—it. He digs the grounds from under his lip and spits and spits and spits and spits. The Gatorade bottle has completed its precious life cycle—container of beverage you drink, receptacle of anti-beverage, now a tiny trash can inside a larger trashcan, Russian bell style. *Doll*, is what I mean. Russian dolls.

He has an audience, and they're waiting to see if he's done for now. Colton takes a swig of hops, spits it out.

"Cheers," says the mangler. "Shall we begin?"

They head north into an industrial sector of town Colton hasn't seen so far. Thin chimneys jet tongues of flame into the night sky, latticed by metal staircases and catwalks and tangles of pipes and gauges Colton hopes somebody knows the purpose of. Stairs twist around three smokestacks like candy cane stripes, while a fourth is bent back on itself in the shape of a U-lock, a fundamental misunderstanding between structure and function. There's white, polyhedron things you'd expect to find at an arctic meteor–… meteor–… meteoro////– an arctic weather station.

This is not where nights on the town are supposed to wind up. This is where *Terminator* movies wind up. All this metal's a magnet for the Terminators!

"Dude, chill out."

Darkened signs and faded awnings, the ghosts of gone jobs, lots of home-style cooking and zero-denomination churches and rogue electronic repair. Bright lights up ahead herald a few blocks' holdout against the tides of economic unviability.

Here be strip clubs, and tonight we are moths. Cammo pulls into the least disgusting of the venues, Valhalla, and their shoes grind glass into asphalt.

Colton spits. "I don't think they're gonna let us in here." Colton spits again.

"My bet is they will."

"Here." Cammo hands Colton and CC what must be fifty bucks each in ones. "Make this disappear."

No neck, but the bouncer manages to nod and head-point the high schoolers girlward. Is Colton just imagining a cooler reception from the clientele—grizzled veterans still in that day or night's blue collars, distracted from their glass-bottom oracles by this intrusion of young bucks into their territory? The crew has drifted into an Old West saloon wearing all black clothes and jangly spurs. Colton scouts for safe spaces to puke.

But the newcomers hear a cheer from teammates already assembled at the edge of the stage. Hoodie orders another bucket of green bottles, Boots slaps Colton on the bicep and almost gets puked on, and Tina resents the brief cessation of money getting tucked into her thong. She clomps to the pole in Lucite platform shoes, and– Who's more flexible, him or this stripper? Colton doesn't know how to *think* at a strip club— how to *not think*—how to assemble his face for these ass cheeks now jiggling inches from his eyes. He checks CC, and CC's braindead, so Colton goes stupid too. Through smoggy bass, infinite mirrors mirror disembodied body parts in case four stages of strutting tits aren't enough.

"Not enjoying the naked women?" Protein asks him.

"Huh?" Has he been doing it wrong? He throws bills onto the pink-lit stage.

"We didn't get you dressed down for nothing."

"Oh."

Oh.

"There we go," Cammo says, cheersing him. "Sweatpants night."

But is a boner that fun with miles to go before… you know? *Stop* thinking. Down this beer. Now's not the time to question the entire cultural institution of strip clubs, these venues for losing—as-opposed-to-using—it.

How long is he expected to broadcast his frustration?

Turns out Vanessa has interesting things to say about her student loans.

JV = EG = elephant graveyard. Driftless junior varsity is the place where hockey players' careers go to quietly die, Colton realizes in a shock of lucidity. It's a team that practices and puts in the hours and travels to play games all over the state of Wisconsin, a team that celebrates triumphs and suffers heartbreak—but it's not really hockey anymore.

Boots chases Vanessa away and replaces her with a newer model.

"Shouldn't have worn your Lulus."

"Chelsea," the only name Colton's sure is not Chelsea's name. He hopes she doesn't discover his arm's all bloody. "You're not the one who's stripping, cutie." True. People don't make out with strippers, right? Chelsea tells him he doesn't need to bring another beer with him if he doesn't want to. That's not what I meant, Colton (nice guy) clarifies, you're not the reason I feel like puking.

Chelsea: "Lucky me."

9

He's been doing this since he was a kid, going online and customizing the colors and specs of goalie equipment— Rockford Glacier blue/green/white, or Chicago Blackhawks red/black/white, or whatever scheme of whatever team he was then fetishizing. But there was always that letdown when he'd found the perfect balance only to have to close the window without submitting the bags of money that would have brought the equipment to his door. A few years ago, companies had added a feature online that allowed potential customers to save the spec sheets as PDFs, and he still has a folder on his desktop labeled DREAM PADS (changed quickly from the original PAD PORN).

His parents aren't swimming in it, but—*look*—they have the sufficient funds. It was always young Colton's quest to remind them of this fact without saying it outright. (*I know you're holding out on me!*) Although they've been plenty supportive over the years, his dad is convinced that buying equipment on the cheap exercises a muscle of self-reliance that otherwise would atrophy. After he'd convinced his dad he wasn't going to opt for a less expensive position, his dad made sure he had top-of-the-line gear, or close enough, but always previous year models, whatever his dad could find discounted or discontinued.

Once in a while, when they were in the area, his parents would drop by one of the big equipment stores, Gunzo's or

Jerry's Warehouse, and let their son pretend he was going home with something. Colton didn't have enough eyes to see, hands to touch. Better than Valhalla! His excitement was such that his bladder would act up, send him to the bathroom every twenty minutes. At best, his dad was using the trip to see what size skates or pants or uppers his son would soon need—so that he could go home and find cheaper stuff online. (This same ham radio guru who hasn't yet learned how to close browser tabs ascends to hacker-level expertise when it comes to bartering the World Wide Web for cheap hockey equipment or flights with complicated layovers.) The employees knew what his dad was up to, found ways to take it out on the kid—with glares or with refusals to fetch out-of-reach goods.

So, his gear never matched. Sure, he was always roughly blue, but Colton's glove and pads and blocker refused to wear out at the same time, his ensemble coming together in the exact manner of the Frankenstein monster's body parts.

In his frustration, he'd resorted to designing his own line of goalie equipment. He filled a sketchbook with potential designs, his favorite NHL goalies wearing his gear: Ryan Miller, Antti Niemi, Craig Anderson, Roberto Luongo, etc. His brand name was PLUMAGE, a puck-bird logo that would have gotten him sued by NBC. Not half bad a name—but *why*? It's scary how your kid brain *knew things* you don't know anymore.

He dreamed of being wined and dined by equipment reps from Brian's or Vaughn or Reebok (back when Reebok was in the goalie equipment game), being "sponsored"—that was a big word for him. Dreamed of maybe, *some day*—

"Do you want your last name stitched on the pads, or do you have a nickname?"

He's forgotten the name of the equipment rep visiting Driftless today.

There's BIRDY now, and his old team called him CROUTON, but he doesn't want that on his pads. Or KILLER, what Dave DiGiacomo called him when he was in eighth grade practicing with the high schoolers—after he'd written *I'M A KILLER* on the inside of his mask's throat guard in magic marker. Better than the swastika he drew in Routhier's helmet.

"Last name would be great."

"Okay, type it there in that box that says *Name Embroidery.* That's one you want to make sure you get right."

"Got it." He proofreads his own last name six times.

"Alright, let's size you up."

Colton laces up one of his skates while Darren—that's his name, Darren—pulls a pair of goal pads out of a giant bag with the Brian's logo. The first one he hands him is green and yellow and black, the Jamaican flag bisecting the five-hole.

"Don't worry, this is for sizing. Rich guy wanted *Cool Runnings* pads and then re-ordered a pair an inch smaller, said we could keep these."

"They line up with the knee."

"These're the G-Netiks, but since you want a stiffer pad, you'll want the Optik Fly model. But sizing is the same."

Colton goes down into a butterfly position, lopsided since he only has the one pad on. "Could they come up maybe an inch on the thigh?"

"Yup. Thirty-six plus one." Darren types it into the laptop. "What kind of toe you prefer?"

"This lace would be okay, but do you guys make the kind that can slide back and forth on the plastic washer?"

"Sure do." He chooses *Sliding Toe Bridge* on the drop-down.

"It says thirty dollars extra."

"I wouldn't worry about that. And you said all internal breaks on the V-Roll, right? Give up many rebounds?"

"You kick 'em out far enough, they're not a problem."

"Now the fun part. Colors. I'll let you drive."

There are two dozen buttons that highlight various regions of the goal pads to show what areas they control, everything from the big V-Roll to accessories as tiny and specific as laces, binding, and whatever the *Knuckle* is. Below the region buttons are palettes of colors, including pink and turquoise and fluorescent green and a few others he wouldn't be caught dead in. Four materials too: *Defender*, *Flat*, *Weave*, and *Matte*.

"Which one is leather?"

"A couple of them are. You want *Flat.*"

"Glad you've got maroon."

"We can get any color, more than you see there."

"Maroon's fine."

Colton toggles the mouse around the various pad regions, swapping white and maroon. A few years back, the craze was all white pads, the theory being that it created a camouflaging illusion that made players unable to see the outlines of the goalie in the split second taking a shot. Colton is relieved that this trend seems to be going extinct—brightness is important for territorial creatures.

Was *that* the reason he'd called his line of equipment Plumage? You know, get the fuck away see how colorful I am! But that's not why birds are colorful. That's more for frogs and snakes and spiders—though... APOSEMATISM wouldn't have been quite so eye-catching on the roll of a leg pad or the cuff of a glove. Now that he thinks of it, following his plumage metaphor not very far at all makes him further disconcerted by his younger self. No, *it's okay*, the prospective mates are perched in the stands, watching the males peck at one another and chirp.

Now I will be maroon. A maroon Birdy.

The question is always how best to balance it out. As long as it's not white, there's something badass about pads that are all one flat color—the eggplant Pro90Zs that Guy Hebert wore for the Ducks way back when, or Brian Elliott's shiny blue pads when he played for the Blues. But that route would also limit the degree of customization.

Colton opens a new window to start out with a fresh palette, adds maroon here, subtracts it there—the dart graphics, the V-Roll, the five-hole region. Is Darren getting impatient?

"I wish Driftless had another color, for more options."

"You can usually get away with gray. Or silver—"

"Gray's good."

"You can think about it for a couple days and email the specs to me. But we'll need them soon if you want time to break them in before your first game."

That's the downside of getting everything at once—you're stiff as a statue out there for a few weeks. Or so Colton imagines.

"We could also ditch the templates," Darren says, clicking on a link for *Pad of the Week 2018*. Brian's is famous for ostentatious pad designs. Colton scrolls, seeing *Transformers* pads, striped hockey sock pads, country flag pads, vintage pads that replicate the "Air Pack" motif from the '90s, pads emblazoned with logos of twenty teams, some familiar and some not.

Pad porn.

"Those are Sparks's famous sendups to Trevor Kidd." He points at a checkerboarded set with maple leafs stitched into the blue squares. "Darling's… Eddie Lack's… Mine." On Darren's pads, symmetrical green dragons spew red flames toward the crotch region. "We could put the big Driftless D across the five-hole." Wayne Bohatta's set features Bucky the Badger, scratch marks raked diagonally down the pads. "Yeah, or get you a set you can wear through college too."

"I think that would be a little…" But it occurs to Colton his goal is that he'll be doing this again in a year's time—with red and white. "Are those Darcy Traeger's?" The design is super simple, five vertical stripes running the length of the pad, the middle the thickest.

"That's right. Big AHL fan?"

"I'm from Rockford. And I used to play against him in high school."

"Maybe you'll play again with him soon."

"Let's go with that. Maroon on the sides and gray up the middle."

"Classy. I can make that happen. Now, what do you want on your mask?"

Colton stops breathing. "My what?"

"The Al Johansson paint job on your new mask."

Al Johannsson designs the dopest masks in the game. "Are you serious?"

"Driftless must be. You ever had a painted helmet?"

Answer is technically yes, but it wasn't custom. It was a mass-produced Boba Fett helmet his dad had lowballed. Not the sturdiest piece of equipment he'd owned—as one Dave DiGiacomo slapshot to the throat guard had soon proven.

Colton shakes his head.

"But I bet you've had designs in mind since you first started playing."

"The mask was what made me want to be a goalie in the first place." Posters in his childhood bedroom, an invasion of NHL masks on a cosmic background, keychains and hat pins, even a mask-themed metal trashcan: Cam Talbot's Stay Puft Marshmallow Man, Curtis Joseph's Cujo, Eddie the Eagle's eagle, and the coolest of all, Brian Hayward's San Jose helmet where his face was coming out of the shark's mouth.

"What's the first thing that comes to mind? For Shane it was chess."

"Mega Man."

"The old video game?"

Colton nods.

"What boss's weapon made you maroon and white?"

"Drill Man."

"Gotta admit, that could be badass."

"Let me think about this a few days."

"I'll give you Al's phone number. He'll have ideas too, I'm sure. Are we good to go on the equipment?"

Colton thinks about it for one second and nods. "I want it now."

"Here." Darren digs around in the bag, produces a maroon neck guard with the Brian's logo. "Grabbed this on the way out."

"Sweet." Notwithstanding its ability to save your life, a neck guard might seem less than exciting—but it matching the rest of your equipment says more than anything else, *I belong to this company.*

I'm *sponsored.*

Darren keeps rooting around in the bag. "You need a cup?"

"Sure."

"More swag. Can I ask why you're going with Brian's?"

Colton points to the *Custom Hand-Crafted in Canada* patch on the Jamaica pads.

"Good man. Alas, I'm gonna need that pad back."

"This special treatment makes me nervous. I hope I'm worth it."

"Yeah," Darren says, "Driftless always expects a return on their investments."

10
MONTAGE

In a lacrosse field north of Steiner, the beer-gutted man executes an impossible somersault.

"Now, you try." Slava makes a circular motion with his sausage forefinger.

It's that easy. Easy as twirling your finger.

Colton wants to ask how breaking his neck trying to perform kid gymnastics is going to make him better at stopping ninety mile-per-hour disks of rubber, but he's gotten to know his goaltending coach well enough by now that he keeps this question to himself.

Slava is wearing tiny Umbro soccer shorts that Colton didn't know existed outside of *I Love the '90s,* and ringer socks pulled up to his knees as if to compensate for the lack of thigh coverage. His threadbare t-shirt is printed with a phallic rocket blasting off, *America's Space Shuttle* in neon font.

Chin to chest, Colton lands on the base of his neck and shoulder rolls, falling off to one side and ending up on his back in the grass.

"Little girls can do it," is Slava's encouragement as Colton picks himself back up, rubbing his vertebrae.

Slava makes his somersault sign language to Gumby, who flashes Colton an apologetic look before turning a somersault that's graceful as hell.

*

"I hear you're a musician."

Colton stops taping his stick and scans the locker room. He'd learned early on that this isn't the setting in which to flaunt high culture. He nods.

#6 Helmut Zilisch, it says on the guy's Driftless bag. Helmut? So that's why he goes by Zilch—named after a piece of equipment.

"What instrument?"

"Piano."

"Typical."

"What?"

"Pianists are the goalies of the music world."

"Why's that?"

"They like playing all by themselves."

"Fair."

"You might not know this, but"—he lowers his voice—"Shane, our goalie last year, was a damn fine pianist. My quartet still hasn't found a good replacement for when we go quintet."

"You're in a chamber group?"

"Yeah, we're all on the team." He points, "Stoney, CC, and The Plague. The Shorthanded Quartet."

Weird town. "Why're you called– Oh, got it."

Zilch nods. "Because there's four of us. But right now we really are shorthanded. We were learning the Brahms quintet at the time of Shane's accident."

"The F minor? That's one of my favorite things ever written."

"You up for a jam session?"

The racquetball smacks Colton in the back of the head. Again.

Slava frowns. "You must shuffle over."

Colton does as he's told—this time it hits way too close to his junk.

"You shuffle too soon."

Parallel with him, Gumby is so good at this drill that he's got a syncopated rhythm going: three quick thumps as he bounces the ball on the court and smacks it hard with his racket against the near wall, the pause before the ball hits high up on the far wall behind him, the longer wait for the ball to come back his way—to his left side or over his shoulder—before it bounces off the wall a few feet in front of him and he snatches it with his glove hand. In fact… yes, Colton's brain has set a melody to the rhythm.

"We try another version. How you say…" Slava searches for the word.

Easier? Remedial? Beginner's?

"Dummy version."

Slava bounces the ball, hits it against the wall, and catches it without all the behind-the-back fanciness that's intended to mask where the ball is coming from.

"You think you can manage this?"

Colton tries it out, but the ball bounces off his thumb and he has to chase it down.

"You have hands made of crowbar."

Colton tries it again, is successful this time.

"Good, now twenty times in a row without missing, and we'll graduate from dummy level."

Colton does it again, and again, and again, adding a poly-rhythm to Gumby's thwacks and squeaky sneakers.

How's hockey going up there in Wisconsin?
Oh not bad. Getting decent at racquetball.

"Why would we want breakfast?" Zev asks. "It's ten p.m."

Ben has a Switch, and Colton has relapsed via the new *Mega Man 11* into his retro NES addiction under the guise of researching his paint job. He'd gotten Ben hooked too, along with his boyfriend Zev and, luckily, Charlie.

"You guys never do that? To feel all night owl."

"I don't know anywhere that's open this late." Ben jerks his hands around as he plays. His Mega Man explodes in radiating circles of oblivion, succumbing again to Heat Man's river of lava. "I'll never get this pattern."

"Don't you guys have a Perkins?"

"How many corporate restaurants have you seen in Driftless? We chase them out with pitchforks here."

"Baby Dahl's is open."

Charlie doesn't want the night to end, is how Colton interprets it.

"That pie place?"

"That pie place in the truck stop with the giant CHEESE sign?"

"The Big Show dropped the ball on this one." Hoodie kicks two bags aside to make room for his own.

"Again."

"There's like twenty freshmen in locker room one."

"You mean you don't want four lines on every bench?"

"*You're organizing Captain's Practice, right?*" Hoodie tries to imitate Coach Riessen but it's spot-on Patrick from Spongebob. "*Chance for Boots's fat ass to get back in shape.*"

"I coulda killed him. I got five thousand emails the next day, all from freshmen dipshits." He throws a tape ball at a kid who looks bantam age at most. "That's right, Pettit Selects, I'm talking about you."

The kid cracks a smile. He has a Pettit hockey bag.

"Why are you laughing? We hate you and don't want you here."

The smile drops off the kid's face, and he becomes very interested in the rubber floor between and around his skates.

"Why don't you leave? You have *zero chance* of making varsity—you're taking ice time from a guy who might."

"Sorry."

"I'm not joking, Pettit. Take your skates off, pack up your bag, and go put in some more hours at the quarry."

Now the kid's a little pissed, his lips a drawstring pulled as tight as it will go. He turns back to his skates.

"I said take off, not lace up." The room is very quiet. "I'm serious. Leave."

The kid's eyes fly around the room for confirmation this is happening. The other freshmen are in stealth mode, hanging him out to dry.

So Pettit starts unlacing his skates, kicks the second one off with the toes of his other foot. He moves to wipe the ice off the blades. No need—they go into his bag. The breezers come off next, the socks and shin guards. The kid just wears a hockey jock under his stuff, and Colton sees him realizing he's going to be naked for a second with the whole room's attention, sees him wondering if he can shield himself with his towel, if showing his ass will be better or worse. Pettit hunches over as he drops his jock, as if to retract his genitals up into his body for concealment.

"Put your shit back on, Pettit," Protein says.

The kid yanks his jock back up, more mortified than relieved.

"Did you guys notice—" Hoodie starts.

"Pettit, do you seriously have no pubes?"

He's putting his shin guards and socks back on extra fast, worried the guys will change their minds—or want a second look at his crotch. "I shave them."

"Why do you shave your pubes?"

"Girls like it."

Everyone laughs. The other freshmen aren't sure what to do, whether joining in will make them less visible or more.

"Yeah, all the girls you're fucking are super impressed, Pettit."

"Thank God that pussy embargo's over. The girls' demands have been met!"

"Shut up Protein, you shave your pubes too."

"Yeah, but not for the girls."

"Where did you learn these drills?" Colton asks. He's pretty sure he has more bruised skin than unbruised by now. He's all scratchy from the grass.

"Tretiak," Slava says. Russia's goalie in the '80 Lake Placid Games. He squats and kicks out one leg then the other. The Russian Dance.

While juggling three tennis balls.

"We drove twenty minutes to breakfast in the middle of the night, and that's *all you're ordering?*"

"Pie's all I want."

"I'm sorry," the waitress says, "we don't have anything called lemon cream pie. I'm not sure what that is."

"It's some Illinois thing."

"We have lemon meringue–"

"Cough drop pie, no thanks."

"You're the new goalie, right?"

"Yeah, Colton." He shakes the waitress's hand.

She points at her nametag. Sophie. "Tell you what, you figure out what's in a lemon cream pie, let us know—and you mention Baby Dahl's in an interview—and we'll name the pie after you. We don't get a lot of the hockey crowd."

One thing's for sure, the ice at Driftless is amazing. Nobody's skated on it since they painted new lines, a calligraphic D cradling the center-ice face-off dot. The smell is that of a winter morning so crisp it tricks you into thinking this must be a fertile season.

Colton stomps his skate blades against the ice a few times as he does his first lap, shakes out his legs, his wrists. Rolls his neck around. Right now his groin injury is quiet, but he's been dreading the first time he tries to get up from a butterfly.

He's a little surprised that the rafters are free of any banners advertising the team's previous successes. Then he realizes that this is a team so good they don't need to remind anyone. It would be tacky. They don't need anything more than the bodies on the ice. An American flag, a Canadian flag, the State of Wisconsin flag, and handpicked European flags, that's all. Steiner's not a huge place, but the stands run all the way around the rink, like a miniature NHL stadium. The scoreboard is a smaller version of those four-sided monsters that hang above the ice surface at big arenas.

Gumby was the only other tendy in locker room three, and Colton swears as two other goalies step on the ice. One of them is already putting the moorings in the net to claim it's his. For a second Colton worries about the who-goes-first etiquette—until he remembers the Big Show's speech in the D-Club room.

Set my net up, asshole, he telepathically communicates to the other goalie as he skates by. *Maybe I'll let you see some shots today.*

Both of these other goalies know how to skate, and one of them is wearing brand new maroon Vaughn gear. The Birdy/Gumby lock on the varsity spots seems not to be settled in this guy's mind at least. Colton wishes his new stuff had arrived so he could start breaking it in, but he's also a little sad to say goodbye to his old equipment's familiarity.

After a fast lap around the rink and a lap of backwards crossovers, a lap of C-cuts and another of backwards C-cuts, big ripping sounds as he carves sickle-shaped swoops into fresh ice with the inside edge of his blades, Colton positions himself in the referee circle to stretch. Gumby, in his all-white CCMs, gets up a bit of speed and spins on his knees toward Colton to knock him over.

"And that was how Driftless lost both of their goalies for the season."

"These chumps wish." Untangling himself from the goalie heap, Gumby falls into the complete splits. "How long has it been since you've skated?"

Colton pushes his left half-butterfly a little too far, and his groin says *Hi there!*

"A month."

"Yeah, me too. I'm just hoping not to hurt myself."

"You've gotta be kidding me," Colton says under his breath as their chamber music teacher walks into the practice room—and it's Slava.

"He's amazing," Zilch says.

"What instrument does he play?"

"Mostly soprano sax."

Slava, now dressed in a hideous polyester button-down with a collar the size of a seagull, claps his meaty hands together once. "All right, play music for me and I will tell you what you do wrong."

After finally catching the racquetball twenty times in a row, Colton advances to a second pattern, hitting the ball off the floor and *then* the wall.

He was lousy in warm-ups, and he's already reading disappointment on his teammates' caged faces. But he also knows that he often plays well after a crappy warm-up—and vice versa. No explanation. Sure enough there's a dozen guys on both benches. Colton's on the team of all the players wearing white or yellow jerseys; any color darker fills out the other side. A few guys have headed back to the locker room to plumb their bags for different colors. There's an equal distribution of maroon helmets and gloves and breezers between the two teams, but Colton knows he won't be able to tell which way the ice is tilted until they get a few shifts into the scrimmage.

Of course there're no refs, so Protein starts things off by throwing a puck the length of the ice toward Gumby.

The white squad moves the puck around their offensive zone, puts a few shots on Gumby. The saves aren't messianic, but it's enough to fuel the new varsity goalie's anxiety engine.

Great. One defenseman drifts down from his position on the blue line, gets caught pinching, and now there's a two-on-O developing in the neutral zone. Goalies love when the first shot they see with a new team is an odd-man break.

Prove you belong here. C-cuts out to the hashmarks, starts backing up when the forwards hit the blue-line.

One of them's Pettit. Pettit will pass. Pettit won't shoot because he doesn't want to risk further humiliation.

Colton follows the passes back and forth, and their momentum decides it's Pettit who has to choose.

Pettit *will* shoot because he put himself out there on the first shift. Because he wants to redeem himself and his shaved taint.

Pettit drops his low hand off his stick, does his best imitation of Forsberg's move from the '94 Olympics, tries to tuck it around Colton on the far side. Colton doesn't bite. Extends his right leg and kicks the puck to the boards.

Gumby gives him some love from the other net, tapping his stick on the ice.

"Nice save, Sparky," Sparky says as he skates by. Sparky's called Sparky because he calls everyone Sparky—which gets confusing.

*

Colton jumping sideways over an orange pylon, again and again, thighs on fire.

"What's a craniac?"

Zev sighs. "My parents are biologists who study cranes."

"They teach cranes how to migrate. They're 'avian aviators.'"

"Not anymore. My mom used to fly a light, one-person aircraft to show young cranes the route to Florida—"

"But too many of them were getting sucked into the propeller."

Zev scowls. "Nice. No. But the chicks were becoming too reliant on humans, missing out on actual bird parenting."

"Deadbeats."

"Even with the robes and beaks?"

Colton wants an explanation.

Another sigh. "They wear these long white robes and fake beaks around the chicks to try to lessen the chances of imprinting."

"And you mean that didn't work?"

"Chicks, man…"

"This is supposed to be march," Slava says after the Short-handed Quintet finishes playing the third movement of the Brahms. He sings the main theme and high-steps around the practice room. "It sounds like your army gets tired of march then drinks a water and is refreshed."

*

Colton rolling a wooden dowel down his forearms, catching it in the air with both hands before it can fall to the ground.

Lunges.

VOGLER is stitched into the cuff of his new glove, and Colton tries to read it with touch like Braille. His name seen in this context is newly novel—he remembers back to the Blackhawks jersey he got as a kid, customized with his last name and what was then his lucky number, seventeen. We get so used to our names, but once in a while we're reminded of everything a name ties us to—and excludes us from. *I'm a Vogler. I am one who vogles, one who birds, a Birdy birder.*

Most goalies wear number one, or somewhere in the range of thirty to thirty-five, so he hasn't been number seventeen since he moved back between the pipes as a peewee. They've handed out practice jerseys for the first day of Bell and Bucket, half the guys in white, half in maroon. Colton's continued to receive signs that he has nothing to worry about—including the fact that they've given him the number one jersey. Pettit next to him got fifty-six.

As with the alumni room, the locker room is not quiet, despite the nerves that most of these guys must be wrestling. The freshmen especially think that falling silent will single them out from the herd, cause them to be left behind for dead. From a few weeks of Captain's Practice, Colton has a good idea of who's got a shot and who doesn't. It's hard to say what's sadder, the resignation on the faces of the guys who know they're getting cut, or the desperation of the ones on the bubble. No, worst is the confidence, fake or real, those new guys pretending they've already gotten the nod.

"Why *Driftless?*"

"The Driftless Region, or Paleozoic Plateau, escaped glaciation during the last ice age." Ben's tone makes it clear that every Driftless kid has this line drilled into their heads in grade school. "Hence our towering bluffs and deep river valleys." He also just showed he could pass as straight if he wanted to.

"Yeah, not even the glaciers wanted to visit."

"And soon the entire world will be *drift*-less." Zev crunches an ice cube.

"Okay, enough out of you."

"If you catch my..."

"Don't do it!"

"Drift."

"You're walking home."

"And we here at Driftless are doing our part to combat the iceberg menace. Utah has the World's Greatest Snow, for now, but we have the World's Greatest Fracking Sand."

"Fracking? Is this *Battlestar Gallactica*?"

"No, dipshit, hydraulic fracturing."

"Oh, okay. What makes your sand so good?"

"It's like normal sand, except even smaller."

"How small?"

"Extremely small. Almost painfully small."

"Do you know hashtag music note?" Slava asks The Plague.

"Huh?"

"Do you know what happens when you hashtag the music note?"

"I don't know what you're asking."

"What is *this* tic-tac-toe mean?" He stabs The Plague's score with his finger.

"That's a sharp."

"And what does sharp mean?"

"Up a half step."

"Hashtag-*then-do-it*."

Colton's not so confident as to wear his new goal pads. They're glorious but they're stiff as boards—and he doesn't want to repay the favoritism he's being shown by tripping over his feet for three days. They might be playing it up to scare the new guys, but Colton's heard there's *a lot* of skating at Bell and Bucket. He figures he's safe in his new blocker and glove, though—especially because he's been wearing the glove for hours on end while lying in bed, tossing a tennis ball into the air and catching it over and over. It was tough to squeeze at first, but he's also been tying it up with a skate lace whenever he's not using it, sitting on it while doing homework. A Vogler family story is that he'd slept with his first goalie glove for a week after receiving it. This new stuff is drop-dead sexy, but so far he's restrained himself from taking it to bed with him.

Whenever he gets new gear, part of him is reluctant to wear it, to kick-off its gradual transformation into a sweaty, history-heavy thing.

"Nice lid, Sparky," Sparky says as Colton takes his mask out of its bag. "I hope Drill Man's ready for drills."

Now, his helmet he's *definitely* wearing. Colton had dusted off whatever feeble artistic skills had been lying dormant since his Plumage days, producing a few mockups before dialing Al Johansson, sketches he destroyed after seeing what the master produced. On one side of the mask, Mega Man and his dog, Rush, are sleek in action poses, maroon and white from being armed with Drill Man's drills. The other side of the helmet pays homage to 8-bit graphics with a scene of Mega Man fighting the boss. *Driftless* across the neck guard. On the back plate

of the helmet, the gray NES control pad. His sticks had arrived too, more than he could break in two or three years, Vogler likewise printed on the shaft.

Twenty in a row, wall then floor.

Colton flipping Gumby over his back, arms locked together.

"The real question is, what qualifies a merchant to call themselves a cheese emporium?"

"Places which the traders of one country had reserved for their business interests within the territory of another country," Charlie reads off her phone.

"Makes me think of a Cheese Road where caravans from all the great cheese-producing countries know they can safely reach southwest Wisconsin. You know, Italy, Mexico, Greece…"

"Buffalo, New York."

"Buffalo, New York."

"I still think the crenelated barbican is a little overkill."

Charlie knows lots of good words.

"You gotta protect that cheese."

"Cheese siege."

Oh, he's got one. "In case of an escalade, dump the boiling hot queso."

Charlie laughs, catches herself, goes back to unimpressed.

Out on the ice, they skate clockwise around the rink, Lehmann leading them through warm-up stretches. One leg down and back, low to the ice, between blue lines. One knee up to the chest. Stick held behind the back, twisting at the waist to each side. Skating drills are harder for goalies, but Colton's always been agile enough in twenty extra pounds of gear. He should have gotten his skates sharpened though.

There are no parents in the stands, a tryouts rule spread by word of mouth. Except Stoner's dad—but, well, the rink's named after him. Luckily his son's good enough that there's no chatter of him buying a spot on the team as well. The Big Show is up there too, clipboard in hand.

Fast between whistles.

The sheer number of guys on the ice is intimidating—and a logistical problem for Lehmann. Six tendies, all of whom Colton has seen play at least once at Captain's Practice. Gumby's the best for sure, but new Vaughn pads (Mark Schwer) is close. He'd be the starter at any Illinois school.

A triple whistle ends their last sprint, and Colton's legs are already burning. Maybe that's the tons of skating he was warned about. Lehmann brings them all down to one end of the rink, and he's carrying a five-gallon bucket in his hand.

"Welcome to Bell and Bucket. This is the bell." He takes a cowbell out of the bucket and drops it on top of the near net. "If we skate you too hard and you need to get off the ice for a drink of water or to look for your balls, ring this bell first"—he demonstrates how to ring a bell—"so we don't think you're missing and send out a search party." *Lehmann's terms*, his teammates call the assistant coach's bluntness. The bucket adds the sound of a kick drum as it hits the ice. "That's the bucket. Because every year a few people do more than just sweat."

Colton hitting the racquetball against the wall. With the side of the racquet.

Colton in love.

11

"Have you beaten it yet?"

"I thought I did." Ben's still jerking his hands around. "I beat this guy who looked like Dr. Wily but wasn't Dr. Wily, but then Dr. Wily appeared and escaped in his ship and there's this whole nother fortress."

Leo is sitting next to Ben on the couch, holding a controller. That it's not plugged in doesn't keep the kid from pushing buttons and imitating his brother's gesticulations.

"*Mega Man 4*'s the hardest."

"Where you off to all sporty?"

"First practice."

Mega Man dies, and Ben looks up from the television. Leo smacks his forehead with his palm, lets his hand run down his face like a raw egg.

Colton says, "Heart monitors should use that sound when a patient flatlines."

Ben has a weird expression on his face, maybe lingering jealousy or regret that he doesn't play. "Congrats on making the team."

"Thanks. I wasn't great in tryouts, so I still need to prove myself."

Ben glances at his brother, wanting to take the conversation in a different direction. Then he changes his mind. "I'm sure you will."

Passing through the kitchen, he's intercepted by Alma. "Good luck tonight, Colton. We're so proud of you!"

The Dr. Wily music has resumed, but Colton wonders if Ben is fuming over his mom's fawning.

"We're back at the *beginning*!" Leo yells.

Alma puts an arm around Colton's shoulder. "If you need a ride home, call me. Any time of night."

"Okay." How come? "Thanks."

He's unaccustomed to walking out the door for hockey practice unburdened by a heavy bag of gear—Driftless is the first team he's played for that has a locker room no one else is allowed to use. He's most excited about wearing his new pads for the first time tonight, but a little worried he'll move like he's got on the Halloween costume Leo's been assembling for weeks, your basic cardboard box robot.

Climbing out of his car, Colton can hear the thump of bass shaking Steiner.

ICE SURFACE, NO GEAR reads a sign on the door.

"You know what this is about?" Colton asks Gunnar, the best freshman to make the team. Goalies appreciate forwards who play both ways, and this kid always hustles back-checking.

Gunnar nods. "My older brother played for the team."

All the rink lights are on, and the lobby furniture's been moved onto the ice surface. There are coolers of beer and a keg, a couple long tables, one of them stacked with pizza boxes, the others hosting a beer-pong tourney. All four sides of the scoreboard are showing the movie *Miracle*, muted.

"Cool! So that's why tonight's players-only." His pads' maiden voyage can wait another night.

"Yeah, real cool."

The team cheers as Colton steps onto the ice, taking careful steps so he doesn't suffer a humiliating fall—while going quick enough that he won't get called a pussy. Now playing "Thunderstruck," a song the Glaciers warmed up to.

"Drink this," Hoodie says to Gunnar, poking a hole in the bottom of a beer can with a Swiss Army knife.

Gunnar doesn't know why there's beer trickling onto the ice at his feet, but he puts his mouth to the puncture.

"What're you doing? Shotgun it, Shotgunnar." Hoodie's been drinking for a while.

He shows the freshman how with his own can, and soon both stomped cans join the rest of the party detritus littering the ice: paper plates and wadded napkins and red Solo cups and crushed ping pong balls and pizza crusts.

Colton expects a smile when Gunnar finishes the beer, but the freshman's still not having much fun. Probably these young guys who've never had booze will be hearing the words "acquired taste" the whole night.

Stoner presents Colton with the silicon tube of a beer bong, climbs up on a table, can in hand. Colton hasn't drunk a drop since the fun sweatpants nightmare.

Down the hole!

He's pleased with how fast he makes it vanish. Not a single cough.

"You're not done." Stoner is handed a bottle of vodka by Protein.

Colton's mind revisits Shane's car wrapped around a tree on a lonely country road.

"I'm not going to pour the whole bottle in."

Colton puts the tube in his mouth and closes his eyes. This time he doesn't hold back coughing. Three shots?

One drink per hour, Colton knows his stuff, so no more

for the next... three hours and fifty-nine minutes and he'll be good to go.

New recruits! Pettit and Beast and Ober. Ober's a junior, played Graveyard the last two years. Colton's a cheerer this time, a singer of "Danger Zone," a prompt pusher of booze to newcomers.

Pizza beckons, tendrils orange and greasy finding his nostrils and tugging–

But he's administered three more drinks—Jell-O shot, tequila shot, something else—before he can take a single bite. Okay, no more drinks and you're one-hundred-percent fine to drive home at... three a.m. See, sober enough to do complicated math no problem. And in three seconds he'll have a stomach full of food. Sober enough to know food keeps you sober. What food does is it soaks up the booze, changes all the math about drinks plotted on x-axes over time.

"Why is *calculus* required?" Colton asks a guy he doesn't recognize. When am I gonna use calculus?

"They take math and science very seriously at Driftless."

Of course they do. As they should! Colton acknowledges stranger/teammate's reply with a thoughtful head bob.

Colton plucks the plastic dollhouse table from a pizza bullseye, chucks the inscrutable object to the ice. Zamboni will have to do a lap on shithead setting. Pepperonis are red buttons you push to dispense deliciousness. And the tip, ten out of ten surveyed Coltons agree, is the best of all pizza slice bites.

Alright, listen up, God booms.

The music cuts out. Colton stuffs the acute angle into his mouth.

"*I trust everyone's good and lubed up.*" It's Protein, sitting in the scorekeepers bench. "*You're gonna need it. Let me start by echoing the Big Show's greeting from the D-Bag room, back when we were all so young and innocent. Welcome to Driftless Dynasty Hockey.*"

Colton chooses chewing over cheering.

"*And to that greeting, I'd like to extend a special welcome to our fresh blood: take off all your clothes.*"

Another big cheer.

It's a joke, so why are Gunnar and Pettit already pulling off their shirts? Guys, stop—they're just trying to see who'll fall for it.

A word intrudes on this players-only practice. *Hazing.*

Colton had never hazed or been hazed. True, the guys were hard on him when he practiced with the Glaciers as an eighth grader, teed up slapshots when he wasn't looking. He filled water bottles every game freshman year. At Riverview he had to get dressed in the bathroom.

None of that was hazing. They couldn't haze Colton—he was the starting goalie as a freshman.

Horror stories flash through his mind. Elephant walks, wet cookie, branding.

Other tendrils seek Colton's attention, are trying to wend their way through all the calculus. You're the starting goalie here too. You're the new stud, and you're a senior. Yeah they're psyched about this rite of passage they've got going, but this isn't something that can be taken offline with the captains later.

"*Ober, I'm afraid you're a freshman tonight,*" Protein says over the loudspeaker. "*You too, Birdy.*"

Colton goes from the verge of taking a stand to taking off his pants. Why? Because he's here. He left his home and his friends and a team that didn't haze him for a chance at D1 puck. Because it's a team-building exercise, that's all. Because it won't be that bad.

And because he's drunk.

No.

Because he's already marked.

No.

It's because he wants to.

God: *"Too bad, Pettit, a little hair down there would keep you warm."*

Pulling down his boxer briefs, Colton has a flashback to squirts when some brave trailblazers started showering after practice. Quentin Bonk was the first, and Colton showered the next practice. That was the last time he'd felt this exposed. A new concern: don't get hard. It's not the naked guys that makes him worried—more the sense of exhibitionism. Lucky he'd jerked off after school. A flashback to more recent showers. How come every guy on this team's uncut?

He gasps as his bare feet touch the ice for the first time.

"Gauntlet." And all the guys wearing clothes grab sticks that Colton hadn't noticed were lying on the ice, form two lines from the neutral zone down to the hashmarks.

Gunnar, out to prove that he's also the best freshman at getting hazed, takes off in a trot as his teammates pound their sticks on the ice. Zilch deals him a swat on his butt cheek with the blade of his stick. Gunnar winces, does a little skip, but continues down the gauntlet, a crimson blotch blooming on his skin. Not every guy hits him, maybe one in three, and they're not putting everything into it—but Gunnar's bleeding by the time he reaches the end.

"Fly through, Birdy!" his backup calls out, waving a Brian's in the air. It's one of Colton's new sticks.

"Get through this, boys, and you'll be knee deep in pussy by opening night."

Colton takes off, running stiff legged so he won't slip. That would make his night worse, somehow. Enter gauntlet.

Christ!

He knows he can't take another swat, but his legs keep propelling him forward. *Cammo. Zilch. Grimmer. Horse.* Last one, *Gumby*, you fucker. Gumby, who put everything into it.

Gasping, a fish that jumped too far, he joins Gunnar in the goal crease. The freshman is hugging himself, shivering. Colton wants to speak comfort to the kid, but the first thing that comes to him doesn't make much sense. *I'm sorry for doing this to you.* No, makes too much sense.

His feet are turning the same color as the goal crease, and what they say isn't true; blood doesn't so much bounce on ice—it's more like an oil and water thing.

The Goalkeeper's Privileged Area, this section of the ice is designated in the USA Hockey Rulebook.

After all the guys have made the run, the Driftless defensive zone resembles a crime scene.

Is a crime scene, Colton reminds himself.

"*Lie face down on the ice.*"

Will be that bad, Colton edits his hope. Worse.

"*Keep your heads down. For the next phase of players-only practice, your teammates are arranging what we like to call 'the contraptions.' Here's what's going to happen. You'll lie there for three long minutes. It will be very uncomfortable. You're not gonna get frostbite, but your bantams will shrink down to the size of mites. After three minutes, all five of you will try to get your peewees to squirt. The booze won't help—you might not yet know about the phenomenon of whiskey dick. I don't want to ruin the surprise, but I should let you know, the loser has to clean up.*"

Colton is no longer relieved he jacked off today. He can hear his teammates scrambling around, sliding objects on the ice. It's too late to exert whatever power he might have still possessed when he was wearing clothes and wasn't bleeding from his ass. Reaching orgasm seems a bestiary description of some magical creature's special powers.

"Pettit, quit grinding your hairless crotch into the ice."

Charlie.

Colton stops shivering. Charlie LaBoda.

It might be his body giving up trying to regulate its temperature—or it might be the realization that this night will soon be over, and that his reward for surviving it will be asking Charlie on a date. These horrors will mean he's earned more than just a spot on a hockey team.

"Alright boys, stand up."

Colton looks down at his body. His skin is the color of a nipple, and his dick is every weak goal he's ever given up. A new concern: get hard. He steals a glance at his competitors, and nobody is fairing any better. Except Gunnar, a complete player. They're all trying to massage life back into themselves, and Colton joins in. His teammates start hitting their sticks on the ice in unison. The stands are dark and empty.

Arranged on the ice in front of them, pink objects. But the ice crystals clinging to Colton's eyelids blur and starburst the blotches featureless.

Do you believe in miracles?

12

"You're quiet today."

Colton gives his neighbor thirty percent of a smile. This blonde girl goes cat-ass every time Colton's around. Too bad for hot Erika—Charlie's also in this section of calculus.

"Yep, pretty quiet," he echoes back.

Class is about to let out, and Mr. Lasshoff is handing back a quiz that Colton isn't eager to see.

"Guess you're nervous about the big game?" Her eyes drift down to Colton's maroon home jersey.

Wearing jerseys to school on game days, another Driftless Hockey tradition. The other guys are strutting around all macho, but Colton is more like a little kid playing dress-up—since goalie jerseys have to be about XXL to fit over their upper body pads.

"That must be it." Colton turns to face forward en route to showing Erika his shoulder.

"I'll be there," Erika adds. "At the game."

"Cool." Colton's quiz appears on his desk. Ignoring the blur of red ink on white in his periphery, he shoves it deep into his backpack.

"Connor's having a party afterwards. His parents are gone. Did you hear?"

"I don't know who Connor is."

"Yes you do. Green shirt, sitting over there. I'm sure you're invited."

"Depends on whether or not we win."

"Why?" She smiles, her teeth CGI. "You're either celebrating or drowning your sorrows."

He thinks about telling this perfect girl why he hasn't been in the mood to drink much lately. He gives a little laugh guessing how she'd react, which she misreads as a response to her joke.

"We'll see." He maintains his smile, hoping she'll release him from conversation so he can catch Charlie before the bell rings.

He sits to the right of Charlie in the back of the room, a position he secures by racing to calculus every day from German. The creep has been known to lay his head down on an outstretched arm, feigning exhaustion, squinting his eyelids open enough to trace the silhouette of her blurry profile in whatever afternoon light is coming through the windows. Today, as usual, she's using these free minutes to scribble in an elastic-banded notebook, gunmetal in color.

"What are you writing?"

"Poetry."

"What about?"

"What else? Birds."

"If you're ever looking for a reader..."

"If I was looking for readers," she says, but doesn't stop writing, "I wouldn't write poetry." It's like she's reading aloud what she's writing as she writes it, and it just happens to answer the question being asked her.

"Well, if you ever decide—"

She puts down her pen. "Why? Are you a poetry fan, Colton?"

"Sorry, you can go back to writing if you want."

"No, we're talking now. Go ahead, talk at me."

"I'm having a lot of trouble in German, and Ben says you're pretty much fluent."

"So... you need a tutor?" She doesn't sound thrilled by the prospect.

"I could pay you." Oops. The study session/date he'd schemed has wasted no time taking on a prostitution vibe.

"Here's one free of charge: *Wie einige Evolutionsbremsen es schaffen sich selbst zu ertragen, bleibt mir ein Rätsel.*"

"Yeah, see I don't know what that means."

"Incentive to learn." The bell rings. "There, I helped."

She clasps the notebook to her chest and hurries out of the room.

Patience. School year's young.

No. Birdy, you've been *miserable* the past few weeks.

Colton has long held the suspicion that love is a myth propagated by the bored. He remains skeptical about the whole cloud-nine business—since he more often imagines Charlie beating him with a baseball bat than he does the two of them picnicking or connecting mouths or laughing. If this is love, humans are a more fucked up creature than he's been led to believe.

But he knows his brain might not be working right these days. He's still stretched out on needle ice, needing faulty logic to get him through that hazy night. When he closes his eyes, the promise he made is his best defense against other invaders. He won't be able to focus on tonight's game if he doesn't make swifter progress than a minute of pre-bell banter.

He catches up to Charlie in the lobby by a big potted tree, says her name.

She turns to him, radiating discouragement. But it doesn't matter what she says. What's important is to have said it.

Okay, it does matter. But this is for him. Now he will ask Charlie LaBoda on a date.

"Are you coming to the game tonight?"

She shakes her head—at more than tonight's game.

"Charlie. I've been having a rougher time in Driftless than it might seem." Wrong direction. "I promised myself I was going to ask you on a date today. I think you're amazing–" Real poet, Vogler. "But I'd settle for– Please come to the game tonight."

She hesitates, and hope starts to peek out from hiding.

"I know you don't like all this sportsing–"

"It's not just hockey," she cuts him off. "Colton, I don't like you. Ben does, so I'm sure we'll hang out once in a while. But we won't be going on any dates."

The tree is a ficus. There's a little sign on a stick. *Ficus benjamina.* Also known as the Weeping Fig.

She's prepared a little sneer for Colton's hockey jersey. "I'm sorry being top shit at Driftless isn't as much fun as you'd planned."

Then she's gone—and Colton is left trying to come up with a response long after its cue has passed. He's surprised the ficus hasn't withered from that wintry gust. Its leaves need dusting. Colton rubs one of them clean. Weep on, Weeping Fig.

For half a second he tries to play the part of a blockheaded jock who doesn't care about that girl anyway. But that's not going to work. That never works for Colton.

He's angry and confused and ice crystals are clinging again to his eyelids. He's somehow accidentally allowed himself to become convinced of something: that Charlie is perfect. No, not in that dopey angelic way that flies off once you realize they're humans; he's fallen into that trap before. Rather, Charlie is already an adult, bored with all this high school inanity. Her smile and her scowl both are objective evaluations. And with what he thinks about her and with what he now knows she's thought about him all along…

"Fuck you," he directs at himself in a whisper.

He doesn't just want to look suave with this girl hanging off his arm. He's not just willing to tolerate her clinginess in exchange for less and less frequent moments of feeling okay. He wants to be Charlie—for there to be no separation between them. For them to be indistinguishable.

Colton has a problem.

"Fuck you," he says louder, again at himself.

He reaches for another ficus leaf. But there, lying on the tiled wall circling the base of the tree, an elastic-banded notebook. He must have missed her slamming it down in annoyance, missed her missing it in her desperation to distance herself from this oblivious jock. Even in the aftermath of such a scene, he respects this girl enough to return the notebook without so much as sampling its direct access to her mind.

For a second or two, he believes that's true.

After stopping for a drink of water, Colton steps into the bathroom to make sure his eyes aren't red and to see if he's not as cute as he remembers.

Nope, still cute, notwithstanding his barber's bib of a jersey.

A stoner offers him a Visine bottle, but Colton waves it off.

If anything, spurned love has given his face a tragic, almost consumptive air. She could have just said no, said he was sweet, made up an excuse like any non-psychotic person does in such situations. Maybe there's hope to be wrung from the fervor of her rejection. Indifference is the real opposite of love, you know—so what he has to do is find a way to positively charge her repugnance of him

"Seriously, bro," the stoner urges the Visine.

Colton accepts it this time. Why on earth did he think that forcing the question would allow him to focus on tonight's game?

He closes himself in a stall to peruse the gunmetal notebook. He snaps the elastic like a waistband. Unlooping it will break a hermetic seal. Is that the logic behind this feature, one last chance to change your mind?

Colton makes the elastic slacken. He's hoping for a tortured elegy titled "Why I Have To Pretend I Don't Love You," but what he encounters is even more surprising. It's true he has little experience with poetry, but this is more like… schematics. There are aerial maps, landscape photographs, many diagrams of a lumpy sickle moon object. *Allies* and their email addresses. A list of phone numbers for machine rental places, price comparisons for rebar, plywood, truckloads of concrete.

The only words that approach poetry are on the very first page, block letters underlined twice: GATEWAY TO THE MID-WEST.

13

He'd forgotten his parents existed. Continue to exist in his absence. True, he talks to them on the phone every few days, but this postgame dinner is the first real reminder of their corporeality since he said goodbye in August.

"Aren't you hungry, dear?"

He's been picking at his sirloin. He saws off an extra large triangle and stuffs it in his mouth, a way to both address the question and avoid talking. They're at a grill downtown called Strassers, an upscale kitsch place with lots of Driftless and Badgers memorabilia on the walls, Packers and Brewers peppered in. A few of his teammates' families are at other tables.

"Big game not as big as you planned?" Flynn Rentschler asks, downing his second pint and motioning for the waiter to bring him a third.

His parents swap the same side-eye they'd swapped after the game when the Rentschlers insinuated themselves on these dinner plans with their son.

"Maybe that's it." Colton had failed to forecast this particular downside of backstopping the best team in the state. "Sorry you guys made the drive for a blowout."

"Hey, a shutout's a shutout," his dad says.

"That was a nice glove save you made in the third."

"Shot was from the blue line."

"Through traffic."

"Tomah's one of the worst teams around," Flynn says. "You'll get your chance. Wait'll we play Middleton."

"Are you making friends with the guys on the team?"

The sector of ice where his teammates had grouped after the buzzer to pat him on his mask was the same *Privileged Area* where he'd been shivering naked two weeks before. Again, he swallows the urge to blurt it out, startle the table for the rest of their lives, upset his mother's vision of this orderly, miracle-strewn world. The red juice pooling on his plate in the shape of a goal crease reveals a slight slant to the table, to the building, to the world—and Colton starts to feel dizzy.

"Yeah, lots of friends."

"Any plans for tonight?"

Colton decides to get fucked up. "I'm going out with some of my new friends." Whatever's farthest from this dinner's forced politeness.

"Where? Is it a party?"

"Guy named Connor's house."

"Is there gonna be booze there?" His dad's question doubles as a jab at Flynn's drinking.

"Connor Oettinger," Alma intercepts the question. She's spent half the dinner in the bathroom. "I know his parents very well, and I assure you they wouldn't tolerate that. I've also made it clear to Colton that he can call us if he's ever in a situation where a driver's been drinking."

Colton remembers Alma's offer to come pick him up after the players-only practice. Why's she covering for him?

"We appreciate it. But we also don't want him putting himself in those kinds of situations."

"You can stay at our house if you want," Flynn says, "make sure he gets back by curfew. Except our extra bedroom is kind of spoken for."

"I'm sorry if we're being uptight." Colton's mom reaches for her son's hand. "We're still trying to get used to our little man being so far away. If you say the party will be safe, that's good enough for us."

He wants to hug his parents and show them where it hurts.

He wants to ask them not to visit anymore.

There are either ice cubes or shards of glass floating in the swimming pool, but none of the nude swimmers seem to care. Guys are lighting fireworks on the Oettinger's tennis court amidst a game of dodgeball while Connor's pack of semi-feral mutts tries to catch any and all things in their jaws. With all the explosions and the choral music blaring from outdoor speakers, it's a good thing there's significant acreage between the Oettingers and their neighbors. Pettit has taken a break from asking everyone at the party for weed to rearrange the Halloween witches and black cats and pumpkins into compromising positions, sticky with cobwebs. Through the windows, Colton can see people inside playing pool or darts and riff-tracking a documentary about that guy who lived in Alaska with grizzly bears for thirteen summers and then got eaten. The projection screen takes up a whole wall, movie theater-sized.

"You think the best guys made the team?"

Has Colton been talking to this kid? His plan was to get shit-faced, but he arrived so late that everyone's inebriation was a super effective PSA against the whole idea of self-destruction. He's only had five or six drinks.

"I mean, you're good." The kid sloshes beer into a planter of candy corn mums. "From what I saw, you're a good goalie. And you didn't know there were already good goalies here. How could you have known that?"

"Do you play?"

The kid's astonished. "I'm Mark Schwer."

Oh, the JV goalie who thought he was going to get the nod.

But why freaky choral music at a party? A Halloween playlist? He recognizes the new track, *Denn Alles Fleisch* from Brahms's Requiem. Someone's idea of a joke.

"In this town it doesn't matter how good you are," Maroon Vaughns keeps talking. "It matters which side of Driftless you live on. If your last name was on the first state champ roster. Graaskamp and Ober's the only exceptions—"

"Easy there, Schwer," Protein butts in. He takes the kid by his shoulders. "I think you've guzzled too much booze tonight, and you should go crash or find a ride home." He snaps his fingers in front of Schwer's eyes. "You hear me, buddy?"

"I'm gonna go find food."

"Good idea." Protein nabs Schwer's beer. "And a big glass of water." Once Maroon Vaughns is gone, Protein downs the beer and tosses the cup into the mums. "Graveyard guys always talking shit at parties. How you holding up, Birddog?"

"I might head out soon."

"If you don't fuck one of these girls that's advertising, the guys are gonna start wondering about you."

"No they're not."

"You're desperate for that girl with the boy's name, right? What's her name? Henry?"

"Charlie."

"Charlie, that's right. Sure she's not a dyke?"

It's not really anger rising up in Colton. Jealousy? What's there to be jealous about?

Protein getting to say her name. Any human talking to Charlie or holding her image in their mind or brushing by her in the hallway oblivious. Anyone or anything she gives her attention to, even non-sentient objects—of late, Colton has found his sphere of envy expanding to encompass them all.

"You know what gets an uninterested girl's attention real quick, Birdy? Go after her ex best friend." Protein points to a blonde girl talking to a group of slack-jawed suitors.

As soon as he sees her, she sees him. She raises her eyebrows and takes a sip of Diet Coke. Then back to the doofus paramours.

"Or if that doesn't interest you," Protein says so close to his ear Colton can feel his breath, "I can fetch... the contraption."

He flashes Protein a look that all guys know: the joking just went too far. This look is bound up in a whole code of awfulness, its power residing in the infrequency of its use, a handful of times over the course of a life. A tacit understanding that must be obeyed. It is, by habit, poorly deployed.

Protein doesn't obey. "The last person who touched your cock was... Pettit? How long do you want that streak to go on?"

This body will self-destruct in T-minus two minutes.

Walking over to the girl, Colton's had enough alcohol that he doesn't worry about how to trip into the conversation. "Hi Erika. I was hoping I'd see you here."

It takes her a second to notice him.

"I'm not Erika."

No, she isn't.

"I'm so sorry." Maybe he's had more booze than he thought.

"Well, we are both... girls?"

"I'm such an idiot."

"I'm Greta," she says.

"Colton."

"I know who you are. I was at the game tonight."

Her attendees, disheartened, are starting to scatter.

"Not much of a game."

He wants to interrogate this tall, ponytailed girl about her history with Charlie, the drama of their falling out. She knew Charlie as a kid, safeguarded her hopes and secrets.

"Yeah, everyone on the team scored—except you. I play soccer, and in soccer the goalies are either the geniuses of the team or they're super deviant."

"I think I've proven here tonight I'm not a genius."

"What makes a person want to be a goalie? Aren't you the cock blockers of the sports world?"

"Big equipment."

"Oh really?"

"Wanna see?"

She rolls her eyes. "Let's have a conversation first so I don't feel like a total hockey whore." Her eyes drift up. "How tall are you?"

A dollhouse, bisected so it can't hide its drama from the moonlight.

He's woken up in a bed that's too small for a teenager, let alone two.

Lots of pink. Lots of *Frozen* sisters.

Colton's head doesn't hurt too bad. He turns over to inspect Greta, and thank God it hadn't been the beer. He'd never fucked angry before, never been with an athletic girl. Both sides had been guilty of yellow-card-worthy infractions.

Red card, rather. She'd bled. It had surprised only one of them.

Might complicate things.

Then he remembers, he's lying next to Charlie LaBoda's ex-BFF.

Turns out the last puke train of the night might not have left the station yet. In the dollhouse bedroom, a princess sits in a chair facing the corner. Time out.

Well, if Charlie won't put out–

No. He's no good at that shithead character. Try again.

In one of the dollhouse's bedrooms, a smaller dollhouse. Colton squints away the darkness.

His phone is awake as well. Must have been the buzz woke him up.

A text from Nate. He'd sort of forgotten Nate existed too.

His thumb pulls up the picture of a pink shriveled golem.

Proud to announce the arrival of Luka Charles Mayry! 6 lbs 7 oz Mom and baby are both healthy and heroic. Miss you, Crouton!! Let's talk soon about all your feats of strength!!!

The mattress is too small for Colton to pull himself into a fetal position, too small for him to cry without shaking the whole bed. So he crawls down to the carpeted, sound-dampening floor.

14

The floors are shiny linoleum and the air antiseptic, but brown water stains blossom on the drop ceiling. They are the weeds of this place, threatening the wallpaper's repeating floral patterns, the framed prints on the walls that appear to be mere magnifications of what they conceal, the plastic arrangements on ornamental tables that have managed to jut forth into three-dimensionality. The synthesized string muzak is preparing the facility's ancient population for the most saccharine of heavens. Everything is designed so that it can be sprayed and wiped clean of bodily fluids at a moment's notice.

It's called Penthe Meadows.

Shane lives here.

It's bad enough old people get put into these places, Colton considers. At least they have a lifetime of memories to occupy their hours.

Of course, Shane has harder hardships than wallpaper—if he's even aware enough to regret his surroundings.

But still, that wallpaper…

Okay, Colton's anxious. It's as if he hasn't grown up at all since those visits to Opa in Woodland Mews, worried whether or not this would be one of the days his dad's dad's dad recognized him. Now he regrets it, how seldom he visited his great grandfather, but those quiet hours were always a depressing reminder of what waits for us at the end. Or, for Shane, pretty close to the beginning.

Alma is there at the desk, carrying a big bag that must contain supplies for teaching.

"Hedy," she says to a nurse, "this is Colton. He's here to visit Shane."

"Isn't that nice of you." The nurse's eyes disappear when she smiles. She writes Colton's name in a binder. "What made you think of paying Shane a visit?"

"I'm the, um, new goalie on the hockey team, and I guess I was feeling... Well, it seemed like a good thing to do."

"Colton has been a *big* help around the house with Leo."

"Shane may or may not really know you're there, but I tend to think he's appreciative in his own way. He's been alert this morning, already has one visitor."

"Well *she'll* have to leave at eleven when his lesson starts," Alma says.

They walk down the hallway, past an accumulation of walkers and wheelchairs facing a TV. Songbirds in a large glass... aquarium? *Air*arium? Whatever it's called, the birds are singing their little heads off in joy or panic. The windows look out on a garden with a pond and a gazebo and a putting green, paved paths winding around amoeboid flowerbeds. From an open door, the clatter of silverware heralds a beefy lunch.

"One thing I wanted to mention to you, Colton—it might be best if you don't bring up hockey."

"You think it would make him upset I got his position?"

"No. That it exists, the sport he'll never play again."

Alma knocks on a door that's already ajar, pushes it open. Colton's similarities with Shane are so numerous that he's absurdly ready to confront his wasted self in the aftermath of a devastating car accident. *Don't stare at the boy in the wheelchair.* But it turns out that it won't be a problem—because sitting across from Shane is Charlie.

She's as surprised as Colton. His phone buzzes in his pocket, and he's sure that it's Greta sensing her new boyfriend is in the same room with her old enemy. Something is starting to make sense to Colton, Charlie's hostility to the idea of dating him.

"Time's up, Charlie."

"Colton—" Charlie starts, ignoring Alma. "What— Can I talk to you for a minute?"

The two go out into the hallway, far enough away that Alma can't hear. Colton positions himself so that he'll be talking to calculus-class Charlie, framed by light from the windows.

"What are you doing here?" Charlie asks.

"Visiting Shane. You guys are friends?"

"Yeah, we're friends." Behind Charlie, the sun stokes the flame of an oak tree's autumn orange. "I appreciate you giving my notebook to Ben. Did you look at what was inside?"

Colton's reluctance is answer enough.

"Colton, at this point it's unlikely that those plans are still secret, but I need you to not talk to anyone about them."

He didn't know the plans were plans, doesn't know what secret he's keeping, but he doesn't want to admit as much.

"No problem."

She holds his gaze for a second to decide whether or not she thinks he's lying.

"I promise!"

"Colton, it was wrong of me to say that I don't like you. I don't know how I feel about you. The problem is that I don't trust you— No, that I can't trust you. Not yet."

The jokes that enter his head are so stupid he has to be real for a second: "What can I do to prove myself trustworthy?"

"Keeping your word about this, about my notebook, would

help."

"Why'd you say it was poetry?"

She smiles. "Because that's what it is."

Hey, happy fool—*snap snap*—remember Greta? Couldn't you have waited one whole day? Colton tells himself that maybe Charlie won't find out, but he knows it's a miracle she hasn't already.

"You're not going to blow stuff up, are you?"

"Not with a bomb." She takes a few steps back, puts one hand in the air. "Nice job on the shutout."

When Colton returns to the room, Alma's face is ice.

Shane doesn't give any perceptible reaction at all. His black hair fails to cover a hook-shaped scar above his right ear. His head is tilted down at an angle, his shoulders hunched, and it turns out that they're not very convincing doppelgängers after all.

"Hi Shane, my name's Colton…Vogler." He's not sure if he should be speaking louder or more slowly than usual, or if it matters. Alma warms, gives Colton a thumbs up. "I'm staying with the Rentschlers right now, and I asked Alma if I could keep you company during your session today. I know it's tough to respond, so don't worry about that." He takes the seat still warm from Charlie. "I'm playing piano in a chamber group with a few of your friends. Zilch and CC, Stoner and The Plague. Blair, I mean. We're doing the Brahms Opus 34 right now. I think I'm keeping up okay, but they gripe about my articulation, that it's not as sensitive as yours. Or, as Slava put it, *You play piano like blacksmith making horseshoe.*"

"I'm going to run to the restroom real quick," Alma says. "You guys'll be okay?"

"Yeah, sure."

As soon as she leaves, Shane pulls his head upright and

looks Colton in the eyes. He holds his blinks longer than normal blinks.

"Alma said she didn't think I should talk to you about hockey, that it might make you sad. But I tried to imagine myself in your position—" You *are* in his position, you ass. "I know that's not possible, but I think she's wrong. Sorry if I'm the one who's wrong."

Shane makes a noise. Then he makes it louder, deep in his throat. He sounds distressed, but it's not distress. He holds eye contact with those long blinks.

"We won our first game. It was against Tomah, and yeah they're terrible. It was ten to zero early in the third. The Big Show told us if anyone scored number eleven he'd bring back Bell and Bucket. All the guys miss you.

"I heard you're a *Star Wars* fan—it must be tough not getting to go see the new one. Maybe they'll let me take you when it comes out in December. At the very least, I can bring it as soon as it's online. Maybe Charlie will come and we'll pop popcorn."

"Colton." Alma's in the doorway. She motions him into the hall. "I was thinking it might be best for you not to stick around for the session. I'm sure he appreciates seeing you, but I don't want him getting overstimulated."

"Yeah, whatever's best for Shane."

"There'll be more opportunities to talk to him. *Star Wars* is a great idea."

"Alma, I was wondering, Charlie and Shane must have been dating, right? At the time of the accident."

"Not that I know of." And why would that interest you? "Aren't you and Greta von Kempf kind of a thing?"

Colton tries to keep anything from registering on his face. How does Alma Rentschler know this bit of juicy gossip—

when Colton didn't even know Greta's last name? People who are things tend to be secure in such knowledge. Remember, von Kempf. Greta von Kempf.

"Maybe."

"I'd stick with Greta if I were you."

"Let me say goodbye to Shane real quick." He pokes his head inside the door. "I'm gonna take off, Shane. It was nice meeting you—Alma's worried I'll give you all the answers to the surprise pop quiz if I hang around any longer."

But Shane's head is back in its previous position, and he doesn't see Colton wave goodbye.

15

Twenty maroon bags are lined up on the sidewalk in front of Steiner, along with a couple big stick bags, puck bags, a cardboard box that contains their lunches, and a plastic bin of laces and tape and Dr. Zog's Sex Wax and other supplies they might need. A few guys are chatting or messing with their phones or taping their sticks. A few guys are jumping rope or stretching. Gumby is juggling. Cammo is taking a nap on his bag. The first line is playing keep away from Zilch's German Shepherd with their sticks and an orange street hockey ball. The dog's mouth/eye coordination makes Colton feel slow. It uses its paws too. Every time the dog wins the game, the players shout blame at one another. Then the dog growls as they try to pry the ball from its mouth and they have to get Zilch to yell *"Aus!"* Everyone is wearing maroon tracksuits, not those sweatshop CCMs that begin fraying immediately, but high-quality getups tailored by a shop in Driftless, their names and numbers on the left breast, white Ds superimposed over maroon Ds on the biceps of the tatted upperclassmen. The same maroon jacket that, along with a clipboard and an air of superiority, had first introduced Colton to Driftless in August at the Bensenville Edge.

"What's with the chessboards?" Colton asks Protein, pointing at a ragged cardboard box sticking out of a backpack.

"You'll see.

("*Aus!*")

Do you play?"

"Chess?" Do teenagers play chess? "I know how to."

"If that's your answer, you probably don't. Unless you're a ringer…"

"I'm probably not a ringer."

A cheer goes up—("Gerdy, *aus!*")—and Colton sees a bus appear from around the side of the rink. The bus isn't just for hockey, but it *is* just for their high school, *Driftless* spelled out in giant calligraphic letters down both sides. He'd been expecting to sit on cracked vinyl all the way to Fon du Lac, but this beast is more than a yellow school bus painted maroon. He can already tell it has a bathroom and comfortable seats and TV screens on the back of every headrest. The bus driver gets out and lifts up the luggage doors, helps the team load their bags on both sides.

As soon as they get in, there's a marker board Sparky's drawing brackets on. Guys are yelling out "Yep" or "You better believe it" or "Ten-four" or "Doom," their names filling out brackets according to a ranking system on a piece of paper Sparky keeps consulting.

"I'm out," Protein says, and the bus protests.

"This messes up the WHOLE SYSTEM, Sparky."

"Someone's gotta teach Birdy to play chess."

The bus sends up a hoot, agreeing that the excuse is a good one.

Before the bus has groaned to life, the board is unfolded on the armrest between Protein and Colton, the magnetic pieces shown where they go.

And, before the bus has exited the Driftless parking lot, Colton's king is dead.

By the time they reach the go-kart tracks and water slides and frozen custard shops of Wisconsin Dells, Colton has learned how to not get beaten in the first five moves. His personal best is fifteen. The Dells, only marginally pre-apocalyptic on a good day, is even sadder than normal because most of the attractions are closed for the season. The ski slopes are clinging to their green, but the trees have already put on their Halloween costumes.

The Plague is upset because he bitched last year about Lorna Doone cookies and now he has a sack lunch with nothing but Lorna Doones.

"You play chess like a tendy," Protein tells Colton. "Do you even know what goes on in the offensive zone?"

"The best offense is a good defense–"

"Checkmate."

Protein clears his side of the board and arranges the pawns in a square around the king. "This might look safe, but it's not. You're trapped. You have nowhere to go. Would you want your D all up in your shit like this?"

"Box defense on the penalty kill."

"Okay, then you're on penalty kill the whole game. Let's try again. This time, send pieces into my zone to fuck with me. Yeah, they're going to their deaths—but don't worry about that."

Cheers and groans fill the bus as another one bites the dust. ("*Aus!*")

The Plague is resorting to charity. Lorna Doones are not trading well on the market this trip.

"What's the deal with this? Does Driftless have a chess team?"

"Yeah, we've won nationals a bunch of times. Me and Sparky and Boots are on the team—none of these other fools are good enough, or they're musicians and their parents won't let them take on anything else."

The game commences, and Colton starts throwing knights and bishops down the board. He takes a pawn.

"Congratulations," Protein says. "You made me think."

"It wasn't on purpose."

"I know. But a rookie can make moves that trip you up cuz they don't know what they're doing."

"Yeah, sometimes I play terrible against bad hockey players. I've already anticipated three moves based on their body language, and they're just trying not to lose the puck. It's like trying to hit a changeup."

"No, it's like a baby with a hand grenade. All bets are off."

16

Heading toward his locker, Colton sees Greta's head periscope above the after-school dispersal. Heart pounding, he ducks into the men's bathroom.

More like the little boy's room—he knows you shouldn't break it off with a girl right after sleeping with her, but it's been tough etiquette to follow. Granted, he's supposed to have significant say in the matter, but his most recent attempt to counter Greta's advances resulted in immediate sex, a resetting of the clock.

Poor guy, he consoles his reflection in the mirror. *Poor, poor high school boy.*

But somebody's having a worse day than Colton. The closed stall door offers little privacy to the person puking their guts out. This isn't a one-and-done *that feels better* type thing. At this stage in the battle, the sick kid is pretty sure that capillaries are bursting in his brain and his GI tract is wrung out and his eyes are about to plunk into the porcelain. He has *nothing left to give,* he's doubtless begging. He'll found a new church if God gets him through this storm.

Now spitting, now muttering "Fuck everything," now the sound of toilet paper being unspooled.

Nope, not done yet.

Colton doesn't want to be here when the guy emerges, doesn't want to have to arrange his face into *We've all been there, bud.* Opening the bathroom door, he pokes his head back around the corner.

Greta's still staking out his locker. She checks her phone, and Colton feels a buzzing in his pocket. Greta's ears prick up as if she can hear the phone through the noisy hallway, her boyfriend's quickened heartbeat.

Did she– Did she *sniff the air?*

He retreats back to the vomitorium. It had to be today, of course, the very afternoon he's perfected a foolproof way of convincing Charlie to come to Saturday's game. In other words, Greta's stalking is keeping Colton from Colton's stalking.

Puke-face thinks it's safe to go back for the toilet paper, and—aren't we getting arrogant?—to flush. Colton should have locked himself in a stall. But now the door is opening, and Colton starts washing his hands at the sink. From behind him he hears the shuffle of feet too leaden to completely break contact with the floor.

He didn't want to see, but now he *has* to see.

Pettit.

They make eye contact in the mirror, Colton's surprised eyes and Pettit's monster eyes that have sucked all the blood from his blanched face.

Make sure your teammate is okay, Colton tells himself. Advise the kid to hang around for a while so he doesn't get busted. Dispense upperclassman wisdom about taking it easy so he's ready for Middleton on Saturday.

But he doesn't. Nor does Pettit say anything. Nor do they break eye contact in the mirror—which at least would have allowed either one of them to think: he didn't recognize me. Pettit passes from one periphery to the other, but Colton doesn't turn his head as the freshman opens the door and stumbles out into the judgmental hallway.

Colton shuts off the water. Greta's text reads, *Tried to catch you after school. No worries. Doing anything tonight?*

Slinking back into the crowd, Colton finds the coast is clear.

Down in the lobby, he spots Zev lounging and sharing an iced coffee with a kid named Andre, the principal clarinet in the school orchestra. Zev laughs and gives Andre an *Oh stop it* swat, and Colton feels a flash of protectiveness for his host brother. But then he reminds himself that gay guys always look like they're flirting.

Colton approaches the two. "Hey Zev."

See, a big smile comes across Zev's face every time he talks to Colton, the highlight of his day.

"What's up, all-star?"

"You seen Charlie?"

"She's got theater in a bit. And you better come to the show in January, or Ben'll be devastated."

Ben will be devastated, not Charlie. Colton laughs, "Then come to my fucking hockey games."

Colton sees a buzz cut he may or may not love vanish down the hallway that leads to the theater, and he leaves Zev to his clarinetist. But Charlie is nowhere to be seen when he rounds the corner. As Colton searches the halls for the back-stage entrance to the auditorium—it's gotta be around here somewhere—he runs his lines. *So, this Saturday's my birthday, and we—oh, thank you—and we're playing against a decent team for once. What I want to know is... What I wanted to ask you was...*

The backstage door is locked. Even as he's swinging around to the front of the auditorium to try the main doors, his fool-proof plan is starting to feel pretty fool-prone. It'll be hard, for one thing, to convince Charlie that he'd just happened to be passing through the auditorium. And if she's found out about

Greta she might be more in the mood to give him a birthday punch in the face.

But the unlocked door *urges him onward!*

The stage is lit up green and gold, a respectable forest scene with a soundtrack of birdcalls and waterfalls, but Colton can't see any people. Maybe they're backstage? He finds himself drawn toward the glow, trying to make as little noise as possible as he climbs a set of stairs to the stage. He's never done any acting, but he gets the attraction—this slipping into an alternate reality is not so different from sports. He gazes over the lightless rows of seats, a stirring in his gut as he remembers the Shorthanded Quintet's upcoming recital.

The set reminds him of the Rainforest Cafe at Woodfield Mall he used to beg his mom to take him to. He fends off Spanish moss and a big spider web, wending his way around papier-mâché tree trunks. Petrified animals issue their warnings—a glassy-eyed squirrel, a rabid raccoon, a parrot in mid-squawk.

And he hears it better now. He'd heard it all along—the noise that lured him to the stage—but now he knows for sure. Through the recorded ambience, a counterpoint of real animal sounds. It's an afternoon of hiding; through a scrim of branches, he sees two students making out in the dark recesses of backstage.

Yikes. Good for y'all. Time to make an exit.

Turns back, waits for his eyes to adjust, render this groping mass of backs and hands distinct. The guy pushes the girl against a row of scenery ropes, and they break apart for a second to lose themselves in each other's eyes before going back in–

Ben and Charlie.

The jolt that wakes you up before you hit the ground in a

falling dream.

Charlie and... *Ben?*

Which of the two does he need more time to process?

Escape. How can he focus on stealth with thoughts as loud as these?

But he makes it. He's free of the forest. He stands for a moment, four feet above the front row, absorbing the power of the stage. The dark emptiness appreciates Colton's performance better than any spectators could.

His phone comes alive again like a swollen forest insect trapped in his pocket, and he begins composing a reply text to Greta in his mind.

Sorry I've been so busy. Tomorrow night, after the game...

17

Newcomers to a language, it's said, go straight for the dirty words—which is exactly what's interrupting Colton's homework tonight: betrayal (*Verrat*), jealousy (*Eifersucht*), confusion (*Verwechslung*), and heartbreak (*Herzeleid*).

He's having a hard enough time in German on his least distracted days. The class is treating the textbook like a flipbook—Colton learned less in three years of Spanish at Boylan. The gendered articles are his biggest annoyance, way less predictable than they are in the Romance languages. "Think of them as the first syllable of the word," Frau Richter told him. Okay, but in English our words don't all have twenty syllables, and the first syllable isn't constantly changing depending on whether it's accusative, dative, genitive, *und so weiter*. That feels like the closest he's gonna get to speaking German, memorizing phrases that keep coming up in classroom discussion, *zum Beispiel* for example. And how is it that his classmates—lazy Generation Zs, the lot of them—have such a knack for it? Every time he tries to produce German noises, he hears them checking their laughter in deference to his seniority and social standing. Today he'd butchered a list of German words that have no English equivalents. *Weltschmerz* when you don't care about the personal tragedies of others or civilization coming to an end because Charlie was making out with Ben not you. *Verschlimmbesern* when you try to snub Charlie by getting yourself a girlfriend, only to realize that now you have to pretend to be happy. *Fernweh* when you should maybe have stayed in Rock Bottom. And, of course, *Schadenfreude* when you derive pleasure from scorning your girlfriend because that's all Greta's good for because you're awful. Tomorrow, a quiz on adjective endings. It's feasible that he could memorize this table of strong, mixed, and weak endings, but not that he could naturalize the rules to such a degree that he wouldn't have to try and recall this chart every time he collides with an adjective in conversation. "Don't worry." Rare compassion from Frau Richter. "You're not going to fail this class." Like Spanish, she said, there's a logic to the gender of nouns. Ends in –e, usually feminine. Ends in –ung, always feminine. Nounified verb infinitives, always neuter.

Also always neuter, *das Mädchen*.

The—neuter—girl.

"*Sag nicht,*" Ben says, entering the living room, "'*Meine Freundin ist heiß.*'"

Speaking of gender confusion. Ben's full-on *schwul* tonight, trying to make up for his earlier lapse.

"What's with the glower? Fix your face."

"Sorry," Colton says, "I'm pissed off at German. I've got a quiz tomorrow."

Ben leans over the back of the couch and starts giving Colton a shoulder massage.

"Nope."

"You're tense. You need to have some fun." He heads toward the garage. "*Tchüss!*"

"Where are you going?" It comes out more paternal than he'd planned.

"Zev's. I'd invite you, but…"

Then I might find out you're not going to Zev's?

"I'm just not sure what you'd do during all the loud sodomy."

Colton thinks about calling his bluff, seeing how far Ben would go.

"Zev might not mind. I'm suspicious he's in love with you."

"Dude."

"No, I mean it, it's Colton this, Colton that—"

"Not during the loud sodomy, I hope."

"Bitch would owe me *serious* ice."

Colton hears the garage open, the car start, the garage closing. *Zugzwang* when all your moves are bad ones, like in chess, but move you must. On second thought, Colton runs back for his flashcards before jogging out the front door.

Headlights off at night—so far only the second most hazardous way he's traveled the Rentschlers' driveway. Between the lamps' hazy spheres of illumination, branches scrape alternating sides of his car. Fifty yards in front of him, Ben takes a right on Osprey. It's the direction of Charlie's house, Colton shouldn't know but does. A rookie at this or any type of sleuth work, he's unsure how close he can get to the car he's tailing. No way to explain his way out of this one if he gets caught. Except the total truth.

The making of a playlist had also disrupted tonight's studies. *Fuchsteufelswild*, its closest English equivalent: easy there, Sparky. The first song, "I Can See For Miles."

Visibility in truth not great tonight given this inconvenient witch fog, making half of Colton's task easier, half of it harder by the exact same degree. The first thing he'd done after coming home from school was call Greta and apologize about what an ass he'd been. He was hoping they could get together after the home game on Saturday, which, coincidentally, is his birthday. She took it well, apologizing for being so needy herself. She wasn't sure she'd have time to go shopping before Saturday, so maybe he could think of some *other present* she could get him *wink wink*.

Ben takes a right on a street up ahead, heading east, and Colton drops back so Ben won't see him make the turn. Charlie's house is the other direction—guess he really is going to Zev's. Huh, disappointment (*Enttäuschung*). Entering a stretch of commercial zoning that resembles a space colony from planet Ski-Doo, Colton sees Ben pull into a self-storage lot and he positions his car on the side of the road with a view of the facility's exit.

Maybe he's running an innocent errand on the way to Zev's house. Or maybe… Zev's craniac parents are super conservative and this is where the loud sodomy takes place. The name of the self-storage is, in fact, Bottomless Closet.

Next up on *Fuchsteufelswild*, Wagner's *Liebestod*.

Soundtrack music for Charlie finding out Colton knows her secret, stabbing him in the heart with a knife and holding his gaze as he dies so the last thing he'll see is her hatred.

Again he goes over the possibilities in his head. 1) The cool kids are all bisexual these days and Ben casually fucks his friends. 2) They were running a steamy Shakespeare scene and were not enjoying themselves at all but are, instead, very dedicated and talented actors. He'd speed-read *As You Like It* online—Charlie or Ben are both well suited for Rosalind/Ganymede, but Shakespeare had included no stage directions with regards to face sucking. *Or* 3) Charlie's boyish nickname and boyish haircut are her attempt to make herself guy enough for her gay friend she's hopelessly infatuated with.

No and No and No.

He checks the time, pulls out his phone. What was that first sentence Ben said walking into the room? *Sag nicht meine Freundin ist… Don't say my girlfriend is hot.* Did Ben know? Was that a threat? Was he secretly warning Colton away from the exact mistake Colton is currently making? *Was bedeutet… "heiß"*? He Googles the word. (Everything could be a clue.) *Heiß* means hot, but not like *That chick's so hot*. In that context, *heiß* would *bedeutet…* horny. Don't say *"My girlfriend is hot."* In other words, Say *"My girlfriend is attraktiv, hübsch, bildhübsch."*

He pulls up his last texts with Greta, trying to figure out what sexual favor he wants for his birthday. The standards are all in his repertoire. His mind wanders to soccer socks and role-playing—too bad locker rooms are ruined for him by now.

He types, *Got it! For my birthday buzz your hair short and start writing cryptic terrorist poetry and stop wanting to be my boyfriend.* His thumb hovers over SEND for a second before deleting it. Greta's probably watching her phone, saw the ellipses, is waiting for the text to appear. What's taking so long?

Now playing "Under My Thumb."

Nope—that song's too much, even for tonight. He skips to Radiohead's "Lucky."

Ben's Jetta swings out of BOTTOMLESS CLOSET, and it's only been three minutes, so this building is in fact a storage facility after all. *Ohne* bottoms. Ben continues west, continues to put miles between his car and Charlie's house. He gets on State Highway 35, and Colton wonders if his host brother *und Verräter* is leading him back to Rockford, doing him the mysterious mercy of extricating him from this drama. Nope, south now on State Highway 53, a stretch of road Colton has never travelled. They've been gone forty-five minutes now, and Colton's beginning to think he should give up.

A text from Gumby. *Where is you? We have weight training tonight*

Oops. Too far gone to make it back now.

Big Show's already pissed cuz Pettit showed up wasted

Ben takes an exit for Onalaska, home to a team Colton thinks Rockford played in a tournament when he was a kid.

Now Ben's blinker's on, and... and why is Ben turning into the parking lot of an ice rink? The Omni. Colton parks, watches Ben pull in closer to the front entrance. Did he get his Jettas mixed up? He did not. Ben opens his trunk, and Colton *knows*—knew two minutes ago, maybe way earlier—even before he sees his host brother pull out a pair of sticks and shoulder a hockey bag.

Still, Colton has to see for himself.

A screen in the lobby says there's *Platinum drop-in* from 9:00-10:30, locker rooms one and three. It feels weird to walk into a rink and not be going on the ice. When's the last time he'd sat in the stands? It feels... neutering, and Colton fast-forwards to the end of his competitive days, a hazy future when this route will become habit. Just another day at the rink for this hockey dad, former contender.

Torschlusspanik what you came to Driftless to stave off.

Ice rinks are not associated, for Colton, with waiting, and his German flashcards are doing little to ease the *Langeweile* of watching a few figure skaters twirl around, a slow Zamboni do its circuit. There are vertical rows of frosted glass bricks in the cinderblock wall opposite the stands, and now Colton is sure that he's played at this rink. Peewees, a bad game, he thinks. A memory of sitting on the sidewalk outside, hiding deep in his goalie cave from the cruel hockey gods. *You didn't have your mind on your business,* his dad had probably told him. Sure it could have been another rink, the fusing of another two or three games, a dream he had on a night of no hockey whatsoever. They all start to bleed together.

The Zamboni leaves behind its puddle and bank of snow as it exits the ice surface, the driver returning to attack them with a snow shovel and squeegee as the first of the players step onto the ice. Here's a goalie in the new Bauer Supreme OD1Ns that Lundquist wears, and Colton bristles with a territoriality that makes him want to yell out what team he plays for. It occurs to him now that he's the only person in the stands, that there's a good chance the guy whose bedroom is right across the hall from his will be able to spot him. Colton is tempted to say who cares. The hell with it. He would love to see the hitch in Ben's stride, unsure whether to get off the ice or keep playing, knowing that his host brother knows at least one of his baffling secrets.

The part of Colton that convinces him to relocate ice-level a safe distance behind puck-marked plexiglass—this part of him, however, doesn't want to give up this phase of the riddle so soon. He wants to sample Ben's power, the lording of known truth over family and friends.

He wants to beat Ben at his own game for a bit.

But tonight's question: would Ben beat Colton at *his*?

There.

It helps that he's as tall as his dad. His jersey is blue, no logo on it, no name or number on the back. No Driftless crimson anywhere. He can definitely skate. And puckhandle. And fucking snipe—blasting a wrist shot bar down on OD1N.

As they divvy up teams and start play, all of today's anger drains away from Colton—or morphs into a more complex emotion not even the Germans have a word for. Ben dangles three guys and humiliates the tendy with a sick backhand. Some guy chirps him—"All roads lead to bar league"—and Ben chirps back. Colton can't make out what Ben says, but there's zero effeminacy in his tone. It's the voice of a big scary player Colton would have to psych himself up to play against. Stepping on the ice for warm-ups, Ben is the player Colton would identify straightaway, attach a mental homing beacon to. He would know any time Ben came on for a shift and if he was drifting into the slot for a one-timer. Ben is the guy he'd warn his D about. On a two-on-one, take this guy no matter what.

He replays the highlight reel of his clumsiness around Ben's purported sexuality the past three months; he's been making a fool of himself for different reasons than he thought.

He's still disappointed because he still loves Charlie, but the insignificance of Colton Vogler in relation to whatever's going on coaxes him into a state of mind that's detached, far removed from the *Fuchsteufelswildheit* that has driven him to Onalaska tonight.

Also—down on the ice, Ben takes the puck end-to-end again, dishing it to a teammate for an empty netter. They raise their arms and hug in an exaggerated celebration to annoy the goalie.

Also, he's beautiful.

18

Siebenthall picks up the puck, the freshman Riessen resurrected from the Graveyard while Pettit does penance. Protein went to bat for the kid, but he'll be watching this one from the—

Charlie.

Charlie LaBoda is in the stands with Ben and Zev, north of the face-painted, sign-holding, alphorn-blowing student section.

Happy birthday to me.

She notices his noticing her—Colton's sure of it—starts clapping her hands for no reason in particular, and Colton is healed body and soul until he remembers Charlie has a boyfriend... who also has a boyfriend. Ben and Zev are holding hands, out of place—one of them not on purpose.

Middleton guy launches the puck from their zone over the heads of the Brothers Grimm, and Colton puts his arm up to signal icing. But no whistle as the puck crosses the goal line in the corner, the ref not whistling it down for some reason.

Power play. Middleton can ice it since there's a minute left on your power play. Get your head back in the game, Birdy.

Colton makes eye contact with the ref, puts his glove on his chest to signal *My bad*.

Third line getting a rare shot at PP cuz Riessen is fine wasting the man advantage to send a message he's pissed about the score, two to one Driftless with shots twenty apiece. Twenty-one, Middleton's goalie pulls ahead, freezing a backhand from Gunnar.

Colton falls down in the splits, full Gumby, under the guise of stretching at the stoppage in play—but in reality wanting to see those faces turn toward him—one guy on the bench, a few fans, smacking their neighbors' shoulders because a guy should not be able to do *that*, strutting peacock or no. But Charlie is busy with a kitten video on Ben's phone. "Look at me, goddam it," he whispers.

There we go. Good ol' Zev, who come to think of it is single and might be in love with Colton after all. But who cares, because now Charlie is thinking about his body. Has to be.

Goal in the first period was a little soft. Colton wonders if sports-hating Charlie knows enough to figure he shouldn't have let Fishbowl #14 draw him off the short-side post. Or if Ben had enlightened her. But he'd made good saves too, that point-blank blocker save with five seconds left in the first to avert a disastrous momentum swing.

The ref drops the puck, and Colton snaps to his feet. His groin says don't do needless splits please. Girls aren't like *Ooh, is that crutches and Icy Hot?*

Sports: where the things you do to prevent injury injure you.

Driftless holds it in the zone. Thirty seconds—twenty-five—twenty. High shot goes wonky off the stanchion right to a Middleton D who ices it again. Wiped, they think this gives them time for fresh legs.

Not in the second period with the long line change. Not with Colton in net.

Poehling coming on for Gunnar at the far bench, Colton crosses over behind the net and throws his body against the boards to stop the puck. No time to double check, he fires a risky wrist shot through the slot at face height, vaulting the blue line right onto Protein's tape.

"Alright, don't fuck this up Polio," Colton says out loud.

Middleton's goalie slides his blocker hand up his stick, faking a poke check, and Poehling says yeah okay and fires it right through the wickets, no deke.

The rink enjoys the breathing room by using up all their breath on screaming and whistling and alphorns. Dustin points back at his goalie to acknowledge the assist.

Charlie is clapping, and Ben whispers in her ear. *That was even more awesome than it looked,* is what Colton imagines.

Flynn and Alma are behind the glass with Leo. They always sit in the first row. Colton's parents are seated elsewhere.

The Brothers show up to dispense taps on pads and headbutts.

Good dog. Very good dog.

"I can play offense too, if you guys need it."

"We got it from here, Birddog."

"Yeah, stay in the blue paint—that's your home."

Happy birthday. Happy *Bird*-day to me.

The Driftless student body aimless in the lobby after a win—ready with a cheer for peers emerging from the locker room hallway, bad hospitality for battered visitors, and high hopes for the scoop on a victory party. He guessed Charlie would vamoose right after the game, too cool for such caveman antics, but still Colton spent longer than usual on his hair post-shower, on knotting his tie. Now the lobby has spotted their goalie and they're starting to crowd around and make noise. He's craning his neck to see beyond the screaming bodies.

There she is, off to the side, by the display case of memorials to Shane and the dead Driftless. She's embarrassed by her presence at the athletic event or pretending to be, flanked by Zev and Ben. The crowd's keeping him from the *Good game* he really wants to hear, forming a back-patting gauntlet—

Don't use that word.

Then there's a tall, tall girl kissing him on the cheek and somehow his mom and dad saying, "Oh Colton, who's this?" He steals a moment from the hugging and introducing to glance Charlie's way. The expression on her face is in fact nowhere on the spectrum between: severe jealousy that Colton is dating my ex-best friend vs. indifference to the whole sloppy scene because I feel nothing for this dumb jock. She sees Colton seeing her, and, if anything, there's a flash of fear, or warning.

Then the trio is gone.

To Colton's horror, his parents invited their son's new girlfriend to dinner, where they proceed to fawn all parochial over her. Colton despises this parental... *participation* in teen dating. How it laces young fun with everything genteel and acidic, everyone joking away the unfaceable reality of teen sex. But maybe it's because he's never dated a girl he loved (he's realized this only in the past few weeks), a girl he wants to forfeit his identity to, a girl he wants to breed rampantly with some day, quarantined from millennia of human ideas about family as an institution. He experiments swapping Greta with Charlie in tonight's on-going TV movie, but the urgency to abscond with her beyond all reach of his parents' approval is even stronger.

After his parents have finally received the bill and Colton has finally received his birthday gift—his parents got him Christmas break Blackhawks tickets (which includes at no extra cost to any of them an unsubtle summons back to Rockford for the holidays)—Greta lets Colton drive her Mercedes and offers him road head. Which sounds great in terms of eradicating all traces of piety with which the dinner had stunned the young couple. But Colton knows road head would lessen the chances at better pleasure down the road ahead, and a vestige of decency also whispers to him that a quickie is not the present this girl wants to give him.

"Well, I kept waiting and waiting for a hint," she says, "but I'm in the mood for something, a little…you know."

Colton can't take sexy talk, foreplay. It's all so sitcom and degrading, his new theory being that nothing is hotter than how the person you love *actually feels,* nothing performative between your body and theirs.

"Where do you want to go?" he asks instead. "The host family's home tonight, and there's parties, but…"

"Turn right at Konigsee Road."

"Ooh, a mystery."

They drive in silence for a minute before Greta says, "It was nice of your host brother to show up."

"Ben used to play hockey, huh?" He'd been racking his brain for a way to trot out Charlie's name, and this is as good an opening as he's gonna get.

"Up until sophomore year when he got the shit kicked out of him. Has he hit on you yet?"

It occurs to him that Greta's purposes might be investigatory as well. "Big time," he fake laughs. "If it wasn't for you I might try it out."

"Gross."

"Nice of Charlie LaBoda to show up too."

The car goes quiet, Charlie's name an anti-aphrodisiac.

"What do you want to know?" Greta asks.

"I heard you guys had an epic falling out."

"Stupid girl drama."

"What happened?"

"Turn right here."

The gate's timber crossbeam reads INSEL IN INSEL. *Insel* is island in German, an involuntarily celibate tract of land. "On the dirt road?" Small plaques hang down on either side, each one painted with a name.

"Yeah, take it easy."

There's von Kempf—and Trautsch and Bielenberg and Steiner, plus a bunch of names he's never heard. And Rentschler.

And– *Vogler*?

He reminds himself to drive by the sign more slowly on his own time, to check the names against the current roster of Driftless Dynasty Hockey.

Greta doesn't say anything for a bit, and Colton gets the impression that the Charlie conversation is over. Maybe tonight's chance at sex too. The dirt road is long enough to make you worried your loved ones won't be able to retrieve your remains. Every fifty yards or so he sees the light of windows off to the left, the glint of the moon off Lake Konigsee.

"A lot of it was our parents. My dad owns a sand company, and he bought the LaBoda's property back when we were chummy, before Charlie's mom died. After my dad's company moved in, I guess Charlie's parents regretted the deal, and they all joined up with an anti-mining group in town. She said nasty things about this very car in which we're riding, which I got for my sweet sixteen, and we had a big argument. Then she stole Shane away from me."

"Shane… the goalie?" Christ. I'm the replacement goalie, pianist, and boyfriend?

She nods. "I mean, we were sweethearts, but our relationship wasn't going anywhere."

"Why not?"

"Shane's pretty religious. Eagle Scout, you know." Mischief creeps back into her face. "He wouldn't put out."

Unprecedented. "So, Charlie dated Shane?"

"That dyke? No, he just started hanging out with them a bunch. That's why I get uncomfortable that you're friends with them. Don't get me wrong, do what you want. I'm not going to be one of those crazy controlling girlfriends." She points up at the next driveway. "But I couldn't stand seeing her broadcast her mopiness after idiot Shane's accident. That's when I decided we weren't going to patch things up. Especially when the whole thing was her fault."

"Especially… what?"

"We can either talk about shit that makes me depressed, or we can have some fun."

Colton doesn't want to stop driving until he hears the whole story—but there's no more driveway. The lake house's windows are dark, and Greta's already stepped out of the car.

There'll be another time. "Nice house."

The front door is an elaborate bas-relief, a castle or a walled city. Carved into the door, words. The family crest? *Know when you're winning.*

"The whole thing's made of candy."

19

The nurse at the nursing station doesn't look up when Colton opens the side entrance of Penthe Meadows. He haunts the end of the hallway, pretending to wait outside one of the resident's doors, a bored family member checking his phone, until the nurse gets a call, stands and disappears behind a partition. The residents in the bird-infested TV lounge are watching highlights of last night's game. *"Birdy shows he knows how to fly, launching a puck to Dustin Poehling who makes no mistake, burying it on Middleton's Aimard to put the good guys ahead three to one."* A few of the residents send up feeble cheers, thinking it's live.

The door to Shane's room is closed, and Colton realizes it's stupid of him to be knocking. Maybe not—stupid to wait for an answer at least. He opens the door slowly, hoping Shane's not asleep. He's in his chair, watching *The Clone Wars* and trying his best to identify the surprise visitor.

"Shane, it's Colton. We met the other day."

Colton hadn't noticed the big crucifix on the wall before, the Merrimack pennant, the pictures of Shane with his family, with his friends Charlie and Ben and Zev, Shane in his Drift-less crimson CCMs, frozen mid-save. And there displayed on the chest of drawers, his mask, his Al Johansson paint job. Jaw down is the field of battle, black and white checkerboard disappearing into the distance. On one side, a maroon bishop chopping a white castle in two with his hockey stick crozier—the figures are half like chess pieces, half caricatures. On the other, a calligraphic D hovers over the wake of war, pawn pieces leaking oily blood. Colton has the irrational desire to put on the helmet, to see through his predecessor's cage.

Shane makes a noise, but Colton can't decide if it's anger, annoyance, the best hello he can manage, or none of the above.

"I hope this is an okay time to visit."

Hard to get information when you can't put anything in the form of a question. How to ask: Charlie is responsible for your accident; your relationship with Greta wasn't going anywhere because you began to realize that her interest in you was not motivated by attraction; you were hazed, and you hazed.

Colton sits down across from Shane, and as far as he can tell the kid's okay with his visit. He holds up the remote, and muting the TV is met with no audible complaint. One sleeve of Shane's sweatshirt is riding up, his wrist atrophied, skeletal. A child's arm sutured to the hand of a man. Long eleventh-interval-reaching fingers—probably better hands than Colton's, even, for piano. He can't imagine that arm capable of the acrobatic miracles Colton takes for granted every day. Can't imagine it supporting the weight of a goalie glove.

Colton, who's so worried about a pulled groin muscle.

Colton, who's never not healed.

"We beat Middleton last night, and I had a pretty sweet assist, flew the puck up to Protein for a breakaway. I checked your stats, saw that you'd registered a goal. I bet it's that puck framed on the wall."

You got that right.

"Scoring a goal's my dream—too bad most Driftless games are blowouts. No reason to bother with the extra attacker when you're down by five goals. I know this is small beans in the grand scheme, but I've got this pulled groin I'm hiding from everyone, hoping it'll go away." Colton had forgotten about Shane's slow blinks. Like a sleepy cat. "The local news channel rebroadcasts our games—maybe we could do a video session some time. You could let me know every time I do something boneheaded."

Sounds fun, Colton translates. Or maybe it was *You're doing something boneheaded right now.*

"The Shorthanded Quintet has a recital this weekend. So if I puke or curl into a weeping ball on the floor, that's why. We're doing the Brahms. Actually, we're doing the Brahms last. We're opening with the Mendelssohn Trio, then they're doing a Bartok Quartet without me, then the Brahms." Colton's eyes move up to the hook-shaped scar on Shane's head—he can't help it—and images he's never seen flash through his mind. One day he'll go visit the site of the accident. His only experience losing control of a car had been in adrenaline-ended dreams. "That piano at the recital hall—"

Those slow blinks. A cat that couldn't be more in love...

On the wall next to the crucifix, Shane's Eagle Scout certificate, gold BSA fleur-de-lis catching afternoon sun.

Colton reaches for another sentence, grabs silence.

The blinks become more deliberate. Colton thinks of his dad sitting at the piano playing one-note songs, each note one of two durations, short or long. Usually too tired or busy to work the rust off his translation skills, Colton would ask him what the song was about, and his dad would say something like *The lineup of the Chicago Blackhawks* or *What we're having for dinner tonight*, or he'd launch into a poetic recitation of "Mary Anne With the Shaky Hand."

Shane sees Colton seeing, makes a noise.

−·· · −· −

Dent?

−. − − − − .−

Dent nota…

Shane is now sure Colton understands.

−. .− −.−. −.−. ..

Dent not—that must be *an—annn—*okay, *Cs—an acci*

So, *Dent not–*

Christ.

Not an accident.

"Not an—"

Shane cuts him off, the loudest noise he can make. Why use blinking, not vocalization?

−.. − − − −. .− − − −. −

Don't

− .− .−.. −.−

talk.

Colton nods.

−.− .− − − . .−. .−

Camera

.. −. / .−. − − − − − − − −

in room.

His stealthy entrance, pointless. That door could open at any second. Admitting… who? Catching Colton in the act of what? There's more, such a slow method of communication. Two ships passing in the night. Colton gets out and shields a pad of paper to take down a few more complicated lines, puzzle pieces as riddling in their shorthand as they are terrifying in their potential implications. But both boys know that their time together is for now coming to a close.

"It's been nice visiting with you today," Colton amps up the saccharine innocence for the alleged camera. "I wish I didn't have to get to practice."

._.. . ._ ..._ . / _. _ _ _ ._ _

Leave now

.. ⌐_. ._. .. . _. _.. / _._. _ _ _ ._.. _ _ _ _ _.

friend Colton.

20

Colton sinks into the bubbling pool, lays his head back and counts the stalactites. The fabrication is artful enough to trick bathers into believing the grotto is naturally occurring— or would be, if not for the waterfall. He kneads his damaged groin muscle, which had tightened up with the ice bath Dr. Bielenberg had prescribed after practice.

A soak is even more satisfying with the season's first snow falling outside, piling up on the windowsills.

Opposite the hot tub cave, a man cave, filled with memorabilia from Flynn's NHL years. On the walls are framed jerseys, every team Flynn had played for, giving the impression that the room was designed by a colorblind and very indecisive sports fan. One wall, however, is dedicated to Driftless crimson, the 88 on the back of teenage Flynn's jersey reminiscent of pummeling fists due to the bloodstains. How do you get blood on the *back* of your jersey? The framed displays of all the Flynn Rentschler hockey cards ever released must have been cheap to assemble, since they're all commons. His only card worth over a dollar—Fleer '11 "Hitmen" foil insert—is in its own frame with an exaggerated matte border and a track lighting spotlight. There's a pool table with a New Glarus stained-glass lamp, a wooden dart cabinet, a sand-strewn shuffleboard, and a bubble hockey dome.

The back door leads into the sunroom, which Flynn calls

the "winter garden," but there are a number of orchids scattered about this part of the basement as well, like an alien race biding its time to slowly assimilate the high schooler.

To his right is a well-stocked bar constructed of broken hockey sticks. Its glowing sign reads THE PENALTY BOX, and on a flatscreen above the bar, a sweaty Hugo Trautsch is giving a postgame interview on the NHL Network. The interviewer wants his opinion on the NHL withdrawing from the PyeongChang Olympics.

"It's disappointing for sure. Even though we love our fans, very few of us in the NHL have any ties to the cities we play for before we're drafted or traded." He looks like his brother, blond hair flatter and darker from three periods in a helmet, a cut under his eye from a high stick last week against Winnipeg. "I'm from Wisconsin, which means I could have been a Hawks fan, but as a kid I admit I cheered for the Wild. So for most of us, loyalty to a place is something we're in a constant process of learning." Ever since he first became renowned for not resorting to the strings of clichés favored by most athletes in interview settings, for actually pausing and crafting thoughtful replies, Hugo's exaggerated it into a caricature that led ESPN to put him number three on last year's list of the Fifty Smartest Pro Athletes. He was the only hockey player who made the list (which says more about ESPN than hockey players). "But the Olympics are totally different. Suddenly you have this love of the jersey and what you're representing, a tribal bond with guys who're your enemies the rest of the time, and you don't have to try to make yourself feel that way. It's cool how automatic it is."

Or scary, Colton thinks, eying his tattoo.

Leo's door opens. The kid is wearing swim trunks and a scuba mask and carrying an armful of toys—which he proceeds to dump into the hot tub.

"Hey, buddy."

Leo gives a solemn nod. "Hello." He turns his back and walks over to the sound system, plucking the remote off the dock. The "Queen of the Night" aria from *The Magic Flute* descends into the basement on a loud cloud scouting for war.

"Do your parents let you in here?"

"Televised," Leo replies, and begins drizzling too much of what may or may not be bubble bath into the water.

"I think we already have plenty of bubbles going on."

"Ship soup." He stirs the water with his spoon arm before climbing in.

The bubbles are already cresting the lip of the tub. The Queen's clipped, arpeggiated call to arms thunders to a close… and starts up again on shuffle.

"You really like this song, huh?"

This question is too much for the kid, and he goes into what Alma calls his "Thinker" pose, palm to his forehead, fingers splayed.

"I've been learning a Mozart sonata. Have you heard me playing it?" Colton hums the theme from the second movement of the G major.

Leo shakes his head. Then, on with the goggles, under with the body. The snorkel is protruding from the foam, but Colton isn't totally comfortable with his role as hot tub televisor. He works to resituate his swim trunks.

Just when he's decided that Leo's been submerged long enough and the bubbles are about to find their way down the snorkel, Leo resurfaces, drawing big lungfuls of air. The bubbles are spilling over the edge now, and it's time to put an end to all this fun.

The basement door opens, and Colton is paralyzed by the

sight: goon descending a staircase. Flynn seems unacquainted with this new technology, holding onto the railing with both hands and taking very careful sideways steps. Is he drunk? The one thing he'd never seen in the man cave was the man himself—making all the jerseys and framed *Hockey News* articles more of a memorial than a tribute to the man's living presence.

Colton rises, dripping and covered in soap foam, switches off the jets and begins throwing towels down around the base of the tub.

"I thought I heard the ship soup song." Flynn picks up a pot of orchids that's ready to go upstairs, approaches the hot tub.

"Sorry." Colton bends down to mop up the water. "Leo thought we needed more bubbles."

"No worries," Flynn shushes the Queen's fury a few notches. "Hey, seriously, Colton."

Colton stops mopping.

Flynn makes a peace sign. "*Hakuna matata.*" Setting the orchid on the edge of the hot tub, he de-goggles his son. "Dinner's in twenty, pal. And I think you need a real bath first."

No, doesn't sound drunk.

"You know where we get the word *orchid*, Colton?" Flynn asks.

Colton does not.

"It's Greek for *testicle*. This is the Hanging Man Orchid. See each flower's little face? Their little cocks?"

Colton is all ready to report that, no, he does not see the flowers' cocks—but he does.

"Colton's hurt," Leo speaks up.

It's the first time the kid has said his name. Colton wasn't sure he knew it.

"Oh yeah? Colton's got a boo-boo?"

Leo's knee rises out of the water like a little iceberg, and he points.

"Just a bruise." Colton shows Flynn. And, no, I was not making your damaged son look at my damaged leg. "Slapshot from Ober."

"Really? That pussy?"

Dinner is a fancy spread from Metzger's. Rouladen and a variety of wursts, plus sides of spätzle, potato salad, and red cabbage. Black Forest cake for dessert, Alma promises. Celebration dinners—Colton's been treated to a lot of them the past few months—are less special when you're trying to stay lean for hockey. His calorie counter app has no idea what rouladen is. A can of Stiegl, with a mug in the shape of a boot, runs a surprising 205 calories.

Leo is freshly showered but is still wearing the goggles on his forehead.

Sitting down, Ben is not impressed with the beer. Colton avoids eye contact with his host brother, unsure what to do with his jealousy, with the information he's learned visiting Shane, with this new theatrical challenge. Turns out being 100% cool with having a gay host brother who makes occasional passes at you is a way easier part to play than acting like he doesn't know. Pretending there's no pretending. He can't stop scrutinizing Ben's every word and movement, spotting flaws in Ben's performance. He was sure he'd seen Ben check out Emma Nylander at school the other day, whispering *That ass...*

Why would Ben pretend to have the very appetite so many people pretend not to? Why would he come out of a closet he was never in?

Ben had caught Colton as well, caught his host brother

staring at him, deep in some uncanny valley of sexual orientation. *You okay, man?* he asked one of the times, failing to hide his concern that his mock passes were starting to work.

Tell him tonight, Colton decides. What's a little awkwardness when Shane's life might be at stake? Friend Shane.

Alma frowns at the portions Colton is arranging on his plate. She takes up spoons and starts doubling all of them. "No sir. We need you strong."

"I need me fast." Well, he can always skip lunch tomorrow. Or see if Pettit's stall is free.

"We play this team tonight, the Screwheads," Flynn says. "Last time we played them dude told me he wants to trade their goalie for me. Does that mean– do you think he was calling me a bitch?"

"Maybe it was a compliment, dear. He wants you to play for his beer league team. That's nice."

"I bounced around the league, I get it, but at least I was there."

"We don't need you getting your bell rung."

"You don't think I could take him?"

"Don't you remember, honey, our more… important news?"

"Yeah, yeah, make your announcement."

Everyone stops eating.

"As you know"—Alma directs this at Ben and Leo, not the non-Rentschler at the table—"we've been trying for a while to give you guys another sibling. And I'm far enough along that we can share the news… It's a boy!"

"Brotherrrrrrr!" Leo yells, pounding both hands on the table hard enough to make everything rattle.

Flynn gulps beer.

"That's really great," but Ben's voice is flat. Another lackluster performance. Another baffling concealment.

Maybe don't tell Ben tonight. Shane's not going anywhere.

"Congratulations!" Colton tries to sound genuine without upstaging Ben too much. "Guess you guys'll be needing that extra bedroom back."

Alma shoos away this concern, flushed and radiant.

"You kidding me?" Flynn says. "You're our good luck charm, Birdy. We might never let you leave."

21

First movement is a stately rendition of evil. But adolescent, too, mistaking outset for zenith, minor key for dissonance—which is the same as confusing physical pain for emotional or vice versa, or nothing like that at all. It's too solipsistic wallowing in its angsty jingles to comprehend that there are three movements to come, more life and fireworks, discord it can't imagine. Then, a moment of stillness—Brahms can't sweat, so he has to pant—a sustained high note on the violin pianissimo enough that the fourth movement can be heard whispering, *Just wait.* Then the opening theme recrudesces, but all sticky—the violin bows trying to extract theme from development like pulling taffy from hair. It should sound, Slava explained, "as if you're trying not to play the theme," are doing so "with gun to your head."

None of these thoughts during the performance, of course. Hectic scraps, maybe, flashes of ghost note narrative. Nor the pure glut of passion non-musicians suppose it, access to a transcendent plane of existence. This is the paradox of the more rigorous performing arts: the hours of practice are both what tricks the audience into imagining you raptured away and what keeps you moored in the routine. Mostly it's muscle memory, the brain operating like the eyes of a driver, not locked on the pavement speeding under your front bumper—the keys that you're about to press, are pressing, now and now and now—

but roaming the middle distance, alert but undistracted. There are a few bookmarks for Colton to remember, street signs. Exit here for development instead of going straight to coda. And places where he needs to make eye contact with Zilch or one of the other guys to time an entrance. A remembered exhortation from Slava about dynamics or pacing—he warns himself not to let the image of the large European flapping his arms and soaring hawkish around the practice room break his focus. Rule number one, don't think *focus*. If he does, he'll start second guessing notes that have been under the complete jurisdiction of muscle memory ever since he learned the piece.

For example, *What I'm playing right now feels familiar and true, but there's that bass note coming up in two measures and—what finger have I been playing it with?—and what* exact note *is it and here it comes and… fuck.*

As a musician, and as a hockey goalie, the scary thing you do is create all new instincts, and thinking too much short-circuits what should be automatic. The performance anxiety is different, of course, because with hockey you're planning for surprises, for other people's blunders, but with music—classical music, at least—you drill it over and over and over so there are no mishaps. In hockey, you can make a big mistake or several of them and still win the game. The comparison is over.

The second movement is the only one in a major key, so it has always been Colton's least favorite. Tranquil, tranquilizing. Any musicologist would disagree, but, to Colton, the Andante doesn't have a main theme. It's a satellite orbiting around a thematic planet for nine minutes without ever coming any closer to it, a moon that vanishes by degrees as its path around the theme exposes it to a rim of light, the blinding sun, the shine of the absent theme off the moon's cratered surface.

The Davidsbund—"Club David," even Colton, with his

meager German, can report—got lost in Wisconsin en route to Bavaria, circa King Ludwig. The Davidsbund, in its struggle against the indifferent Philistine Goliaths, had painted its vaulted ceiling with naked babies. It was armed only with a slingshot and lots of porcelain, gold foil, and private donations. (There is industry in Driftless older than the sand boom.) Big distractions during rehearsals yesterday. "Do we come here to play music"—Slava—"or do we come here to ogle obese women?" Replacing Stations of the Cross, alternative mythology: Wotan in Valhalla, The Dragon Fafnir, Siegfried Learning Birdsong, The Wild Wälsungs, The Twilight of the Gods. Sublime music can transform the most humdrum setting, but when space and sound vie for ascendency, it's hard not to thrum with higher callings, to momentarily forget the distractions of Taco Tuesday and the Marvel Cinematic Universe.

The third movement is the big single off the album that gets the radio play—but all the kids who were into Brahms way before he was cool know it's a little overrated. Powered by excitement rather than lasting energy, the Scherzo is bound to burn out, another tourist of despair like the first movement. The kind of anger– oops, CC botched that entrance bad. Okay, back on track. The kind of anger you feel at a fly buzzing in your face, an agitation that's really a balm because it distracts you from the facts—that the water is rising, that people die in misery, that you'll see a nuclear weapon detonated in a major American city in your lifetime, that a fourth movement prowls the tree line.

The Mendelssohn went well, the Bartok too—even though Colton sat that one out and doesn't know the piece that well. Or, as Slava put it, "Could throw darts at string quartet and would sound good." His parents are back up for the performance, Alma is doing her best to keep Leo from cheering when he hears something he likes, and Charlie's presence with Zev and Ben is again causing Colton to forget Greta in the front row with the quintet's teammates.

For Colton, piano and hockey have always been at either end of a seesaw—up and down, skill and shame. He's still getting used to how this weird town and its high school have muddied the highbrow and the low, but he's almost more excited to show Charlie his piano chops than he was to have her see a game, proof that he's not just some dumb jock. Since she's here, hopefully that means she doesn't hate him after finding out that he and Greta are a thing—not that he wants her to be at total peace with this revelation either. There's been no good chance to tell her about Shane. He's been too occupied with school's nonsense and extra rehearsals and entertaining the parents to confront larger menaces.

When the third movement collapses in exhaustion and the eerie, weary opening of the Finale begins—it sounds how an orchestra from another planet might tune their instruments—you realize that every emotion you've savored in the first three movements have been ruses, their sole purpose to tenderize you for the fourth movement's evacuation of the soul. Now you'll pay for gleaning whatever you've gleaned. The fourth movement of Brahms's piano quintet is a malignancy, impossible to play any one passage of it in your *Kopfradio* without being ambushed by other phrases, creating a roiling, schizophrenic canon. Now you're infected—and banishing the gigue so you can get on with your day is no easier than extricating yourself from barbed wire. Such hatred. No coherent program is possible, the Finale a montage of unlinked, hyper-personal images: running up a stairway in pursuit of a human you love or hate, screaming their name; standing on a high place, gazing down on a landscape and a people that belong to you and you alone, the trees, grass, water, the cloud cover spiraling from the imprint on the eyes of prior motion; *the die is cast* and is perpetually coming to a rest without ever revealing its dire result.

It's a different species of applause than Friday's game. All of them are having trouble not grinning like idiots, except CC, whose face is drained bloodless. The audience insists that the quintet come out on the stage again, and again, and one more time, and *oh no you don't*, for a series of stilted, uncoordinated bows.

"I'm so sorry guys," CC says as soon as they're backstage for good.

"For what?"

CC looks at his goalie like he'd spit on him.

The Plague's grin is gone as well. "Dude, we were *recording* that."

"I know. I'm sorry. I fucked up."

"You mean in the Scherzo? That was one little mistake."

"Birdy, don't make this any worse."

"Is okay, is okay." Slava appears through the backstage door and approaches the group, hands in the air. "I find you new violist. Gimmick of name won't make sense, but I have been watching tiny freshman girl with great interest."

"What are you talking about?"

"Mark." Slava puts his hands on CC's shoulders. "At least you still have hockey. For now."

At the reception in the lobby, Colton is hoping he'll get a chance to talk to his defenseman, but CC doesn't stick around for snacks and punch.

"You play adequate today." Slava is assembling cheesecake squares on his plate into a precise grid for maximum coverage. "But your technique needs improve for beating Orientals at state chamber competition." He's run out of plate space, and so, frowning, he begins a second layer.

"State competition?"

"Is what I say, yes. Milwaukee, Wisconsin, champagne of beer of cities. Weekend of April twenty-fifth. We do Shostakovich with tiny freshman girl."

Before Colton can tell Slava that his spring is already booked solid with potential catastrophes, he has to again fend off congratulators. Greta has been crying, which makes Colton want to fall down on his knees and confess everything. His mother would have everyone in earshot know that *her son* had wanted to *quit* piano lessons as a kid, that *she* had the idea of bartering practice time for packs of hockey cards. Seesaw goes up, seesaw goes down. His dad makes a joke about sports and broken fingers. Leo wants to give Colton multiple high-fives and then examine the effect it's had on his hand. Alma persists in being pregnant.

Eventually the crowd disperses enough to allow Charlie, Ben, and Zev to approach.

"Well well well," Zev says, "doesn't somebody *love* to have large groups of people clap for him."

"No words," Charlie says, and Colton makes an immediate resolution: write a string quintet. For Charlie.

"You okay?" heterosexual Ben asks. "You tried the cheesecake squares yet?"

You okay? The most lied-to question in the history of human discourse. The game is over, the recital is over—and there are games and recitals still ahead, endlessly propagating. Add to that Shane watching TV the rest of his life (*Friend Colton*), the image of Ben skating big crossover strides on an empty sheet of ice, Charlie alone in the stands.

"Guys," he whispers, and all three of them lean closer. "I know everything."

22

"It sounds like you know *three* things." Ben is driving, heading northwest through an industrial zone of Driftless Colton hadn't seen.

He'd convinced Ben to drop the act once they'd gotten into the car, but he's gotten so used to Ben's performance that the real thing sounds voiceover. Fake macho anger.

Zev gives Colton a halfhearted smile. "Still gay."

"I told you this would happen, Charlie."

"You became friends with him too."

I'm in the car, Colton wants to call out. The parents are arguing.

Wait, he *has* seen this part of town—back on sweatpants night. No Wotans in this Valhalla, its neon libido made flaccid by daytime's hangover.

"It was inevitable," Zev mediates, "once your family was chosen to host him."

This calms Ben down. He makes eye contact with Colton in the rearview. "How'd you find out?"

"You're not that good of an actor." Colton is still hesitant to admit he'd caught them smooching.

"But… hockey?"

"I followed you to the Omni one night."

"Goddam it!" He hits the steering wheel and Charlie puts a hand on his arm.

"If it's any consolation, you *are* that good of a hockey player."

Charlie turns in her seat to face him. "Colton, does anyone else know? Did you tell any of the guys? Your parents?"

They leave behind the strip clubs and cross into the hinterlands, everything dead for the year or pretending to be. Today's drear is a temperate spell lodged between last week's snow and the Indian summer sun that had melted it.

It's clear they're not going to out-with-it. "Can I ask why?"

"No."

"I mean, it's kind of fucked up. Kind of disrespectful."

"First of all, maybe I'm not one-hundred-percent straight."

"He does enjoy it way more than he should," Zev jokes.

"I just pretend to be further on one side of the spectrum, and there's a very specific reason why."

"And that is?"

"It's dangerous for you to know certain things," Charlie says. "Dangerous for you and for us."

"Especially now that you're with Greta von Kempf."

"Then I'll break up with her—"

"No!" all three friends in synchrony.

"Why not?"

"Colton, listen to me." Ben finds his eyes in the rearview again. "This is going to sound crass, but if you're with Greta— if you've been with Greta—then you're going to have to stay with her for a while."

The road is terrible, like a washboard... that's been firebombed. A firebombed washboard. Ben can't go any faster than forty, slower around its winding curves.

"How long?"

"For as long as you're in Driftless."

Charlie turns again in her seat. "Please, Colton. You'll know a little more after today, but, if you care about us—about me and Ben and Zev—you'll stop investigating and carry on as if everything is normal. For now."

The views here would be scenic any other month of the year, bigger hills than people would expect to find in the Midwest, limestone bluffs rising above the wide, sluggish Mississippi.

"I know four things."

Colton has everyone's attention.

"I know Morse code."

"Congratulations. So?"

"Who learns Morse code?"

HAM RADIO dads. "Eagle Scouts," Colton says, and there's two seconds of silence before–

"Oh my God."

"Shane?"

"How could we have been so stupid?"

"And…?"

Colton considers trading info for info…

No.

"It wasn't an accident."

Zev closes his eyes, and Charlie puts her hands over her face.

"I'm sorry. I didn't know what to do with the information."

"We have to get him out of there. *Now*."

"We can't take care of Shane, not until we're eighteen."

"What else did he say?" Zev asks.

"He said way more Driftless players have been killed than the guys in the memorial case. They cycle new jerseys and photos in there every few years. And not just athletes. This place kills kids."

"And we have to stop building the Gateway."

"Ben, we can't just let two years' work..."

Gateway? "Shane also said his room is bugged."

"Fuck!" Ben hits the steering wheel again.

"Maybe this car's bugged," Zev says. "Maybe they're following us. Ben, I hear you're pretty good at getting tailed."

"Okay, guys, so what have we said to Shane in that room? Anything incriminating?"

"I can't remember every single word I've said to him."

"I've talked about the Gateway. But I think we can forget about that being a secret."

"They'll know I snuck in the last time I visited," Colton says.

"What do you mean snuck in?"

"We need you to cease and desist on this double-O bullshit pronto."

"Should I go and visit him with Alma again, or pretend it never happened?"

"Here they are. They're coming for us. Here come the shitty Vikings."

Ben starts doing an angry rendition of "Ride of the Valkyries," showing each dump truck a middle finger as they lumber by, twelve of them total. The dust cloud they chariot is so thick that Ben, coughing, has to slow down further to keep from running off the road.

The dust clears to reveal, through chain link and razor wire, a wound being wounded. Angled conveyor belts peak mounds of sand and gravel as other trucks subtract from the base. Giant glassless hourglass. Chemical lagoons are slicked rainbow, the workers dressed for warfare. A sign on the fence reads

VON KEMPF ROCK PRODUCTS

"Frac sand?" Colton asks—but nobody answers because they're all holding their breath.

After they've left behind the mine, the trio exhales as one.

"Superstitious?" Colton tries again.

Charlie: "Silicosis."

"Is that Greta's dad's mine?"

"One of them."

Colton still hasn't met Greta's dad.

"Here's one got separated from the herd—check out the name on the side if you didn't before."

Another dump truck, RENTSCHLER in maroon letters on the driver side door.

"My uncle," Ben clarifies.

"Makes a racket."

"*Is* a racket."

"I guess that's why the roads are so terrible."

"This road is less than five years old," Charlie tells him.

They drive for a couple more minutes before Ben pulls into the driveway of a house that's perched on the edge of a vast nothing. Its architectural distinctiveness is so incongruous with the blasted backdrop that it comes across as even more scablike than a humbler house would, like it was dropped here by a tornado. Its design is a harmonious battleground; everywhere you look, it's all angles, and then a series of graceful curves turn wood and stone to waves, return human dwelling to natural growth. But the big windows are dark and dusty, the yard overgrown, the water fixture run dry. It's the right address, but it doesn't match the Google Earth image that Colton (total creep) had saved on his desktop under the name parnassus.jpg. It gives the impression of being so utterly exposed to the elements, to the sun and wind, the last human holdout clinging to a road that had strayed too close to an uninhabitable frontier.

"Believe it or not"—Charlie reads his thoughts as she keys in the garage code—"the frame used to match the picture."

"What happened?"

"Sand equaled jobs."

Colton remembers back to a cluster of signs he drove by a few weeks ago, carried by dudes in Carhartts and their families, black letters on bright yellow. The laborers were horded opposite a smaller group of mostly young people and elderly people protesting a land development deal in front of city hall.

"Don't they say *equals*? Sand equals jobs?"

"They do indeed."

"At least they're honest," Ben adds, "about their trade."

Zev touches Colton's hand. "Wanna pretend to be gay with me?"

"Maybe later."

On display inside the house is a similar bafflement of form and ornament. A big flagstone fireplace, hardwood floors, tall ceilings, open floorplans—stagnant air, looming vacancy, general disrepair, accumulated clutter. It's as if it had been hastily vacated after a pinpointed apocalypse, Charlie and her father as squatters in their own home. No photos on the walls.

Charlie's relationship with Ben has not exiled her from Colton's pre-dream dreams. Tonight he will fall asleep playing in his *Kopfkino* their most epic love drama to date, a daring escape from Driftless to save Shane's life. But what will the revelation/confession hinge on? Ben will have to be sacrificed, that much is clear. The last two weeks, Ben has fallen out of a few windows, been involved in untold car accidents, and discovered too late his terminal shellfish allergy. He's been forced to move to faraway lands. He's been a total jerk to Charlie, leaving her in need of a shoulder to cry on. He's even realized once or twice that he is in love with Zev after all.

Colton wants to see Charlie's bedroom, but he cannot imagine the request sounding appropriate coming from his mouth.

She instead leads them to the basement door, yells "Dad, I'm here with friends" down a flight of steps.

A weak voice makes a reply Colton can't decipher.

"Don't talk too much," Charlie tells Colton before starting down the steps.

All the lights are on, but the basement huddles in half-light. It's not a basement, Colton realizes, not really—more like the walkout bottom floor of a ranch. But still the light is sickly and claustrophobic, all the windows blinded by blackout curtains. Cracks of daylight sneak through where sections have come untaped from window frames. It's the species of space where most American families put a poker table, dartboards, a big TV, a hot tub grotto. This basement, on the other hand, is a domestic collision, a breakdown of demarcation: a family room's couch and TV and framed photographs, a dining room's table and plate of picked-over food, a bedroom's bed and chest of drawers, a rod for hanging clothes, a makeshift kitchen with crock pot, microwave, and mini fridge. On a flat surface that is still technically a pool table are strewn blueprints, some of which reproduce the lumpy sickle shape that once had perplexed Colton in Charlie's gunmetal notebook. And a model of the house in which Colton currently stands, just as dusty but with greener landscaping, an unfalling waterfall. If he were to look through its back door, would he see an even tinier model?

Charlie's dad is seated in an armchair, hooked to an oxygen tank, a toy train engine and a screwdriver in his hands.

"Hey, Mr. LaBoda." Ben is back to being gay.

The man sets aside the train, removes the jeweler's glasses

that made his eyes all googly. "Hello kids!" He pulls the oxygen tube thing over his head as well. "Who's this?"

"My name's Colton." He shakes Mr. LaBoda's hand.

"He's a friend from school," Charlie says. "Moved here in August."

"If I'd've known you were bringing a boy to the house I woulda made myself more presentable." Mr. LaBoda coughs. "Sorry there, Ben, Zev."

"No offense taken."

Oh, so the part he's playing is that of the potential boyfriend... He looks at Charlie for directions—only to be deflated by a glare that says *Don't encourage him.*

"And sorry about the state of my little nest down here." Mr. LaBoda grabs a wadded napkin off the table and tosses it near an overflowing garbage can. "Those damn machines—I don't know how Charlotte can stand it."

Charlotte! Charlotte LaBoda, who brought a boy home (Colton) to meet her father. He improvises variations on this theme: *Hello my name is Charlotte* name tag, the glowing anonymity of LABODA, CHARLOTTE on a teacher's attendance sheet, her full name—she has a middle name!—Charlotte _____ LaBoda on a tax form or driver's license or, or... The clouds open and, the *Ch-* that has always tolled her signification can morph at whim into a *Sh-*, and (lo!) a *-lo* anticipating the *La-* cut short by a pair of savage *T*s, the unbearable vulgarity of the plosive *-Boda.*

Old man, tell me your daughter's middle name!

"How's the train coming?" is Ben's ludicrous follow-up to the name Charlotte released into this stuffy air.

"Better than the real thing." Mr. LaBoda hooks the engine to a set of cars on a track—Colton's eyes move around the room—that runs on platforms affixed to the walls at eye-height. He flips one switch on an elaborate panel and the thing springs forward. Its path traces bridges and cliffsides, a muddy meandering of paint on the wall that must be the Mississippi, threads a Styrofoam tunnel turned on its side. It leaves the wall for a ping pong table where it winds around a green hill spotted with trees and a miniature version of the house in which Colton finds himself standing at the present moment.

The three friends start clapping as the train says goodbye to the table and starts back along the wall. Colton joins in.

"Thank you, thank you." He gives a pained bow. "You see, today I had to fix—"

He's interrupted by rolling thunder, and for a second Colton thinks it's another truck armada—until he hears the whistle and remembers the train tracks that jarred Ben's Jetta not far from Charlie's house.

"Never come between a momma train and her young," Mr. LaBoda yells over the noise.

Colton smiles—but understands it's a joke that gets less funny with each telling.

And, as the noise is dying away, "Hard to believe I used to admire trains."

"They used to be once a day," is Charlie's reply. "Dad, we're gonna walk around, show Colton the Gateway."

"As long as he's not with the enemy."

"You know I wouldn't do that." *Right?* her glare interrogates Colton.

Outside, they cross a lumpy flatness of cracked mud pocked with the dead chaff of grass and thistle. Deep tire treads crumble under their shoes, bearing witness to the recent passage of vehicles. Big ones.

A rise in the land, a fall. Jagged metal, ribboned plastic wrap, and pieces of jugs jut from the ground, blighted crops.

Here and there, pools of brown liquid show no intention of evaporating ever. Looming there in the valley is a massive structure that resembles a very abbreviated rollercoaster, just the first hill. Or a device built by a cult to receive alien ambassadors. Or a big allegorical ship to save the LaBodas and every species of animal from forty days and forty nights of rain.

"Colton, you told me one time you wanted to read my poetry."

A crane sits idle, its boom raised in greeting or warning, inquiry or inactivity.

"What is this?"

The proportions are so disorienting that Colton, rather than making his approach, feels himself to be walking in place as the structure itself quickly grows. Its metal poles, horizontal support beams, and X-ed braces shift from latticing landscape to latticing clouds as the four friends reach a ledge, about three feet high, three feet wide, that runs the length of the installation. It's concrete, chalky white in color—but it hasn't been painted. Its surface is textured from the plywood panels that had been used to frame it.

Charlie boosts herself onto the ledge, and then all four of them are walking with their arms out like it's hard to balance on something three feet wide and barely off the ground. Above them the girders are the remains of an unnamed megafauna that surrendered its bones to pre-Wisconsin wilderness. The sight is so vertigo-inducing that Colton almost stumbles off the ledge. He considers asking if they should be wearing hardhats, but he knows the answer is yes.

"How could you build this?"

"With a lot of help from a lot of malcontents. We have secret meetings."

As they approach the end of whatever this is, the distance

between their heads and the narrow ceiling supported by the beams shrinks, to the point that Charlie can put her hands up and touch it, to the point that they can go no further. Dismounting, Colton can see the ledge's terminus. Metal rebar gropes upward, the concrete's exposed nerves. Before him, looking up the length of the thing, climbs a path of wooden planks Colton could ascend were he not so uninclined.

"Do you still want to stop construction?" Charlie asks Ben.

"My goal was always to survive until the age I could escape this place," Ben says. "I'm not sure how that came to include building a giant beacon announcing my revolt. Especially now that we know for sure about Shane."

"Don't you want to get back at them? *Especially* for Shane?"

"We're so close to pulling this off," Zev adds.

"The way I see it, they'll think this is just about the mining—and that's not the big secret here. Maybe this keeps us safe?"

"How?"

"When they see us scheming, they'll think it's just some land art project."

They walk back toward the house without having reached a decision—which is, perhaps, a decision.

Before it disappears from sight, Colton turns back around to face it head on. "I still don't see it."

"You will, Colton. Everyone will. It'll all be white concrete."

"What will happen to the... the..."

"The falsework. It'll all be gone, and hopefully the arch will stand once the centering's stricken."

"Why an arch?"

"Do you remember my dad's train set, that big green hill?"

"Yeah." But his mind is still browsing the blueprints on the pool table.

"Welcome to Fort Mountain," these lunar badlands, "site of a very happy childhood."

Music begins playing, a faint interval, a minor seventh. A piano enters, thickening the texture.

"So this," Colton says, tracing an arc in the sky.

Charlie nods. "Police chalk outline of a killed hill."

23

Consider something in your life you think goes unnoticed and write about why it's important to you.

There, he's already up to seventeen words. No more blinking cursor and forbidding white expanse more treacherous than an arctic expedition. Granted, all he's done is paste in one of the hokier prompts from UW–Madison's application, but words are words. He types:

The smell of an ice rink. It forces even the most one-track mind synaesthesic. A rink smells cold. A rink smells blue. To me, equal parts musician and athlete, it smells like a diminished seventh chord awaiting resolution—listen to the opening of Brahms's Symphony No. 3. When the Zamboni leaves the ice and there's a clean sheet in front of you, marred only by the palimpsest of previous battles, the whole atmosphere is a compressed spring, and what you smell is the upcoming pain and disappointment and, on nights it all pays off, triumph—

He rewards himself by pressing the social media lever. Turns out he checked Facebook so recently that zero of his 732 friends have posted anything new since the last time he was on. He refreshes the page to make sure it's not a glitch. He clicks on a link that he scrolled past minutes before, back when he was choosier about his distractions, an article about how we as Americans are more tribal than ever. The article blames the recent rise in tribalism in America not on Trump or identity politics or social media, but instead on the degraded state of professional athletics. Baseball is slow and old-fashioned. Football won't be around much longer. Eugenics and other race-based discomforts make any real enthusiasm about basketball seem suspect. Professional soccer has been roundly and inexplicably rejected by the Americans who love playing it. We have no decent proxy tribalism, the article claims. Pro sports in the U.S. have embraced militarism and the most excruciatingly hollow displays of patriotism. The athletes almost never hail from their team's locality, and they are bought and sold as commodities. The article demonstrates the less popular status of the NHL by not mentioning it; Colton displays hockey's subsequent self-consciousness by getting sore and seeking other distractions.

Like, how come none of his new Driftless friends are on social media? Are they ahead of the trends or really, really far behind? He's noticed a preponderance of flip phones among his teammates. He searches *Charlie LaBoda* again to be sure. *Charlotte LaBoda.* Nothing. Nate sure is posting a lot of photos of his offspring on Instagram. *Love this little guy!* He's gone from making fun of social media nonstop to joining all of it at once. *Boys and their dinosaurs!* Nate used to say he didn't want any external manifestations of himself floating around the ether, acting independently of him, trying to decide whether or not the time had come to rise up and destroy its host organism. *Can't believe it, two months already!* If Colton had a kid—a shiver courses up his spine—he wouldn't post any photos of it until the kid was old enough to decide they wanted their image in the pockets of strangers. *This little guy let us sleep in till 5 AM today!*

He deletes what he's written, tries to convince himself that this, too, is progress. Too many mixed metaphors. Palimpsest?

Giving thanks is easy with this smiling sweet potato-smeared face at the table!

Fighting magpies are raucous right outside the window at a lady's piano recital as she's playing the angry birds movement of Ravel's *Miroirs*. She stops playing and knocks on the window to scare them away. The audience laughs. She sits back down, starts over, super solemn, but the birds return and now there are three of them.

Baby's first Halloween costume. Raaaaar! says the most cowardly of littlest lions!

Werner Herzog offers more evidence to back up his claims that chickens are "abysmally stupid."

Look, I'm Colton Fucking Vogler. I go to Driftless High School. After I'd won three Illinois combined high school state championships, the Big Show took notice, and now I'm posting a GAA under two, with three shutouts and zero losses on the season. But I'm no dumb jock. I got a 32 on my ACTs, and I'm already taking AP English, Psych, and History. You assholes like that? You're gonna love this. I'm also a classical fucking pianist. I played the first movement of the Grieg concerto with the Rockford Symphony Orchestra for a crowd of about two hundred. No mistakes. Yet here I am, shopping my talents to your institution, and you have me WASTING MY TIME on bullshit essays when I could be on the ice or learning the Shostakovich quintet. Here's my essay: mention my name to Coach Salonen and see what happens. What goes unnoticed in my life? Nothing. I fucking go noticed.

Colton holds down the delete key, and it takes eighty-three Mississippis for oblivion to eat his pride backward.

He has a fifty-dollar Amazon gift card burning a hole in his wallet, and it would be a very responsible use of his time to do a little research. His Mac power cord has been disintegrating over the last few years, and the electrical tape starts to unravel and get sticky after a few months. Seventy-eight dollars for a new one. It'd be nice, but it's an old computer and won't last much longer anyway. Can he hold out until they give him a power cable with a new one? Speaking of disintegration, how about shopping for running shoes? He could start jogging outside in his gym sneakers, but then they're no good for the gym anymore. Mizunos are all he can wear because they have the highest arch support. Wave Creations, $99.89-$159.99. Quite a price range.

He opens parnassus.jpg, Charlie's house, and squints through the watermarks for new details he might have missed, signs of life. Charlie must have been in grade school when this eye in the sky espied her home one day and blinked. Her best friend was Greta von Kempf. Her dad had not yet been driven into the basement. Her mom was alive.

He changes the photo's filter to grayscale, and the whole scene goes spectral. Save as killedhill.jpg.

Googling *blink morse code* brings up grainy footage of a guy named Admiral Jeremiah Denton blinking T-O-R-T-U-R-E while imprisoned during Vietnam. Instructed to tell the camera that he was being treated well as a prisoner—"I get adequate food... and adequate clothing... and medical care when I require it"— he feigned trouble with the lighting and snuck the truth to Naval Intelligence.

Damn. Suddenly, filling out college applications does not seem so harrowing.

They tell us that student is first in "student-athlete" for a very important reason. They are wrong. They're wrong because the delineation between the two roles—like most attempts to categorize human identity and experience—is not as strict as they make it seem. Namely, academics are an athletic endeavor. Success calls for the same stamina, self-care, mental toughness, camaraderie, and sense of competition that ice hockey, my sport of choice, requires. And there's a more accurate cliché that we (hopeful) Division One athletes embody: we truly are "students of the game." We do not switch from one role to another when we step into the classroom or the ice rink, and if anything important about us goes unnoticed, we're the ones who have to fix it. Because everyone is watching, and the game is always on the line.

Okay, here we go—

24

Fracking, fountain in reverse, pool born
at Arethusa's fretful feet, second-rate
metamorphosis fleeing river god rape.

Colton hates poetry. How it avoids saying the thing it wants
to say, how every word seems to turn back to the reader to ask
if you think it's pretty.

So why is he writing a poem on the drive back to Rockford
for winter break? Maybe it's momentum from the creative essays he's been forced to write for college applications. Maybe
it's recent events that have left him feeling isolated, in search
of solace. Maybe it's inspiration from the Gateway, his fledg-
ling attempts at translating Fort Mountain into wordless music.
Or maybe it's this brand-new gunmetal notebook—with elastic
band—that needs its pages filled, an early Christmas present to
himself he's been hiding from the person who inspired the pur-
chase. The center of his steering wheel was not made to double
as a desk, and his new notebook is doubly diminished—by the
words and by his handwriting.

How can we trust a genre of communication that's found-
ed on vagueness and obscurity?

He crosses out *Fracking* because that provides readers with
the cypher too soon. Keep it ambiguous so the reader has to
figure it out on their own.

See?

Okay, so they read "The Waste Land" in English class, and Colton thought it was pretty cool how Eliot pieced together scraps of other people's language to achieve his version of a Grail legend, a desiccated world in dire need of renewal. (Even if Charlie told him that "Eliot was a shithead.") So last night was another baffling hopscotch of hyperlinks, starting with a Google search of *fracking* and ending on an Onion article titled *Poet Announces Plan to Use Water as a Metaphor*, stopping along the way at an English/Latin translator, Netflix to add *Gasland* to his queue, and *biblehub.com*.

Will his parents make him go to church on Christmas?

Zap!—Ovid morphs into Jesus Christ.

> The water I give them, a spring
> welling up within, eternal life

He knows poets have a fancy word for it, the putting of one thing next to another with no transition. This millennia-spanning, globe-hopping antecedent of the hyperlink by which you dump bold equations into a reader's lap and wish them luck. This alternative approach to time/space is what must be the privileged realm of poetry–

No. There's nothing that keeps you from doing all those same things in prose.

Poems are no different than other forms of writing except you leave out certain words so the sentences aren't sentences, and you press enter at random.

Zap!

:

> destination spot, Ponce's apocryphal
> spring break.

Apparently you read it differently too, when you read it

out loud. He tagged along a few weeks ago to an open mic with Charlie and Ben at Driftless's only hip derelict building. After suffering through much heavy-handed slam and lilting affectation that made every line sound like a question—how about you let the *audience* decide whether or not your words are precious?—Colton realized that one of his big problems was about to be solved. If Charlie went up there and lilted all non-human, he would no longer be in love with her. Fortunately/unfortunately, Charlie did not transform into a different person when it was her turn. It went by too fast for Colton to evaluate the actual poem—it was indeed about birds—but his problem remained unsolved.

Today's snow almost delayed Colton's departure. He imagines it piling up on the Gateway, which has grown since the first time he saw it, the gap between the arch's arms shortened by the return last week of the concrete mixers and pump trunk. Colton was less help than the grizzled and disgruntled miners who showed up to lend a hand, but it was gratifying to be making some small contribution to this larger act of defiance he still didn't entirely understand—and to know his new friends were trusting him more and more. These hours, stolen from homework and hockey and piano, had made life no less hectic.

On a family trip to Yellowstone, he once hiked up to the meager spring that eventually became the Missouri River.

> Chide hydro for skipping
> the middleMan, hellroaring
> power for the disempowered.

It's too warm for icy asphalt, and driving conditions are okay so far. The low cloud cover and accumulating roadside snow seem determined to meet in the middle, returning the state of Wisconsin to a white spot on the map. It's the first of many trips home for the holidays, and Colton wonders what landmarks and impressions and habits are solidifying each passing mile into ritual.

> The fuel they give us, springs
> forced down through confused crust

Visiting Shane for the third time, he did as Charlie advised, striding by the desk like he owned the place. "Um, excuse me," the nurse called out to him. *Who… me?* "Are you visiting a resident? You have to sign in." "Oh, my bad." He complimented the Christmas pattern on Hedy's scrubs, and she blushed.

Shane had been waiting for him—a thought immediately followed by how daft it was. Shane was always waiting for anything. Colton held up his laptop. "I have Saturday's game against Janesville."

Shane blinked *Hello.*

The cross on Shane's wall, a rosary he couldn't reach for.

> *—In profundis clamavi ad te Domine—*

"You are about to see the most unbelievable own-goal in the history of the game." He found the seven-minute marker of the second period. "I mean, tell me this is my fault."

After five seconds, mild panic that Shane was choking and a nurse needed to be called. Then Colton realized Shane was laughing.

"And of course it's Hoodie. But let's watch it again, because you'll see he had help. It's a coordinated effort." He plays it in slow motion. "So Sparky, my teammate, without any clear impetus, takes my legs out from under me as he skates by, right when their D-man is cranking a slapper. Now, the puck is on the ice, so it would've hit me. For everything to work, Hoodie had to come in and deflect the puck up over me. Watch me reaching for it like it's a cheeseburger." Shane, laughing so hard that Colton almost cried. "And that shit fucked my shutout."

enema for Gaea.

First, contaminate the contaminant
—cleansing agents, sand equaling
jobs—

The line break. The stanza break. Paragraphs, no doubt about it, are different rooms than stanzas. But *rooms* is the wrong comparison.

Music. Of course music. Line breaks and stanza breaks and white space are just another instrument or articulation or harmonic progression unavailable to straight-up prose. Then again, prose knows tunes that are off-limits for poets. Poets are impatient, lack symphonic stamina.

So why not use everything?

Colton pulls into a Pilot station. It's the shit version of those sci-fi settings where characters live in a single building that accommodates all their needs. It has showers, laundry machines, a barber shop, an arcade, an Arby's, a country diner named Country Diner, and a gift shop specializing in Tim Allen DVDs and pewter dragons glued to chunks of amethyst. Colton can already tell that this will become one of those important road rituals, stocking up on provisions. It's not that he can't get this stuff elsewhere, but that he wouldn't let himself. No, it's something about how the act of buying and eating makes it real, the unreal experience of traveling hundreds of miles in a few hours. Stopping reminds you you're driving, reminds you you're stuck in a body too.

As his eyes are roaming the illuminated Arby's menu, he realizes there's nothing he wants.

That's not true.

Maybe he's not hungry?

No, he's hungry.

It's one of those menus that lists calories—that's the problem. Beyond all biological wants and needs, Colton simply *knows* that he's not going to get anything. His pep talk had failed. The calorie digits aren't going to start ticking downward. So he slinks off to the refrigerators, where he browses the glowing rows like a kid with no money at a window display.

Plenty of money in his wallet, but he can't afford a Red Bull.

He tries to congratulate himself for his willpower as he slumps back behind the wheel, but it doesn't work. He anger-writes lines that came to him while peeing.

> here in Driftless take advantage
> of glacial neglect to end glaciers
> for good. You know, spend to make,
> gut to glut, convoy Wisconsin ever westward,
> pushing killed hills into tillable Dakotas.
> Eat peaks to squeeze your base.

"So, as you can see," he told Shane his practiced lines, looking him straight in the eyes, "the team is in quite the predicament. Despite everything we know, I'm not sure we're going to be able to fix our offense until after winter break, especially without number eighteen. I don't see why we can't get more aggressive–"

─... .─.─. .─ ..─ ... .

Because

– .... .– – ... / .– – .... .– – / .. / –.. .. –..
that's what I did.

Step two, fail to contain the contaminant,
you delved too greedily and too deep

That one's *gooood*. A real rhythm to it, a phrase that feels like home–

Fuck, there's a reason why. *Lord of the Rings,* the dwarves in the goddam mines of Moria. He'd stolen elsewhere in this poetic effort—but from places that felt okay: God and gods and other poets. But taking from Tolkien is worse than nerdy. Better not compare it to Balrogs—global warming and water contamination and a rash of earthquakes. Balrogs are fantasy.

~~you delved too greedily and too deep~~
lace aquifers with cancer,
"We deliver cheap natural gas
straight to customers' homes"
via kitchen faucets.

He's supposed to go to dinner at Nate's a few days before Christmas, and he's been trying to ignore the weirdness of seeing Paige again.

Stanza break.

Maybe *avoid* the lines that feel like home.

This is how man insists.
Tools are a mark of our humanity.
Earth quakes under man's might.

Staccato.

He's been switching between a couple playlists trying get jazzed about the idea of being back home—*Freshman Year,*

Sophomore Year, DISASTER YEAR—but he's discovered that the songs had only served to preserve excitements trite and embarrassing in retrospect. Is this why adults stop listening to music?

> *Behold, rebel earth,*
> *I do something new, highway in the wilderness,*
> *desert in the river.*

Is it done? Two words alone glow on the page: *killed hills.* Because what he wants to write more than anything else is a poem with Charlie's words.

Turning into a real pussy, Vogler.

He asked Shane, "I wish the team could take you with us on a road trip."

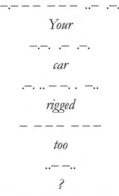

—.— — — — — — ..— .—.

Your

—.—. .— .—.

car

.—. .. — —. . —..

rigged

— — — — — —

too

..— —..

?

Colton realizes he's going five under the speed limit, presses the gas.

He strikes twice with his rig
—heartland heartburn—
and their beasts drank.

25

The traffic lights are all dark on Riverside because of a power outage, and the greenhouse where Colton had spent the last three holiday seasons sheathing Christmas trees in netting has gone out of business. His phone sends him down streets of his hometown he's never driven on before, and heavy winds are blowing the snowfall sideways. A short time gone, but "home" has shown how fragile it'd been all along.

And he hasn't even seen his rowdy friend Nate as a family man yet.

There are two wrapped presents on the passenger seat. What an impossible task. His mom had refused to help him, enjoying her son's indecision.

He shouldn't have worn his Driftless Hockey hoodie. There was the desire to display an immediate, outward sign that he's changed, proof that, aside from his familiar haircut, this is not the Colton they'd said goodbye to in August. His sacrifice has been worth it. However, the calligraphic D might as well stand for *Done with you. I've moved on to bigger and better things, brighter prospects and friends with shinier taints.*

Colton silences his *DISASTER YEAR* playlist, and the sexy-voiced woman on the radio—

"*—Stanley Cup champion and captain of Team USA, will be sitting out tonight's game against the New York Rangers after he was taken in for questioning by police yesterday following a late-night rant against his Uber* *driver, who was transporting Trautsch and a group of teammates from a bar to their hotel. The contents of the rant have not as of yet been disclosed, but it has been made known that the driver is a Muslim American. NHL Commissioner Gary Bettman has withheld commenting about the situation until more details are released, putting out a statement that the NHL, quote, 'aspires to inclusivity.' A spokesperson for Hugo Trautsch has given no set date for return to play."*

Fuck. Having reached a grid where the traffic lights again are functioning, Colton glances at his phone, but Protein hasn't texted him. Nobody's texted him.

Its Christmas lights are showing up all the other houses on the street, and for a second Colton's surprised that Nate's deadbeat dad and busy mother got around to decorating this year—until he remembers that Nate is the dad. Incongruous images enter his mind as he shuts off his car: Nate checking the lights for burnt out bulbs, Nate shoveling the driveway, Nate paying his Comcast bill.

He rings the bell, and someone somewhere screams. But Nate appears unperturbed as he opens the door, grinning. He eyes Colton's bombastic hoodie; Colton eyes Nate's snowflake sweater, unsure whether it's being worn ironically or not. Nate's once long hair is short, domestic paradise having achieved what school rules never could, his face a little puffier than before.

Their man hug is made clumsy by the presents Colton is carrying. "Come on in. Paige and Rudy are already here."

Here goes…

"Oh, hey," Nate stops him, "can I get you to take your shoes off?"

"Yeah, sorry."

Framed family photos on the wall answer his question

about the snowflake sweater. Colton imagines the frames falling off the wall as he walks past, his hellion presence an irritant that can only be expelled by priest.

They step into the bright kitchen. Christmas music is playing, George Winston over-accenting every—single—note. Colton's mom loves *December*. She loves making their kitchen smell like this.

"Audrey, Colton's here."

"Yes," Audrey says, mopping her forehead with a towel, "the prodigal goalie. And you brought presents! I'd hug you, but my hands are greasy."

Colton tries not to make the *You're pretty but not worth it* expression. "This one's food." Colton holds up a wrapped rectangle.

"Great, the fridge?"

Rudy and Paige both rise from the loveseat in the living room for hugs. Of course Paige is blushing– but so is Rudy. Both of them avoid eye contact with Colton after sitting back down. The tinsel on the Christmas tree has been reused, and most of the ornaments are handmade.

"How's hockey going? We've been following online, but give us the updates."

"Yeah, it's cutthroat, but it's going well so far. College apps are out, and there've been scouts at our games. My host family's house is pretty posh—it has a hot tub built into this, like, cave thing. The town itself is a little weird." But he realizes they're not listening to him, just waiting for a chance to talk. "What's new with you two?"

"We were wondering if we could ask you a question." Rudy sorts through a bridge mix, locates the elusive cashew. The chewing makes him sound all casual. "Would it be okay with you if Paige and I went to prom together?"

Colton checks himself just short of bursting into laughter. A clear *Why would I care about that?* might, after all, not be taken well by his friends. He pretends to debate the idea for one-Mississippi, two Mississi– "Yeah, no problem. Thanks for asking me, though." He'd forgotten prom is a thing, that Greta would be expecting an invitation soon. "Are you a couple?"

Both look away. Then, together, "Yeah."

Might have asked me about that first. No, he can't pretend to care.

"Are you seeing anyone?" Paige asks.

"Yeah. Now, I promise she's a girl–" Colton stops himself. Saying Greta now wouldn't make much sense. "Her name's Charlie." A smile spreads across his face, because as far as these two dummies know, it's the truth. He's dating Charlie LaBoda—that's what they have no reason not to think. Thank God his new friends are all so disinterested in social media. Then his mouth, drunk on the freedom he's given it, starts blabbing about the Gateway, his and Charlie's "collaborative land art project." He's already written a piano quintet they'll play at the unveiling.

"She sounds unbelievable."

"Like Amber from summer camp back in junior high," Rudy adds. "Remember Amber with the giant–"

A kid has appeared at the threshold of the hallway, is staring at Colton, frozen. Colton glances at the stockings hanging from the mantel. Cory. That's right—there's a stepson.

Cory is wearing an Ice Hogs t-shirt, those sandals made out of skate laces. He unfreezes and approaches Nate in the kitchen. "Do you need help with anything, Dad?"

Dad? Does Audrey make her son call Nate Dad? This is a very sad or very exemplary kid. Christ, there are guys on Colton's team that are like three years older than Cory. Gunnar… Beastie… Pettit.

Gong Show Pettit.

"For sure. The plates and silverware are all out on the counter if you wanna start setting the table."

The kid moves to do it, but then goes back into the kitchen and whispers something to Nate.

"You know," Nate calls into the family room, "it's hard for me to impress this kid when I'm competing against the great Colton Vogler. Cory here wants to know if you've been drafted yet."

Remember that game of Never Have I Ever when we found out that neither of us had never slept with Gretchen Sommers?

"Not yet," Colton tells Cory instead. *It's a sweet moment, and you have to go and think that. What's happened to you?* "You play?"

"Yeah." The kid starts setting out the plates. "One time I was at a goalie clinic you were running."

"You're a goalie?"

"No, I was one of the shooters helping out."

The baby is produced, and Colton doesn't know what to say to it. *Your dad and I once got drunk and stole a golf cart*—he can't stop himself—*spray-painted it BTTM seeking TOP and left it in the woods.*

Guess that's why people goo-goo at these things.

Dad hands Luka to Mom, and Colton finds himself conscripted into a clumsy nativity scene. He pretends these two smiling food-stained dopes are him and Charlie. Ultimate consummation—making new life, metamorphosis, a merging of identity and DNA the lovers can never themselves achieve. But he can't get Charlie's face right, or his own. Instead they each wear a petrified rictus, a parody mask. He tries working on one face, kneading some humanity into it, only to have the other one go lifeless with neglect.

Where two come together or don't, one will always love more than the other.

They move to the table, where Colton's mind goes to work counting calories. He can't figure out if he's one of the kids at the table or one of the adults. Cory, sitting right across from him, keeps looking at him every three seconds. As Colton starts to pick up his silverware, Audrey clears her throat.

"Do y'all mind if we say a prayer?"

Colton's sure to receive a subversive wink from the buddy who used to ditch all-school mass to get high with him behind the tennis center. But Nate's head is bent, his eyes closed.

Colton didn't give anyone permission to become a grown-up, to transition from keg parties to dinner parties. He feels like he missed– was missing– *is currently missing* a crucial exit on the road of normal human development. It's well marked, the exit, miles in advance. But they'd forgotten to make it reflective, the people who make the signs. It never occurred to them that anyone would be driving this road at night.

Elephant graveyard.

But the most frightening change hanging in this Yankee Candle air is the might of his indifference, as if a fundamental human capacity has atrophied within him.

No, it's nothing that grim– These people simply have no share, no access to Colton's new drama. He has this *thing* he carries around now, safeguards, that they don't know about. Can't know about. He could say her name out loud again, try to explain it, but the secret would remain a secret.

For dessert, he will unwrap Baby Dahl's best-selling new pie. Rudy will say, *Is that… Could it be?* Rudy will cut one slice and then lift the rest of the pie onto his plate. Rudy will cue the laugh track.

The laugh track fixes everything.

26

Because 12-stave notebook paper is insufficient for his quintet's instrumentation, Colton drives to Guzzardo's in the slush for a plastic-wrapped pack of those huge symphony-sized sheets. The names of the greats on expensive Henle Editions and all the nerdy kitsch of a music store make him eager to join the pantheon. By the time he gets home, however, the paper itself is so beautiful with its thin pinstripes and infinite possibilities that Colton is close to deciding he's met his quota of composing for the day. Enter: Charlie's wordlessness after the Davidsbund recital and her anticipated reaction to a sublime quintet composed just for the unveiling of the Gateway, just for *her*. And so Colton is successful in parking his ass on the piano bench. He's gotten spoiled by the Rentschlers' Bösendorfer, and his parents' Everett upright—which they've at least been shamed into tuning for the first time this decade—is sounding extra tinny, the action limp and uncooperative. He's been trying to get into the Shostakovich, but so far it's been awfully athletic for way less payoff than the Brahms— plus he's been feeling unenthused about jamming with Slava and the Shorthanded Quintet, or whatever they're going to be called, since the ousting of CC (who refuses to talk about it), looming Milwaukee competition or no.

He places one of the oversized pieces of staff paper on the music stand. His reward for all this progress should be a

Mozartkugel—is that Mozart *bullet?*—but he can already hear the mixer in the kitchen going to town on whole sticks of butter, and he isn't sure how he's going to keep starving himself in front of his mother and her cooking over Christmas break.

Luckily, Christmas puts him in a musical mood. Part of it is the free time, and part of it is the chance to play holiday songs without people throwing things at him. For the last twenty minutes he's been messing around with "Carol of the Bells," which is what a horror movie would sound like if it was a Christmas song, while waiting for dots to start appearing on the staff paper. Part of it is also the tree, the bounty of only-child presents beginning to accumulate, the snug warmth of the family room contrasted with the other side of the window, strings of lights glow-berrying snow mounded bushes. A shelf next to the piano is packed with yard sale books and binders of photocopies and crumbling sheet music singles, evidence of a juvenile scramble to explore the new world of old music. The setting reverts Colton back to a pajama-wearing, childlike frame of mind, the same room where he'd long ago discovered that a dude named Edvard Grieg wrote a lot of pretty famous jingles. The troll song! The wedding song! The sunrise song!

Which reminds him of one of Zilch's original compositions, a variation on Grieg's "Morning Mood" that he calls "Morning Wood." Same melody, but it gets faster and faster then peters out abruptly. Which reminds him he's not a kid anymore, and he doesn't believe a single word of any Christmas song. An hour ago a tiny bust of a Santa Claus Brahms had made him all revved up to write a piano quintet, a quintet for a girl—a *woman*—he's in love with. But now he's busy flipping through his early primers, trying to locate a song he used to play. Had a picture of a raccoon, cross-eyed at the bee landed on its nose.

Stop. You must write a note.

He hasn't composed that much music before: a bassoon quartet medley of *Star Wars* themes; a legit prelude a little too reliant on rising sequential figures; one page of Piano Concerto No. 1 in A minor, Opus 1 No. 1 by Colton A. Vogler back when he wasn't entirely sure which way the flags and stems went; and a few martial-sounding rock songs before he'd figured out his favorite bands all sing *around* the beat, not right on it. *Cantabile*, syncopated. In one semester, his Advanced Music Theory class at Driftless has matured him far beyond the young composer who once thought he'd invented the circle of fifths. He's been sketching scraps of melodies and harmonies in a notebook, but for the quintet he's decided to jettison all those scraps, pour out his impressions of a ghost hill he loves by proxy, starting with that minor seventh interval that buzzed like a drone over the barren land. He hasn't figured out the time signature yet—all he can hear are the two notes, no pulse to them. 4/4 is always a good guess, but he wants to go stranger. Glitchy. And he needs a key signature, too. Or he could ditch the key signature altogether, bluff his ability to sustain continuous chromaticism—

though tonality is so hammered into him that he knows he'll fall into D minor or G major or something pretty quickly. At least he can write the instrumentation, get graphite on the page. *Vln. 1, Vln. 2, Vla., Cel., Pno.* A line to connect them all on the left side, flat bracket around the string staves, curly bracket around the piano treble and bass clef.

And he can name the piece. Brahms was all about absolute music, the idea that music degrades itself by verging into another art form's territory. Colton gets it. There's something pure about abandoning language altogether, titling a composition with aggressive blandness, for example Piano Quintet No.

1 or Piece for Piano and Strings or simply "1" (thereby burning all his previous work). But the circumstances surrounding this composition call for a more programmatic approach, a title that gives the audience a hint that it's about more than the play of vibrations, like Gateway Memorial or Killed Hill or Song for Charlie—the danger being that the listeners won't *hear* the hill or monument or girl, and will resent this chump for suggesting they should.

Two words appear, and his hand is writing them on the page before his brain has had a chance to vet them, neat enough to look aesthetically pleasing, messy enough that future archivists will speculate that Vogler could scarcely find a spare second to write them down, such was the torrent of heaven sent sounds.

Driftless Quintet

And sometimes there's music on the page before a single note is written.

Now, how does one say "hill"—with music?

[Colton working...]

[Colton working...]

[Colton working–]

Ab*surd.*

One syllable could straightaway bring to mind the mental image. Give Colton a sentence or three and "hill" would be honed into Fort Mountain and its absence. But, since he's chosen a *hard* art—fucking poets—something akin to sorcery is called for. How have composers of the past said "hill" with music?

No, stop—his defenses step in to fend off all influence, worried he'll end up transcribing the melodies of others.

Hey, lay off—just a good whiff to put me on the trail.

But danger and inspiration vanish in sync, as Colton is unable to recall a single piece of classical music evoking hills. Or mountains. Great upheavals of earth, and centuries of composers *hadn't thought* to translate that gasp of disbelief into song? Or are mountains too much, a natural beauty so surfeit as to repulse human efforts of representation?

A big blind spot for an entire artistic medium.

Did Beethoven's pastoral wanderer in number six, that translator of nature into culture, encounter a hill? Colton doesn't think so. A storm, yes, with timpani and sforzandi. There's a reason why it's easier to say thunder in music than lightning. Strauss has a symphony about the Alps, Colton remembers, but he's never heard it. Whispers of a twentieth-century composition in which the line of noteheads traces the shape of the mountain range seen out the composer's window—but that route fills Colton with a greater sense of futility than any other. Can't see the mountain when you're "In the Hall of the Mountain King." He chases off mountainous film scores as too infectious—Jerry Goldsmith's *The Edge*, John Williams's *Seven Years in Tibet*, James Horner's *Legends of the Fall*.

No.

Night on Bald Mountain.

His *Kopfradio* is able to queue up nothing more than snatches. Halloween low brass theme, swirling, infernal strings (again, wind poses less of a problem). He knows the truth, that if he put it on right now, he would only hear hill because of the title. Is it even about the hill, or is it about the night? And... *witches*, he's pretty sure. *Hexen.*

Getting distracted. Driftless Quintet doesn't need to be– needs *not* to be– needs to *not* be about–

Needs to *be*: hill.

He could run to his room for his laptop, pull up parnassus.

jpg, but he knows that this would be yet more fake productivity, another point scored for the inertial resting state. The image is burned into his brain anyway.

He's never seen it from the *side*, he realizes. Texting Charlie for a photo of Fort Mountain would have the added advantage of being an excuse to text Charlie, to initiate a nervy wait for the ding of her response. Her name on his phone's screen, its indication that she'd dallied on his existence for at least the number of seconds it took to send the text. But it would be the depths of hell if she didn't reply, wasn't intrigued enough by this riddle of requested photo to ask why.

Not that he'd tell her. Not yet.

He knows he shouldn't need a photo. The heartbroken polystyrene miniature in a claustrophobic basement is the real inspiration, or the second rendering traced across the clouds as he stood there at the very locus, a transmutation of so many tons of frac sand for Colton's blood and bones and beating heart–

Wait.

Play that again.

Immediately his skittish hands want to scamper off, to banish the melody to the blackest pits of unhearing. While his mind had been putting the task off, his restless fingers and ears had gone ahead without him. He works backward via muscle memory, grabbing the melody by its tail and yanking it into the light of scrutiny. Not a melody, not really—a sequence of pitches that, rather than falling into a cadence, threatens expansion. Rampant development. He twirls the giant tuning knob of his *Kopfradio*, combing every melody he's ever heard to check for theft.

The eureka of jotting down the first notes of the Driftless Quintet—what the hell, give it to the poor viola—is rebuffed by another one of music's torments. Your experience of music as a listener is always tied to time. Even harmony, which seems vertical, can't be perceived without the vibrations that constitute it. Stacked dissonance augurs movement. The space-time of listening stretches during the process of composition, exposing a slowness that goes unnoticed in the concert halls, the music having drifted too near a black hole. You're engaged in a push and pull between the horizontal and the vertical, rushing to fill in harmony, texture, and dynamics without losing whatever momentum you've stumbled upon. Those movies which show a composer's hand racing across the page, and you hear the composition as if one type of stylus were another… that ain't how it works. More like spinning plates, but you're also called upon to simultaneously invent plates and gravity, no time to mourn the countless other compositions you silence with every single mark you make.

27

Carlson Ice Arena is dingier and more dimly lit than Colton remembers. Smaller too, the set of a movie downscaled to make a tall teen appear taller.

Maybe just your big ego, Colton warns himself.

Carlson was a big deal when it was first built—at long last a second sheet of ice in a northern U.S. town of 150,000 people—and a lot closer to Colton's house than Riverview. He remembers sitting on five-gallon buckets and getting dizzy from paint fumes before the locker rooms were complete. Not as bad as the pepper spray the police used after Dave DiGiacomo's dad came on the ice to "break up" a fight. The businesses that share space with the rink are clinging to survival: a Blimpie Subs that Rudy has gotten fired from twice, the nightmarish Kidz Zone play place, a Tae Kwon Do studio trying to demonstrate a more elegant style of fighting, and Scott's Skate Shop—which Colton always hurries past, guilty at having bought his gear elsewhere. Scott, he'd guess, still has that one pair of all white, 32-inch Warrior pads.

He refrained from wearing his Driftless hoodie, but his crimson bag and $2,000 pads broadcast plenty. Bombastic trophies of war, no way around it. He brought his old gear back with him to get crusty in his parents' basement, but he isn't going to risk getting reacclimated.

Skates have worn a roughened, darker path down the center of the hallway's rubber floor, branching left at each locker room and right at the doors that lead to the ice surface. Colton pauses mid-stride at the coach's locker room. Habit had been taking him to locker room three, a room which is no different from rooms one, two, or four, but which had hosted the Glaciers ever since its random selection on the Night of the Five Gallon Buckets. But he's not a Glacier anymore, and the locker rooms are cramped as it is. If he dresses with the coaches, though, they might think *Oh, so he's too good for his old teammates.*

"Crouton!" Someone clomps down the hallway behind him. Lalande. "I've got bad news. We gave your spot away."

"But I've come crawling back."

"Tough shit, traitor."

"Do you think there's room in three for me, or…"

"Yeah, we'll move Virgil to the bathroom."

"Virgil?"

"Foy."

"I can't believe Foy is on the team. I'm so sorry."

"He's even shittier than before. He's lowered himself *beneath* the challenge."

"Why do you call him Virgil?"

"After you left he strutted up from JV like it was finally time for his ascendancy and you'd fled town in fear of your upstaging. He immediately started to bully the freshmen on the team as if it wasn't his first year too. He became obsessed with this new kid, Jeffries, started stealing his stuff and making the kid supply him with shampoo. Then he tried nicknaming him Virgil after finding out through this awkward, forced interrogation that Jeffries is a virgin. But the kid was like fuck you I'm fourteen years old and more of a badass than you and started calling him Virgil back. I'll give you one guess who the team rallied behind. Even Momma Foy calls him Virgil. It's hilarious."

More accusations of traitor as Colton lugs his bag into the tiny room, a third the size of the varsity room at Steiner, no individual stalls with name plates, no flatscreen for video sessions, no *Lehmann's Terms* printed out and taped to the walls (for example, *Human highlight reel!* or *You've just earned yourself an opportunity to improve*, or, of Dustin's more-talented younger brother, *It's obvious who got the quota of athletic talent in* that *family*), no free tape or skate sharpening machine or team logo on the cinderblock walls or crimson carpet. Again, habit causes Colton to step around one wall only to find Foy's gear where Colton had been setting his bag since freshman year. Foy sees Colton's mistake as loaded with aggressive intent, and he scowls at the homecoming of this usurper.

("Virgil!" a teammate calls out.)

Foy's a little worm with a penchant for giving up dump-in goals. Colton can't feel too bad for him about the nickname. He'd been using everything except athletic talent to try to wriggle his way onto the team for years. Once, on an off-night for Colton, he asked if "the magic" was gone. But it's his sorry territory now, and Colton sets his bag down next to Routhier instead, who's gotta be the starter these days.

Routhier. Why is Colton's heart thrumming with joy? Sure, they're friends, and Colton hasn't seen Routhier for a few months, but, has he gotten that sentimental? Is the goalie bond really that strong?

He hasn't seen a black person since moving to Driftless, Colton realizes. He does a snap roll call of his entire high school. The whitest city in America.

"Nice tat," Krpata says when Colton takes his shirt off.

Colton looks down at his arm. "All the upperclassmen get them."

"What's it stand for? Dumbass?"

"Dickhead?"

"Dipshit?"

"A *scarlet* D, so… Doltery?"

Not bad, dork. "Wouldn't be Defense if you got one, Kirby."

"You missed it. I back-checked a few weeks ago. It was unprecedented."

"It's a brave thing you're doing. Usually it's guys with muscles who get bicep tattoos."

"You still working up to a hundred?"

Freshman year, Colton had failed to bench press much of anything during a gym fitness test. Weird that his former teammates have preserved information about him that he himself had forgotten.

"Still working up to your mom."

It's a cringe-worthy joke, but everyone's laughing. These *kids*. He imagines his new squad facing off against his old.

Driftless hockey : Glacier hockey :: Driftless hazing : Glacier hazing

"You getting any action up there?"

"Sure, yeah."

"What's his name?"

Colton decides not to repeat the lie he told Rudy and Paige. Breathe that name in this polluted air.

"Greta."

"Greta? What is she, an octogenarian?"

"When did they start offering a big words class at Boylan?"

A kid Colton doesn't know stops short carrying his bag. Colton gives him an apologetic expression, and the freshman heads for the bathroom.

Routhier is trying on Colton's glove and blocker, admiring the name stitched above the thumb piece. "Dude, I would jerk off with these all the time." He demonstrates what that would look like, jerking off with goalie gloves and exploding in orgasm.

"Wait'll you see my mask."

"*Brutal!*" Coach Cantley shouts his trademark zinger as Colton steps on the ice, and Colton can't help grinning—and feeling super self-conscious about every move he makes as he skates around what seems to him like a miniature rink.

It is smaller, he reminds himself, since Steiner's an Olympic-sized sheet.

Cantley knows Serge Strowbridge, a former Badger, and once in a while he has Serge help out with practice and tenderize his goalies with ninety mile-per-hour slapshots. D1 isn't in the bag for Colton, but the guys are giving him the attention he'd no doubt given Strowbridge in the past. Especially the fresh blood, kids he doesn't recognize. He locates his name three times on the Illinois State Championship banners hanging above the glass. The Glaciers' rosters had always sounded to Colton like a badass marines special unit, but now they're just so many elephant graveyards.

Which makes VOGLER glow all the brighter in that company.

His groin is tight from a week off, and he eases into stretching. Virgil wastes no time setting up a net, staking his claim, and taking shots. Fine.

When Colton does step in, at the other end, the ice tilts in his direction. Everyone abandons Foy, wanting to see what Wisconsin has taught their friend.

Spezak is the first to come down on him, and Colton challenges as cavalierly as possible. There's always this paradox for good tendies at unimportant sessions: stop the pucks without trying too hard. In spite of the tacit rule that you warm goalies up with shots from out far, he can tell Spezak is still stupid and is gonna deke. Let him have his fun, Colton decides—but lunges with a pad at the last second as Spezak goes around him on the backhand. The forward throws his arms up in the air in exaggerated celebration, as he always does when stakes are at their lowest, and Colton loses all sense of perspective for an annoyed moment. Down the ice, Foy is shaking his head a little bit, not believing the hype.

Remember, you don't belong here anymore.

"*Brutal!*"

Kids. Little fucking kids.

28

What 90 West is for memories of youth hockey, 90 East into Chicago is for three years as a Rockford Glacier. Since the Glaciers are a combined team, drawing from three local high schools, there's no limit on the number of games they can schedule in a season, and during Colton's years on the team they played in Central States as a midget double-A team in addition to exhibition games and their Metro Northwest league play. That meant sixty to seventy games per season, most of them in Chicago suburbs. That meant two road games a week at least, his mom or dad always making the drive even after Colton got his license. An apple and an energy drink—Smarties smell of Red Bull—his earbuds battling his parents' talk and talk radio, reading a book or messing around on his phone or staring at the reflection of his face superimposed over the blur of wilderness. Many a Wednesday night he didn't get to bed until one a.m., dreading his six-thirty alarm for school. Why are teens so *moody*?

Past the Kishwaukee River, swollen by snowmelt, past corduroy farmlands framed by a tangled wall of skeletal forest, only Indian Hill rises to meager heights above the soccer fields and outlet malls of northern Illinois. He'd gone through a nature boy phase in early high school, had imagined his tent tucked into *that* valley, safe from all the pressures of a hectic world.

Now he imagines the landmark erased from the countryside, imagines caring enough about a heap of earth to save its memory from the void.

Ninety minutes east to everywhere: home-away-from-home West Meadows where they played most of their league games, Barrington and its student section's proclivity for throwing lighter-heated coins onto the ice, purple and teal Johnny's Ice House wedged Lego-like into prime real estate downtown, the Polar Dome located in a Chernobyl fallout amusement park populated by untrademarked crossbreeds of the North Pole and Black Forest, posh Seven Bridges with its three ice sheets and way better than average pro shop and concessions, home to Team Illinois and the memory of a life-changing opportunity Colton had turned down as a peewee. And Bensenville. They're dangerously close to The Edge, where Colton's life *did* change, *is* changing—here, now—because of the opportunity he said yes to. And, of course, the United Center.

He's never gotten to step on the ice at the United Center, an honor reserved for the real state championships, New Trier versus Mount Carmel or Loyola or Stevenson. But there's a banquet they've been invited to every year they won combined states, tickets for the whole team to whatever game was least likely to sell out that year (always, always Phoenix), vouchers for free hot dogs and pop, their team name on the scoreboard. Colton's dad is old enough to have seen games at the original Madhouse on Madison, the one with the organ in the stands—back when Near West was far from gentrified.

"You're quiet tonight," his dad says as they pass below the arch of an open tolling station.

An observation that forces him to offer proof to the contrary. "Yeah."

"Nervous about going back, I suppose."

The return. First week back home it was all he could think about. Then the friends and places and rituals of Rockford started to render Driftless—the game against Eau Claire, Charlie and her monument, his host family's erratic behavior, the inexplicable straight A's he'd achieved, Shane's secret—more and more some bizarre dream.

Despite Greta's daily phone calls reminding him of its reality.

Colton went whole minutes at a time not thinking about Charlie. He drove Woodward's Festival of Lights, Sinnissippi's ice sculpture competition. He sledded Alpine Park. He ate Swedish pancakes at the Stockholm Inn with his old carpools. Lunch at Beef-a-Roo. Nate even convinced his wife to let him go on a nocturnal Perkins run. At a Boylan basketball game last night, the sight of his friends and former teachers had Colton wishing himself back in the student section with the hooligans.

But preparations for the trip north, homework too, have made him face the unavoidable return. Return to Driftless.

"Crazy about Hugo Trautsch. You can't say anything these days."

You're being tested.

"Unless you're the president."

"Alright, alright…" Millennials. Dark times we live in.

Don't say something you might not regret later. "I'm worried about Protein."

"Who?"

"His brother. Spencer."

"Have you talked to him?"

"No. I keep thinking I should check in, but sometimes people want to act like it's no big deal."

"In my experience, it's better to make sure."

*

"Get whatever you want in terms of food." They're slaloming their way through red and white memorabilia, the occasional clash of navy and yellow, brave Sabres fans throwing their hands up in the air at every jeer like they aren't last in the Atlantic. "That's included in your present."

"I shouldn't go crazy. I've chunked out over break."

"Nonsense. Aren't the Rentschlers feeding you?"

Portals of dizzy vastness open into the arena every aisle. They're so far away the mezzanines opposite each entrance seem not to move at all when Colton walks past. The effect is that of bad green screen. Father and son find section 117 and hand their tickets to a woman in a red jacket for inspection.

"How's everything going with them? The Rentschlers." They make their way down to the first-row seats, on the glass right behind Crawford's net. "Dad's a little spacey, huh?"

"Oh, I forgot—Mrs. Rentschler's pregnant."

"Good for them."

Colton's dad always insists on getting to games early enough to watch warm-ups.

"I guess we won't be seeing Trautsch tonight."

"Did you hear the news?" The guy sitting next to Colton sloshes beer on the ground as he wedges himself into the conversation. His neck tattoos commemorate the Hawks' three recent Cup wins, and his lower lip bulges with chew.

Is there a way he can switch seats with his dad? "The racist thing?"

"No, man, that's just the tip of the iceberg," Neck Tattoo says. "Turns out he has a bunch of gambling debts too. Checked himself into a Betty Ford to avoid the mob."

Colton confirms the news on his phone. Nothing about the actual mob.

He opens up Messages and stares at their names, the last

words of the last texts they'd sent.

Protein: *Sometimes you gotta get your shit fuckin shit fucked*
Ben: *Have you ever gotten the Ryu fireball in Mega Man X?*
Charlie: I *would legit buy hockey equipment called Plumage*
Pettit: *You didn't tell anyone, did you???*
Return.

What happens if you don't? Return, that is. If you lay it all out—your dad loves you—here, right now? It's not your job to save Shane or make a grand statement against hydraulic fracturing, not your job to win a state championship for a city and school you hardly know. If Dad doesn't take it well, then blame him.

Blame him for fooling you into thinking the world was a simple, decent place.

"No Crow either," his dad says.

"Healthy scratch." Neck Tattoo has all the answers.

"Colton." His dad grabs his arm. "Recognize anyone?"

The goalie skates into the crease, takes his helmet off, pulls back his long black hair. For a second Colton thinks they make eye contact, this NHL goalie who doesn't look much older than Colton because he isn't. He puts back on his Rockford Ice Hogs mask and starts taking shots.

"Traeger." Neck thinks they need help reading the name on the back of the jersey. "Hometown hero. First NHL start."

Colton turns to his dad to tell him what's wrong with Drift-less.

"Dad," he says, "notice anything about his pads?"

He thinks for a second. "Oh, same design as yours."

His freshman year, Colton led the Glaciers to an improbable tie with New Trier's varsity squad, the only time Rockford had ever—*would ever*, probably—come close to beating the best high school hockey dynasty in Illinois. Traeger, then a senior, looped back after the handshake line, found Colton. Goalies do this sometimes. *See you in the big show, kid.*

Colton has never told anyone.

29

Colton spends the whole day nervous about seeing Protein. He's not a girl you're asking out or breaking up with, he keeps reminding himself. Still the nerves are the same brand.

They don't have any classes together—he does spot Protein once, passing through the lobby during lunch, but Colton lunges behind the *ficus benjamina* in the manner of a cartoon character who can effectively hide behind an object much narrower than himself. He knows he's been making the situation worse with every passing day he doesn't contact his friend. Now, every passing second.

After school, heading to the gym, Colton knows it's time. There's another locker room for the gym at Steiner, but the varsity guys all use the hockey one. Protein's the sole occupant when Colton enters, everyone's gear spread around their stalls as if they'd been raptured away, leaving these two teammates behind and no one else.

"How you holding up?"

"Fine," Protein says, like he doesn't know what Colton's talking about.

"I'm sorry I didn't call you over break, check up on you. That was shitty of me."

"No worries, Birdy. Save the drama." He laces up his sneakers. "The captain of Team USA versus some jihadist with an iPhone. I think my bro'll be okay."

Colton's eyes dart around the room even though he knows they're alone.

"Might want to cool it with that talk, you know?"

"This is a locker room, Bird. It's a safe space! C'mon get dressed."

Protein is waiting for him outside the locker room as Colton exits in his workout clothes. Teammates are already hard at work in the gym trying to burn off the holiday, and if Protein notices they're giving him the same awkward treatment Colton had, he doesn't show it.

"Is that Pettit, in the *weight room?*"

"Should we stretch out first?"

"Come on, Birdy, I want you to see this."

He leads Colton over to the bench press where Gunnar is in position to spot Pettit. Protein nods him off to the side and stands over the bar.

"You don't mind?" he says to Pettit.

Pettit does, but shakes his head anyway. Furrowing his brow with determination to impress the seniors, Pettit makes micro-adjustments with his torso on the bench's maroon vinyl pad, his hands on the bar's silver knurl. Two twenties on each side—Colton decides not to share the Glaciers' running joke with his Driftless teammates, his weightlifting fail freshman year at Boylan.

Protein cups his hands under the bar, helps Pettit lift it up, draws back.

"Good to see you getting your shit together, Pettit."

Pettit strains. *One.* Not looking good for lots of reps.

"That's what breaks are for," Protein continues, "recuperating, thinking things over."

The freshman's face is purple-red, a vein making itself seen on his forehead. *Three.*

"Why're you wearing long sleeves to the gym?"

"Work up," Pettit puffs, "a sweat." *Five.*

"I heard that you've been chatting with Dr. Hagen."

The school counselor. Pettit's eyes find Protein's. For a flash, Colton's. *Seven.*

"Get anything good for Christmas?"

Pettit shakes his head, arms trembling. *Nine.*

"I got a new phone. The cameras on these things keep getting better and better. Everyone becomes—how does the commercial put it?—a roving photojournalist."

Pettit spits a little on exhale, a fleck landing on his chin. He's not gonna make it to *eleven*, but Protein's hands remain at his sides.

"You can document anything—cat antics, your avocado toast, a pro athlete expressing some red-blooded American fury, you and your friends hanging out at the rink—super high resolution so you can make out *every detail*, then upload it to the cloud, and it's there forever."

"*Help*," Pettit gasps.

Gunnar steps up, but Protein pushes him back. "I'm trying to get you to help yourself, brother."

The bar sinks down to Pettit's sternum, which takes a lot of the weight—at the expense of the kid's ability to breathe.

"Check out this picture quality." Protein takes his phone out of his pocket, thumbs around, and then holds it screen down above Pettit. "Oops, let's mute it. We don't want our star goalie to know *all* your secrets."

Pettit's face goes even deader.

"C'mon, man," Gunnar starts, but Protein brings the phone up in front of the forward's face, a talisman that makes speech fail.

Protein pockets the phone and leans down to grab the bar,

but for a second he puts more weight on it. "I know you don't much like your nickname, Pettit. But let me make this crystal clear—the *last* thing you want in the whole world is for your teammates to start calling you Jonas Graaskamp. The day they start doing that is the day they're not your teammates anymore. It's the day we stop protecting your tweaker ass."

He nods to let Colton pull the weight off Pettit's chest, rack the bar. When Pettit turns to face them, though, it's not Protein but Colton he's glaring at. Wounding with his woundedness. Colton glances around the room, but their other teammates are averting their eyes.

"You should've learned already," Protein adds, "drugs are not our drug of choice here in Driftless. And you," he directs at Gunnar, "you are your brother's keeper. C'mon, Bird."

Protein leads Colton over to the power rack, where he starts loading on plates.

"That seemed a little harsh."

"Bird, the kid's a junkie. At fifteen. Do you want me to let him piss away his career?" More plates, one-fifty on each side and going back for more.

"What was that on your phone?"

Protein starts putting on the lifting belt. "A reminder he needs to get with the program."

"Protein, that's too much weight."

"Why don't you let my huge guns be the judge of that?"

"I mean that's too much weight for me, spotting."

Protein gives a sneer. "If I needed a spotter, no offense, but I'd ask someone else, Birdy. Birds have hollow bones."

He positions himself under the bar, does the micro-adjustments dance, breathes in, breathes out.

Then turns his head. "Aren't you gonna spot me?"

Before Colton can replay the content of their conversation of two seconds ago, Protein takes a deep breath and lifts the bar off the rack. Colton rushes to hook his arms under his teammate's. Spotting squats is like the board game Operation—make contact with the body and you'll get zapped—or siblings pestering each other on long car trips with *I'm not touching you.*

"How was… your break?" Protein manages. *Two.*

"It was good. Sat right behind the glass at the Hawks/Sabres game–" Thus trotting Hugo back into the conversation by accident. *Three.* It could've been casual, normalizing, but the way he stopped himself only goes to punctuate the blunder.

"They're shit… without Hugo." *Four.*

Colton lowers his body along with Protein's, rises back up more slowly—*five*—sensing without touching his teammate's trembling muscles, vibrations of disturbed air.

"At least… he picked… the right time… to be racist." Somehow, *six.*

Seeing Protein's face in the wall of mirrors, you'd think this rack was the torture device.

"The right… religion too."

Sevennnnn– Protein starts to fall forward.

Colton clamps down on his teammate's lats and brings his chest back up. "Walk it in."

"Thanks, brother."

"At least Traeger's been solid. I used to play with him back in Illinois."

"In five years guys'll say that about us. *Used to play with Vogler back in high school.*"

"Let's get through Sparta first."

"You asked Greta to prom yet?"

"Not yet."

"You better get on that shit. I might ask Erika Holz."

"Could be a little awkward."

"Why? You didn't fuck her, did you?"

Colton shakes his head.

"Maybe I'll holler that other girl you're hot for—Conrad?—tell her she needs to get with the program too."

"Charlie." Yeah, she'd love you.

30

Charlie, writing in the sky with fire and steel.

Colton knows he's not supposed to look at the flame, that this risk is the reason the welding mask was invented. Despite the danger, despite Charlie's wastebasket mask, her winter clothes, her heavy gloves—which leave everything to the imagination—he can't help himself from pausing work and stealing skyward glances. The two arms of the arch are reaching out at glacial pace to shake hands across the falsework. He does not hate the idea of becoming the first suppliant in the history of love to be really truly blinded by the sight of his dearest. Because of Zev's engineering skills, his ability to use the tools of the gods, he gets to live up in the sky with the poet.

"It's whistle while you work," Ben says, "not whistle while you watch."

Oops—he'd been giving a sneak peak, or sneak listen, of the Driftless Quintet.

Ben raises his eye protection. "I know you're crazy about her. Charlie."

Bigger oops. Scouting around for the most dangerous of the power tools, Colton guesses the jig is up. Ben is holding the spinning-bladed circ saw; Colton, a carpenter's pencil.

"Look, I–"

Ben lifts a hand to silence him. "Don't be nervous. Look, Colton, my experience with Driftless Hockey broke me as an athlete, as a man, to the extent that I can play the game and I can enjoy the game, but I can't go back to acting like I'm *supposed to*. A good thing, no doubt, but, well, I'm still a teenager."

"Ben—"

"Shut up, I'm on a roll here. I also can't act like a man is *supposed to* when it comes to this." He indicates himself and Colton, then hits his fists together like rams' horns. "With my distance from the whole thing, it's a big joke. Charlie and I have something amazing, a deep understanding, and we're looking years down the line. Decades. She tells me that I don't have anything to worry about from you. Not with words—we don't always need words. But, if that changes, I'll take what I've learned and wish the best for her. Because I love her enough to always want what she wants. And I hope the same goes for you."

Before Colton has a chance to attempt an answer, they are rejoined by a guy who's been helping them out today. Marshall, in an old North Stars sweatshirt.

"It's whistle while you *work*," Ben repeats, covering up their silence. "Not whistle while you watch."

"I don't know," Colton says, his heart still pounding from the confrontation, as he drops off another piece of plywood by Ben's sawhorse setup. "You're the one falling behind."

"Running a saw is a little harder than running a pencil. Wanna switch?"

"Slava would find out." His goalie and chamber music coach is already pissed off at Colton's slow progress on the Shostakovich, not knowing it's because he's been putting so much time into a quintet of his own.

"So you're not going to use the saw because your hands are much more important and delicate than mine."

"That's what I'm saying. Besides, I'm the one having to

make all the precise measurements."

"Yeah, and those re-measurements every time you fuck up are pretty time-consuming as well."

Marshall remains mystified by Ben's adeptness with power tools.

With the unveiling ceremony in the books for April, it turns out that his friends have no intention of letting cold weather or senioritis keep them from pouring concrete. Their ambition has been aided by a few weeks of unseasonably—or, as Zev referred to it, "soon-to-be seasonably"—warm weather. Today is in the high forties, and the only reason Colton feels chilly is because of the sweat he's working up.

They've also been joined today by a two-person documentary crew Charlie had gotten in touch with. There's a camera pointed at them right now, a microphone Jim Henson might have dreamt up. Colton isn't sure whether they're rolling or not since Angie and Lucia are currently arguing about f-stops—but his words and actions are still stilted by the possibility they're being made permanent.

"This is the last section of eighteen," Ben says, clamping the plywood onto two sawhorses and making the necessary quadrilateral emerge with four clean cuts. The workers drop everything to lay out the labeled pieces on the muddy ground and power drill the flat slabs into an angled, 3-D tunnel.

Whistling again.

Hard to keep the music out of his *Kopfradio*, located as he is at the quintet's place of origin. Finale's human playback gets a little more sophisticated with each year's new version, but it's still aggravating that so far he's only been able to hear computer software interpret his work, not living musicians.

He's reached an impasse in the composition. On the one hand, he's super happy with the three minutes of music he's written. It's chromatic but listenable, and somehow it really does evoke a hill, no doubt about it. On the other hand, it feels like it's done. It's fallen into a cadence and doesn't want to budge. He can't *hear* any further thematic development.

Or maybe the problem is that he's terrified to mess it up. He knows he's lucked into something special, and the attitude of *Let's see what happens* that had taken him this far has been replaced by the kind of caution that never creates anything interesting. As impressed as Charlie might be with a three-minute piano quintet, he wants to produce music that measures up to the Gateway itself, especially being here on the site. Calling it done would be the same as leaving the arch in its current state, drawbridged.

"How'd Charlie convince you to help out?" Colton asks Marshall as he angles two pieces of plywood together and Marshall readies the screw.

"It wasn't Charlie. It was her dad. We met at the doctor's and got to talking. I grew up with a backyard beach like this one, and I worked at a mine for a spell in my twenties."

"Why'd you stop?"

"There's no rules—and the ones there are they don't follow. I was working nights at a cleaning facility outside Iduna during this crazy downpour, and the rain washed away one of the ponds. We had to work all through the night sand-bagging the berm. Next day, we covered the sandbags with earth, strips of sod. Nothing could live in those ponds they're so full of chemicals, and it all flooded this creek that never looked right again, as long as I worked there. Our overtime was buying more than our extra hours that week."

"How much longer did you work there?"

He knows what Colton's asking. "The money's good, and there's not much else going on around here. So it's no blinding light story. My dad—he owns a dairy farm—his cattle started dying off, from the water or stress from the noise, I don't know. A big crack formed in our kitchen wall from explosions they'd set off underground in the middle of the night. I got a cough that never went away. So the anger creeps up real gradual, the realization that your neighbors and your buddies, that you've all been used. If it was just our hours and our land and our health, that would be bad enough. But it's worse than that. They figured out how to get us to believe in it, against our best interests, to defend it with our dying breaths. And so... *angry*. We're so angry. I've lost friends over it."

"Sand equals jobs," Ben says.

"Shit, an equal sign is the most complicated argument most people can handle. It matters a lot who's drawing those two lines. Things can equal a lot of things."

This section of frame is assembled, reinforced, and the three guys carry it over to where the hook of the crane swings lightly in the breeze. After securing it to the hook with tie-downs, Marshall gives Terrance in the crane a thumbs up. It begins its ascent, eclipsing the sun for a second, up to where Charlie and Zev have advanced the rebar bones beyond the section of arch the frame will cover.

The Driftless Quintet is again interrupted by the *beep... beep... beep* that has been scattering his notes like frightened birds all day. Ben says he thinks they're about to pour the concrete, and the three of them decide they can take a minute to go watch. At the other arm of the arch, where a larger portion of the frame is complete, a concrete mixer has backed its ass up to a truck that is exactly what a little kid would draw if you told him you needed to pour some concrete way up high. Like the lure of the ugliest fish on the ocean floor, its boom extends up and angles toward the arch, where two workers clipped into climbing harnesses wait to guide its hose into each of several access points cut into the top of the frame. It's a few minutes before the concrete starts to flow, by which time Colton has convinced himself that the first section of frame that he helped build will explode from the pressure and send a ton of gray goop glopping down the side of the falsework. But in not too much time the worker has capped the cutout in the tunnel and is moving the dripping hose to the next opening. Globs of concrete plop onto the ground below.

Colton and Marshall head back to the stacks of plywood.

"Is that sweatshirt real-old or fake-old?"

"Real real-old. Met Center, 1991, versus the Quebec Nordiques."

"Double extinction."

"You like hockey?"

"Yeah, I'm a goalie."

"Where do you play?"

"Here, in Driftless."

Marshall stops walking. His expression is that of a bad epiphany, one that doesn't make sense.

"Don't let that worry you, Marshall," a voice booms out. It's Mr. LaBoda, limping toward them in sweatpants and rubber boots, lugging an industrial coffee urn. "Colton's no shitty Viking. He's our spy, not theirs."

"Hi Mr. LaBoda," Ben calls out, taking off his gloves.

"Rations for the troops. Zev's parents are on their way with food, but they couldn't keep up with me." Marshall takes the urn from Mr. LaBoda. "There's those craniacs!"

The two adults walking their way from the direction of the house are carrying bags of food from Strassers. Colton hasn't met Zev's parents yet, and he imagines them dressed in white capes and beaks, bobbing their heads as they approach, scrutinizing the giant machine named after the birds they study.

The crane operator, Terrance, helps Mr. LaBoda transform plywood and sawhorses into a table for the food and coffee urn. Angie and Lucia decide that eating lunch is more important than filming it.

"You're Colton?" Zev's mom asks.

"Yeah." Maybe it's because he's ravenous and they're handing him a hot meatball sub, but Colton likes Zev's parents right away. And wants them to like him.

"Zev speaks very highly of you."

It strikes Colton as newly novel, being spoken of at all. "It's nice to meet you."

"I guess their food is going to get cold," Zev's dad says, gazing up at Charlie and Zev. They've started on a new section of rebar.

"It's hard to tear yourself away," Colton says. "The work is addictive."

"I know the feeling."

Colton receives a plastic travel mug of coffee, takes a sip. "So, you're the avian aviators?"

They smile. Guilty as charged.

"What's it like, flying with the cranes?"

"It's so strange," Zev's mom begins. She waits and waits for this question but is never prepared. "My first thought when I saw these birds—they're big, with six-foot wingspans—flying so close to me, trusting that I would lead them to a home they'd never seen before… Pardon me, but my first thought, the thought I could never keep from having, was: now I'm a parent." She looks up at Zev and Charlie, likewise wearing climbing harnesses for safety. "As if I wasn't doing this same thing every day for creatures so much more complicated and breakable than these birds."

31

Need to get him off the ice right now. Refs know. They're watching him.

Never all of a sudden, the big penalties. There's accidents of course, checking a guy into the boards from a little too far away, or realizing at the last second you're staring down a victim's back. But more often there's a red glow around a guy, a froth to the way he moves, his mask pointed with intent.

Most of the Sparta guys have done the calculus—in a 5-0 game it's not worth getting between Trautsch and whatever he's dealing with.

Except number seventeen, all five-foot-eight buck-fifty of him. He's devised a new version of hockey where all you do is pick out one player on the other team and see how pissed off you can make him. Slashing, hooking, late checks, chirps. Three trips to the box so far haven't taught him any lessons.

Or maybe Seventeen is the *only* Spartan who's figured it out. Driftless (playoff-bound) and Protein (Badger-bound) have way more to lose, after all.

Good, Protein's off the ice. Colton realizes he's been holding his breath. Yeah, throw those water bottles, spaz.

The one who seems most clueless is the Big Show. Colton keeps checking to see if Riessen will at least give his winger a pep talk—but it looks like he's gonna keep crossing his fingers.

Guy coming in bad angle shoots it far side and the puck

glances off the knob of Colton's stick. *Would have sailed wide anyway, but how about let's stop watching Protein?*

The three completed minutes of Driftless Quintet have been looping all game in his *Kopfradio*. With all the hours he's been spending at Gateway ground zero, still no budging, no further ideas or thematic development. Colton's not sure if the quintet's on his list of "acceptable soundtracks" for hockey games. There's those nights of pure instinct of course it doesn't matter what song is going through your head. It could be and has been Taylor Swift and it wouldn't matter. Wouldn't need to shake it off. Other nights Colton isn't quite so zoned in, "Hey Ya" or "Ya Hey," and it will be very important that the song is eviscerated stat, before it starts vamping whatever's left of his focus. The more he thinks about how important it is not to have a song playing in his head the more his brain is pretty sure he's selected it lots of times in a row on the mental jukebox. (For example right now, Colton's *Kopfradio*: *Baby shark d-do d-do d-do.*) An aural palette cleanser is necessary, so Colton has a list of songs for such occasions. Banish the baby shark, "Change Clothes" or "Laika," "Shadowplay" or "Seven Nation Army." Anything by *Radiokopf.*

Protein back on the ice. Seventeen on the bench but standing.

No Charlie in the crowd tonight. Ben and Zev in attendance makes it worse. Ben might be repaying him for going to see *As You Like It* last weekend. Or, well, Ben enjoys watching hockey. Looks bored right now. And conflicted, must be, like Shane watching video with Colton at Penthe Meadows.

Colton slides from one post to the other, whipping his head around to follow Seventeen, back on the war path, behind the net. Pushes off the post to challenge Seventeen going wide around the circle toward the high slot, D not letting him get close.

Baby shark d-do d-do d-do—

Stop it.

No, don't order it to stop—that makes it angry. Stop the puck.

He'll go for the screen, shoot it when a Brother Grimm eclipses Colton's vision. Gets low to see through legs, commits to shuffling a little early so he can crane around Grimmer, leaving the short side vulnerable.

Safe at last! Violins soaring—cello exploring its lowest depths—viola remaining inconspicuous—piano trilling: we've reached the top of Fort Mountain, and you can see the whole Midwest from here.

Drops it to his D, locked and loaded.

Where can you go from the top of the hill but back down? Repeat the whole quintet retrograde?

Find it. High. Arms in. Spread low for deflections. Chest tall.

Puck hits Colton right between the eyes—

And the rest of the Driftless Quintet leaps fully formed into Colton's brain.

They don't believe you smell smoke, but you do.

His ears ringing the quintet.

Falls to his chest to cover the puck. Gets a whack, snow shower.

Not that he hears it, not in his *Kopfradio*. He can't hear it. But he knows what to do, where he went right and where he went wrong.

You were trying to evoke a hill with music. And you did.

But there's no hill there anymore.

"Okay Birdy?" someone asks him. Grim Reaper.

Can you die from a good idea? Like being scared to death. The lightbulb's wattage so hefty it zaps your plain brain? Maybe the number one cause of death for artists—killed by the perfect kernel they were seeking out their whole lives.

The ref does the SportsCenter theme, and it almost finishes Colton off.

Turns another knob of the *Kopfradio*, checking for flaws, for staleness, for logistical problems—but the revelation keeps returning elated. Within days his quintet could triple, quadruple in length.

And he won't even need to write a single new note.

Protein and Seventeen, off to the side by the boards. Someone might think they're just chatting, but masks a little too close. Refs occupied with debris on the ice.

It happens so fast, Protein ripping off Seventeen's helmet, then his own. Punches—real punches—he lands *real* punches on Seventeen's face. Immediate blood. Seventeen crumpling to the ground and trying to turtle, Protein falling on top of him, keeping him from turning over. Sparta players are all like good luck with that. The refs taking a little too long to decide how best to enter this tornado.

Finally the heftiest of the stripes pins Protein's arms. Once refs enter the scenario, players tend to give up, but Protein wants more.

"Fuck you! I'll fucking *kill* you!"

A Sparta player sidles up to Colton. "Pete probably deserves it."

Colton enjoys these truces that form between players on opposing teams who don't have any interest in fighting. For a second they're all spectators.

"I don't think anyone deserves *that*."

Seventeen's face is flayed. No movement.

"Pete kept talking about Trautsch before the game, Hugo Trautsch, like he was obsessed. I bet he said something."

"Social justice warrior?"

"Yeah, right. If there's one guy on our team most likely to

be dragged out of an immigrant's taxi by the police, it's that asshole."

It takes both linesmen to escort Protein, and one of them follows him to the locker room to make sure he stays there. Cleaning Seventeen off the ice is going to take a while, and the referee calls the game. In his excitement over the quintet epiphany, Colton hadn't realized there were only forty seconds left. The rest of both teams are dazed and sedate, but still the refs cancel the handshake line and keep Sparta on the ice while Driftless heads off. Colton receives a paltry two or three taps on the pads for congratulations on another shutout. The fans file out silent, a small crowd sticking around to see whether or not an ambulance will show up.

In the locker room, the supply cart has been dynamited, a mirror has dispensed all its bad luck, and three $200 sticks have been split to kindling. Guys step around the mess without commenting on it. Protein is sitting in his stall, head in his bloody, broken hands. They can all hear that he's crying.

Maybe these idiots are stupid enough to think it's about his brother.

32

Colton's hand finds but doesn't flick on the mudroom light switch. Opera is playing—Strauss?—and a faint glow reaches out through the dark house.

Yup, *Der Rosenkavalier*. A fourth voice joins the famous Act Three trio. Alma's voice.

Groping his way through the kitchen, he finds her sitting on the living room couch. A single sandalwood candle burns in the vicinity of the flatscreen. He was hoping for Bösendorfer time tonight to test the veracity of the musical revelation slapshotted into his noggin.

"Ulrich and Winifred Rentschler née Abendroth begot Klaus Rentschler, oldest of eight. Klaus and Gisela née von Grimmelhausen begot Lütold, third of four. Lütold and Solvig née Metzger begot Volker, youngest of six, who left the old country. Volker begot—"

"Mrs. Rentschler?"

"Colton Vogler," she replies in the same tone, as if he were just another entry in the line of succession.

"Can I switch on a light?"

"By all means, more light." Alma doesn't blink in the sudden brightness. Her hands are crossed over her stomach, and she notices that's where Colton's eyes go. "I'm trying to imagine myself in the cave of a womb. They say it's good for a baby to hear his parents' voices."

"Do you know it's a boy?"

"Of course it is. Say something to little Fritz. Tell him your grandparents' names."

"Well, on my mom's side are Eric Geiger, and my grandmother's name is Lana. They're both still alive. On my dad's side is George Vogler, and my grandmother—she died in a car accident before I was born… I'm blanking on her name. That's terrible–"

"Flora."

"That's right. How'd you know that?"

"I think it's important for children to know their lineage, where they fit into the grand scheme. More and more young people get so wrapped up in friends and gadgets that they forget about tradition. They know the names of everyone on their favorite sports team, or every song by their favorite band, but you ask them about their family and they're stricken with amnesia."

"I'm afraid that's me." He's only pulling up two of eight great grandparents' names. At least Opa in Woodland Mews had an excuse for not remembering Colton.

"I'm sorry we missed your game. I was wiped and Flynn has a bar league game tonight. A late one."

"No worries."

"I assume you won?"

"Yeah, but I think Spencer could have used one of those pep talks you give Flynn when he's all riled up."

"He got in a fight?"

"A bad one. He broke his hand."

She takes a sip of tea. "That's not going to help his family."

The trio reaches a climax, the Marschallin realizing she must let Octavian go.

"What do you think of those Baby Mozart theories," Alma

asks, "that playing music for kids when they're young transforms them into virtuosos?"

"There might be something to it. My mom was sold on the theory."

"I think it's nonsense. It's all genetics. Fritz will be a great musician because it's in his blood—and a talented athlete as well, healthy and well-proportioned, a real ladies' man."

Gross. Gross enough when they're pre-pubescent, even grosser when they're prenatal.

"Maybe you'll play a song for him?" She mutes the Marschallin. "A lullaby."

He wants to say no, but he's living in these people's house, and the awkward silence coaxes him to the piano bench. It's not a lullaby exactly, but he opens a book to Grieg's "Arietta."

Ben's mom thinks Ben is at Zev's house. Ben is staying at Charlie's tonight. Ben's mom thinks that Ben, despite his blood, is not much of a ladies' man.

He finishes the short piece and Mrs. Rentschler says nothing. Her eyes are closed but her mouth is moving over silent syllables. He begins Schumann's *"Träumerei,"* another instance of an adult artist misremembering what childhood was like.

Colton's ears have been ringing on and off all night from the head shot. Schumann had tinnitus, a persistent A5 singing in his ears. Schumann was gifted angelic and demonic visions by syphilis. Schumann tried to kill himself by jumping off a bridge into the Rhine.

When he finishes, Alma hasn't moved.

"Do you mind if I go take a soak?"

"By all means," she says, keeping her eyes closed. "Soak away."

"Do you want me to turn the light off?"

"Please."

After he plunges the room back into night, one hand on the doorknob to his bedroom, Alma says, "Colton, we're so glad you've come into our lives."

33

He'd been looking forward to a very rare Saturday without hockey. He hadn't expected to end the night playing beer pong in a garage in Madison with a college girl hot enough to make him forget what's-their-names, one step closer to D1 hockey.

His lazy Saturday plans were upended by the appearance of Coach Riessen at the Rentschlers' front door.

"Pack your stuff," was his hello. "Time for a campus visit."

At least no sweatpants. As Colton tried to think up an excuse why he couldn't go, he realized he was supposed to be excited. *Was* excited, in a way. Flynn, cycling pots of orchids up from the winter garden, wasn't fazed by the impromptu trip, but Ben found a moment to communicate a grave nod of the head.

"Shouldn't my parents be involved with this?" Colton asked.

"You're not signing any papers."

Colton found himself in his room, packing an overnight. Why an overnight for a campus visit?

He would have to call the chamber group to cancel the Driftless Quintet rehearsal scheduled for 3:00. He'd emailed the faculty at Saint Mary's University in Winona, right across the river, and they'd recommended four talented students who'd agreed to make the drive and not charge what they were worth. After both the cellist and violist had asked Colton if he'd accidentally sent an incomplete draft of the quintet, he'd emailed the whole group explaining his idea. Today it was supposed to be Colton making the drive into Minnesota's sliver of the Driftless Region. He'd have to throw a little more money at them to keep them from getting pissed about the cancellation.

Cammo was already sitting in the front seat of Riessen's SUV, so Colton got in back with Boots.

"Guys, your goalie wants to know why his parents aren't coming."

"I think this is the fun trip," Boots said, "not the business trip."

"Hey, no blowing," Colton's beer pong partner yells at Brenda. Colton's been this guy's partner for at least an hour and hasn't retained his name.

"Wisconsin rules," Brenda counters, scoping Colton up and down again. "Girls can blow."

Colton examines the contents of the cup he's been told it's his turn to down. The ping-pong ball appears to have been rolled in an ashtray. It bobs in foam like one of those red and white things you use fishing. He emerges from the cup with the ping-pong ball suctioned to his lips, lets it fall into his hand.

"Doesn't matter." Colton, booze-cocky, throws a line drive that all laws of probability and rules of strategy are powerless to keep from finding the Capitol dregs at the bottom of his opponents' last cup.

The garage cheers, his partner high-fives him, and Brenda can't believe it.

Colton has advanced to the semi-finals of a tournament he didn't know he was involved in.

His phone buzzes in his pocket. Greta's been trying to reach him all night.

"How are we feeling about next Wednesday?" Riessen asked once they'd gotten on the highway.

"River Falls shouldn't be a problem."

"No, they shouldn't. How about our goalie?"

His groin hurt. "It's tough not having Protein."

The car went silent, and Colton wanted to explain himself. He wasn't talking about the empty seat in the car, where Protein would be sitting if he'd kept his shit together, wasn't talking about this SUV of star seniors driving south to schmooze with the Badgers.

But it was all he'd been thinking about since getting into the car, so maybe he was.

"Spencer made his choice," Coach Riessen said. "I don't want you thinking about that—or getting too stressed about states either."

"Hard not to," Cammo answered for everyone.

"Of course it's hard. If it was easy for you three not to get worried, I wouldn't be telling you this. But you're seniors—you know this doesn't mean anything. Sure we've got a town counting on us, sure winning or losing is a memory that will remain with you the rest of your lives. But that's a boy's game. This, what we're doing today, this is the important thing. It's a paradox, but I bet you're beginning to figure it out: when it's not about the sport anymore is when the sport becomes important."

*

"Have you ever been to Strassers?" Brenda asks him.

"What's that?" He can't believe this girl. She's a music major at UW, plays the harp. He's been pulling himself back from the brink of angel-based pickup lines the entire night.

"In Driftless."

"Oh yeah, we go there after games." They've been talking shop for hours. She told him who to study piano with, and he's pretty sure he wrote it down. Must be this... *Ramlevvzk* on his hand. "You know Driftless?"

"I told you already, I grew up there."

No way that's right. Either he's being shallow or she's a liar, and Colton's never felt so deep as tonight. Sophisticated, ready to leave behind childish things, burn incense while sipping tea in his reading nook, street music filtering in through the night window.

"Sorry, it's noisy in here."

"I used to be a hostess at Strassers. When the hockey crowds would come in we'd call them the Shitless. I'm not sure why. Get ready, the Shitless should be rolling in soon."

"What does this say on my hand?"

"It should say Pawlewski. You know, Colton, if you want college girls to fuck you then you actually have to listen to them."

They met for a good half hour with Coach Salonen and his head scout, Will Tremblay of the bad poker face. Unbeknownst to Colton, Tremblay had been at the Eau Claire game, the sole game so far this undefeated season it could be argued he'd stolen for his team. The whole whirlwind was reminiscent of the fateful night Riessen had shown up at Bensenville—the tour of campus and training facilities and the promises of free gear and bright futures and scholarships *déjà vu*-ing his first weeks in Driftless—but all of it exponentially intensified.

The last six months in Driftless had been nothing more than a rehearsal for this wooing, the peak he'd summited just another tier of a limitless future, a lucky life in which everything goes right. Every second an elixir of forgetting.

He'd known in his gut why it's a joke when his teammates call Riessen the Big Show, but now he could write an essay about it. A poem, a symphony.

Wearing a portion of the memorabilia they'd bagged on a shopping spree at the Badger bookstore, they attended the UW/Bemidji game that night, seats right on the glass with all the free concessions they wanted. The farther you sit from the glass, the more elegant hockey gets—but in a bad way. Ten rows up and it's already slowed down. From the balconies, everything's choreographed and the players look automated. You have to get down to the glass to see the danger of collisions that from higher up seem collaborative, the chaos of a bad bounce, the speed and desperation and hatred.

The recruits had a guide, a lackey named Chris, who informed Colton that Bohatta was going pro next year, signing with Nashville. He didn't need to tell Colton (but did anyway) that Haney, his backup, would be a senior. "I'm not authorized to promise you you'll get varsity games your first year or two, but I know for a fact it's Sally's plan to groom you for that spot."

Colton's phone buzzes in his pocket, as if jolting the words out of him. "I have a girlfriend back in Driftless." The way he says it, he means Greta this time.

"Yeah, back in Driftless." Brenda's picked up on it too. "I

mean, sports don't impress me. But you're this jock who writes disappearing piano quintets—that's unusual."

He told her about the quintet?

"All I'm saying is I picked you out and we've been talking for three hours, and I was thinking I had you locked down for the night. Imagine me binge-watching the new season of *Fuller House* in my apartment, and that would be your fault."

He's trying to imagine it's Charlie he's staying loyal to— but that makes it worse. As they've been spending more time together because of the Gateway, he'd hypothesized that *being around* Charlie might be enough for him. No, it's taken his envy to a lightless place. The other day all she had to do was act distant to him, no excuse prepared for why she'd missed his game, and that night he stared at himself in the bathroom mirror, lights off. He whispered the word: *survive*. More than winning states or committing to a school or wowing everyone with his quintet, *surviving* is Colton's exclusive goal for the next few months.

The best years of his life.

"Look, if you love her, whatever." Brenda's still talking. "But I came here with a boyfriend from Driftless and it was awful. I had this opportunity to start fresh with all these amazing new people and ideas, and I was chained to this prior version of myself. God, I mean, haven't you noticed how *fucked up* that place is?"

After the game, Chris took the three recruits into the Wisconsin locker room. It was strange to be fully dressed and rested in the same space where they were always exhausted and sweaty with everyone else, to be tiptoeing onto equal footing with players they'd been fans of minutes before. Colton wondered whether, in his outsider status, he should be quiet and respect-ful—or channel his inner Protein. But the players had made the recruits feel relaxed. They were used to it, had been in the same position a year or four before. The two Driftless alums would be their guides for the night, Max Abendroth and Kurt von Kempf. "No relation," the latter said when Colton mentioned Greta.

After they'd retreated to the hallway to let the players finish getting undressed, Coach Riessen said his goodbyes.

"Where're we staying tonight?" Boots asked.

Coach Riessen laughed and shook his head and walked away, and Colton was grateful not to be the one asking the stupid questions for once.

"What place?"

Brenda's becoming concerned he's an idiot. "Driftless."

His phone dings in his pocket, a text message this time. Greta: *Emergency.* "I should take this."

"That your boo?"

He grimaces yes.

"Driftless girls…"

Colton walks out onto a sod lawn that won't be turning green in two months. The slab seams show, a dead checker-board. Supposed to stagger them, he knows from his years at the greenhouse. Red cups and fallen soldiers litter the turf like a misguided hydration idea. It's a clear night, but only a few stars make it through the urban purple murk.

Sophisticated and adult. Parisian. In a few months I'll be having heated discussions in coffee shops with lifelong friends—real characters— and chumming with profs who've taken an interest in my intellectual devel-opment—

A girl's voice pierces the street's noise pollution: *"Get out!"* Colton sees a barefoot guy shoved out the door of a neighboring house. *"Get the fuck out!"*

The guy begins to slink away, turns back, disappears into the weekend.

"Where *are* you?" Greta asks, when she picks up.

"Not Paris."

"I know you're in Madison. Are you at a party?"

"Yeah."

"I wish you were here tonight so we could celebrate. I got my acceptance email today."

"That's great." Is that the emergency? This college town has been singing *escape* to him the entire day—even just something about being in a state capitol, with all its heavy granite and purposeful people, the breeze over the lakes and the lofty flags. He hadn't thought about Driftless following him here. A number of other D1 schools suddenly submit competing offers. "We'll have to celebrate when I get back."

Then Brenda is standing right there. *Break up with her*, she mouths.

The idea is such an immediate relief that he knows he can't do it over the phone but is about to anyway. A few minutes of agony and then he doesn't have to pretend anymore to love somebody he doesn't. He can move on to other, more fun mistakes as soon as tonight.

"Greta–

"We might have more to celebrate than schools–

"I've been thinking–

"I'm not sure if you'll feel the same way, but I hope you will–

"When I get back we should probably talk–"

"I'm pregnant."

In a split second he lives out a thousand clichéd futures. He bullies Greta into getting an abortion *I'll pay for it* then does or doesn't leave her. He goes on a public speaking tour of private school gymnasiums about waiting until marriage *Don't make the same mistake I did* or back further to damn the wiles of a temptress *From woman cometh evil into the world!* He tears up and grows up and his heart is filled to bursting with love for Greta and the baby *Filled to bursting* whether it is or isn't. He reverts to a childlike state of dependence and crawls back to his parents *You guys were right about everything* so they'll fix his problem for him. He hangs up the phone and gets in a car *Get the fuck out!* and drives forever.

"Didn't we always use something?" he asks, trying to elongate time and, through sheer act of willpower, stave off the breakneck future.

Brenda, wide-eyed, chooses *Fuller House*.

"You know what they say…"

Yes, Greta's disappointed in her boyfriend's reaction, and both of them are saying what they say, slipping into roles in a scene that has been reproduced too often in human history to allow for new reactions.

Or, failing that, total honesty.

34
COUNTDOWN

*S*HE'S *a brick and I'm drowning slowly–*
       No. Anything but that song.
For the life of me I cannot remember–
       Goddam it! For the life of me it's fucking playoffs.

       What's the game before quarterfinals even called? Do they bother giving it a name?

       First goal was a shot wide from the point, bad bounce off the boards to the guy with an empty net. Okay. Nobody could say that's your fault. I won't be held responsible–

       Don't replay your goals. You don't want *failure failure failure* on the mind. Visualize yourself making the save. You're big, the size of a country. Nowhere to shoot. Mentally he conjures a River Falls duo breaking free, passing back and forth up the ice. But Colton knows all the dance moves, imagines gliding into a graceful leg extension blocker side, feeling the thud of a puck on his shin.

OFF the coast and I'm headed nowhere–
       Maybe don't fight it. Let it play. A song has no power over the body.

       Good guy. You're a good guy who comes up with good guy responses. *Greta, I'm… bursting,* he told her, that beer pong night on the phone. *Colton shrapnel is flying every which way at in-*

credible speeds. Not verbatim. *Part of me's thrilled—me, a dad—us, parents—*

Every day one day closer to human, the procedure less like a procedure—that word he hasn't spoken yet and that doesn't seem to be in Greta's vocabulary.

They call her name at seven thirty. I pace around the parking lot.

and part of me, part of me's terrified—ditto—and all of me's shocked. A good guy with good guy words, he was, that night of recruitment. A bird who mates for life.

For life.

And the second goal? I cannot remember the second goal. Third was the two-on-O tap-in I almost got a toe on. Again, not my fault. Nothing's my fault. I'm not playing half as bad as my shrapnel mind and badger stomach would have me think. I just haven't given up three goals in a while. If only I could—

Greta, can I beg you: as I learn how to live in a state of exploding, over the next few seconds or days, don't expect a coherent, consistent response.

Six a.m., day after Christmas—

But of course I'll be there for you.

Not verbatim.

Ah, the second goal. Yeah, five-hole so close to the nuts it's like it went right through me. That's why I suck. The second goal. Frozen, didn't even move. How couldn't it hit anything? Up by three goals still—no reason to freak out. Zero chance they'll come storming back. Hark, no footsteps.

Zero chance? That's how disasters happen, Bird.

That's right, zero chance. I dare the fates.

She was touching her face—

Guy centers the puck from down in the corner, Colton challenging— Hits Cammo's skate, stops there on a platter for a white jersey coming in hard. Colton tries to stop his momentum the other direction, sprawls out for a pad save to steal the empty netter, a twinge in his groin as he pulls himself back up to his feet, hugs the post.

There we go. Good guy with good guy words, big as this country.

How did you know? he showed concern for his girl.

I've been throwing up, Greta said.

I won't be held responsible. She fell in love in the first—

So have I, he did not say.

Does she look any different? Glowing? Puffy maybe? *That's right, I'm talking about you,* he projects Greta's direction. She sits in the first row next to Alma Mater, all four of them. How to tell one's newly inseminated prom date that—whether or not he's drafting his proposal—he'd rather her not attend his important hockey games because the gravitational pull she exerts from the stands throws off his ability to center his body on the puck, cants the whole ice surface to one side like a listing icebreaker.

SHE'S A BRICK—

Question: Is this hockey goalie in love with me?

Other words to battle flaccid *I Love the '90s* schmaltz rock. Turn to other words, your own words, when the playlist of acceptable soundtracks is offline.

Colton had inflicted a second poem on his gunmetal notebook, forced tainted introspection into the deepest parts of himself, fracturing his guilt and desire so that wieldy utterance could rise to the surface. From the second stanza, verbatim— he'd worked so hard on every line that he'd memorized it:

We goalies know our hearts

are no bull's eyes, know better

than to use

as theodolite

the body's dire asymmetry.

Daylight, opponents call it,

the holes in us.

Breaking out of the zone, Grimmy passes it up to Pettit on the boards. Pettit's mask points, telegraphing his pass, and Colton sees the next five seconds play out before they happen.

Answer: Probably not.

Track instead our noses, our navels, the V of muscle going down.

A River Falls forward shares Colton's prophetic powers, intercepts Pettit's cross-ice lob. Pettit, the maroon jersey closest to Colton, has time to fix his fuck-up—but trips on the cross-over, sprawls face down on the ice.

No one you'll meet is more prepared

to see the very thing that centers us

The forward, remembering his team's second goal, doesn't bother with a deke, firing for the sliver between Colton's right arm and his ribs–

slip right by.

"Great moments… are born from great opportunity. And that's what you have here, tonight, boys. That's what you've *earned* here tonight. One game. If we played 'em ten times, they might win nine. But not this game. Not tonight. Tonight, we skate with them. Tonight, we stay with them. And we shut them down because we can! Tonight, we are the greatest hockey team in the world. You were born to be hockey players. Every one of you. And you were meant to be here tonight. This is your time. Their time is done. It's over. I'm sick and tired of hearing about what a great hockey team—"

Colton turns off the movie. He knows the rest of Herb Brooks's pregame speech to the 1980 Lake Placid squad, as depicted in Disney's *Miracle*. He thought it would get him revved up for tonight's playoff game against Amery, but it's backfired.

Colton is sick, and Colton is tired.

Miracle used to function as prescribed. Even though Rockford had been the powerhouse of a powerless league every year Colton played for them, he'd never allowed his ritual to be infected by tonight's realization: comparing his big game to that big game, he's never been ragtag Team USA. More than ever—Driftless is the Soviet Union of Wisconsin. Amery is no Red Army. It's Amery who're the doomed fuckers possessed by a whole history of underdogs tonight, thinking maybe, just *maybe…*

Meanwhile Colton's full of shitty little proverbs, for example *Losers should keep losing.*

The tragedy overdogs feel when they're brought down is stronger than any joy the winners can know.

Great moments are born from great opportunity. God, what a stupid string of words. Hollow, throwaway. Chewing gum communicates more.

And it's up to Colton, more than anyone else. When they win, he'll be only one of many contributors on the team— "team" will remain devoid of *I*—but it's totally within his power to give Amery fans the chance to trumpet *Do you believe in miracles?* Every goalie has a horrendous game once a year or once a decade, those nights the hockey gods have chosen to punish you for all your sins. There's no hiding, not in the most cramped recesses of your goalie cave. You're a funnel—they could shoot it anywhere and you'd make sure it goes in.

What if tonight's the night? This, of course, the exact type of thinking that aligns those planets of catastrophe. Another new proverb for their inspirational posters, *The sooner you pity, the sooner you're pitied.*

And now that Colton has realized he is in fact not Jim Craig but Vladislav Tretiak—or Vladimir Myshkin, more likely—his brain is snatching all the other ways he's an overdog. A straight white kid from an upper-middle class family (a.k.a. an upper-class family), tucked away in the safe center of a Goliath country. Everywhere else, all kids are starving. And how terrible would it be to be an insect that feeds on dead things? It wasn't that long ago we crawled out of the ocean. But yeah a hockey game is *so* important, so worth the gasoline for a team bus and a hundred cars packing the lot of a refrigerator the size of a building. He tries to remind himself how he did yard work in the neighborhood to save up for his first goalie pads. How he's starved himself and tortured his body. All the sacrifices he's made. How he's earned the right, is *meant* to be here tonight–

Nope. The problem is, he's already experienced *Miracle* in its perfect venue, poisoning all other viewings of the film.

Survive.

Remember Tyler Bianchi returned from Minnesota with horror stories about playing for John Harrington. No place is more resistant to being Disneyfied than a hockey locker room. Imagine the tonnage of sickness that had to be scrubbed from that team so they would serve our country's purposes.

Imdb.com informs him that the charismatic athlete-turned-actor-turned-Green Beret who played Jack O'Callahan shot himself in April, and tears spring into Colton's eyes.

After squeaking past River Ralls 8-4, Colton thought about telling the Big Show to start Gumby against Amery. Between his pregnant girlfriend, his wavering loyalties to Driftless, and his growing suspicion that everyone around him is conspiring to situate him as a tragic hero, Colton's head isn't in the game.

But he won't. He'll play tonight, and he'll do fine.

There's no such thing as a team sport.

And in other news, there is no other news. Our Driftless boys are going to the state championships for the eighth year in a row. They did not disappoint tonight on their home ice in front of a packed crowd wearing the crimson and white. Badger-bound tendy Colton Vogler gave us a scare at the beginning of the game, letting in the first shot he faced—a snipe, but one he'd like to have back. Echoes of River Falls? Birdy was slow getting up on the play, but quick to wake up, flashing the leather on a shot ten seconds later from Appleton's Sanjay Bhatt. There you are getting turned to stone by Coach Riessen's serious face. But, no fear, Driftless quickly countered with a power play goal. The Brothers Grimm dangle an apple in front of Appleton's goalie, older brother Greg demonstrating brotherly love by letting younger bro Rob finish it off. That opened the floodgates. Here's a pretty goal from another Wisconsin recruit, Dustin Poehling. Team calls him Boots—not sure why. Check out this series of passes from our third line—tic-tac-tac-tac... um, tac-toe! That's freshman Gunnar Zieglbein with the tally. "Do not doubt me," Birdy says as he absolutely robs Appleton's Travis Morales with a desperation paddle save. That got the crowd fired up. We're not worthy. Final score, Appleton: Two, Driftless: Five. Join us for the state championship game at the Kohl Center in Madison this Saturday night versus the winner of Hudson/Superior tomorrow. Here's to our boys fulfilling the destiny of Driftless Dynasty Hockey.

*

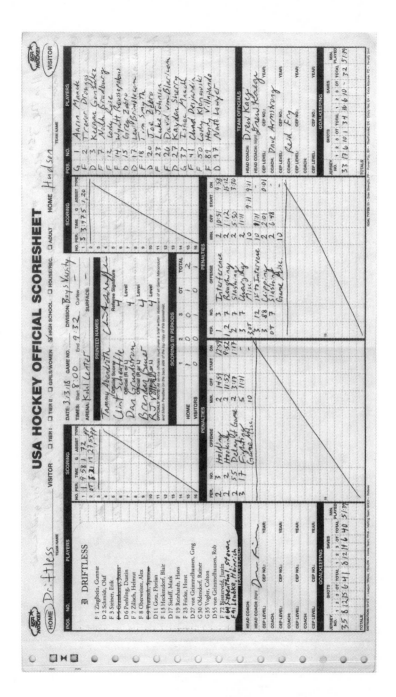

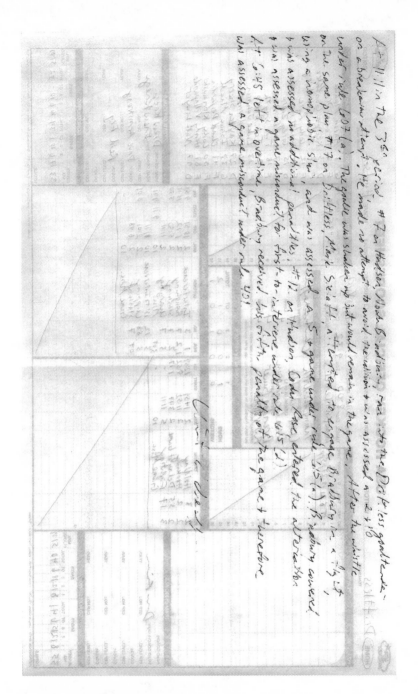

At 11:1 in the 3rd period #7 on Hudson, Mark Bradbury ran into the Battless goaltender—on a breakaway attempt. He made an attempt to avoid the collision & was assessed a 2:10 interible goal (a). The goalie was shaken up but would remain in the game. After the whistle on the scene play #17 on Battless, Mark Sviatt, attempted to engage Bradbury in a fight using a monopoly stick and was assessed a 5 + game under rule 3:15(a). Bradbury covered & was assessed no additional penalties. #12 on Hudson, Cole Rose entered the altercation & was assessed a game misconduct to first-to-intervene under rule 93(a).

At 5:45 left in overtime, Bradbury received his fifth penalty of the game & therefore was assessed a game misconduct under rule 451.

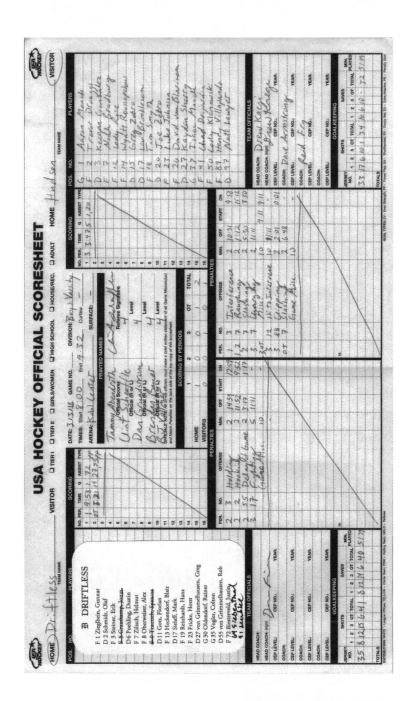

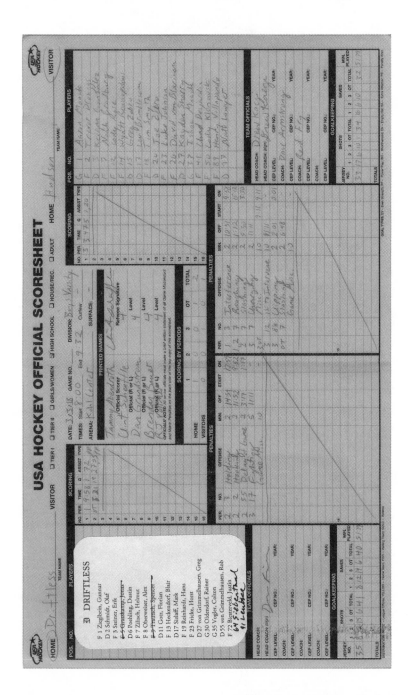

DRIFTLESS QUINTET 245

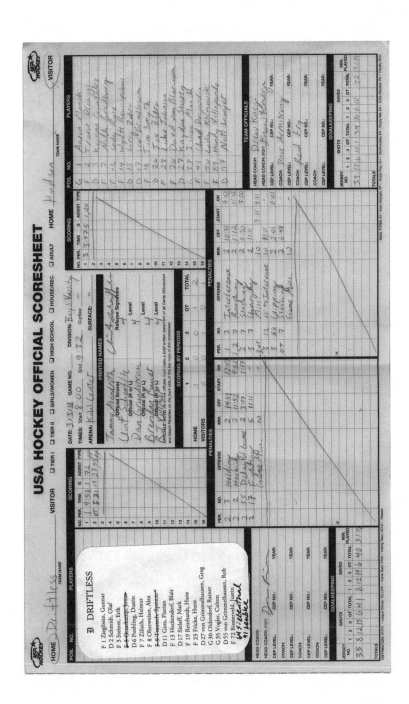

DRIFTLESS QUINTET 247

35

They hadn't publicized the event, but the crowd is big enough to growl nerves into Colton's stomach. The news had spread throughout the same network of families who showed up to town hall meetings with signs protesting frac sand mining in the region, the same donors of money and materials, the same construction veterans and rookies who'd leant their widely varying skills to help speed along the completion of the Gateway. The documentarians, Angie and Lucia, are hard at work committing the potluck to posterity. Charlie's dad is there, Zev's as well. Colton doesn't see Zev's mom.

The evening began with a feast spilling over the LaBoda's back deck, lots of casseroles, slow cookers, secret family recipes, and beer. The chatter turned strategic, groups voicing their hopes that the Gateway would help galvanize awareness of hilltop removal nationwide. How, they speculated, would the SAND = JOBS people respond? Colton was kept from eating much because of his nerves and because he was busy with the upright piano that had fallen horribly out of tune while being transported to the base of the arch. A smartphone app had saved the day, aided by a tool Mr. LaBoda had been able to rustle up that suitably approximated a tuning key. (Colton does not know how to tune a piano, but he's learning.)

He feels himself pushed to the margin in another way as well. Aside from volunteers he'd encountered on the job site, he doesn't know many of these people—but they all know him, and are treading with care in his presence. Like Marshall the first time he learned what hockey team Colton played for. Their hellos do not include the state championship congratulations Colton is growing accustomed to at school and in town. Whether by design or by chance, it's a community that has remained for the most part hidden from him.

The four string players from Saint Mary's huddle together trying to keep their hands warm. Colton did his best to prepare them for the unique venue, but they're very obviously stumbling through what future stories will describe as "Weirdest gig I ever played."

The arch doesn't really need any further unveiling. There it is, hunched over the visitors, playing tricks with the eyes. Hard to tell how far away it is, hard to hold the whole thing in view without running your eyes along the contours like a hiker, hard to be sure when you're facing it straight on, at what moment it will begin to crimp in on itself, winking the sky away. The darker it gets outside the more the arch glows pallid.

"You brought the wrong instruments," a voice interrupts Colton's ruminations.

It's Terrance, the crane operator.

"Why's that?"

"If you're going to use European instruments to grieve a Ho-Chunk hill, let them be drums, the flute."

"I don't have a lot of experence writing for drums."

"Will there at least be singing?"

Colton shakes his head. "It's a piano quintet."

"I don't understand this. You have voices, so use them. Has an evil spirit taken your powers of song?"

"I'm afraid it's a little late for rewrites."

"I'm fucking with you, goalie-man. But one of these days

I'll take you to hear music you don't need to write down. Can't write down."

"What made you decide to work on this project?"

"The filmmakers asked me that as well, Lucia and Angie. First, money. Second, I've had to do a lot of work I'm not proud of, building outlet malls and condos. When I got my own machines, I told myself I'd help out people doing good work. Abomination though it is, I like this arch. We have our effigy mounds—this is what America's should look like. Empty, concrete, annihilatory. On the websites about frac sand mining, they list all the hazards with bullet points. But you never see a big one: they dig up bones."

"Bones?"

He nods again. "Cultural relics too. And they know they'd have to stop digging if anyone found out about it—so they bury them elsewhere, bury the bones with the bones of strangers, enemies even."

Dusk is approaching, and it's time for the group to move into the field behind the house. Luckily it's been dry and warm for April. There aren't any chairs, but people lay blankets on the ground. More beer appears. A guy wearing his dress Carhartt chases after the cellist's sheet music. The cellist is given paperclips to keep it from happening again.

Charlie approaches the microphone in a black dress and sports jacket. She comes across more comfortable in the formal attire than Colton would have imagined. Still has on her boots though.

He told her about the quintet the night they won states, right after the game. Unlike back in peewees, this time they'd gotten to dress in one of the Kohl Center's big locker rooms. When he saw Charlie placid in the mob where autograph seekers usually awaited Badgers, he wanted to increase his joy to a level that would leave no room for fear and guilt. He'd completed the Big Thing he'd been brought to Driftless to do, told the Kohl Center's rafters *See you again soon*—but new timelines had cropped up in the interim, Greta standing there next to his parents, wondering if tonight would be the night they'd share the news with their families. Maybe his parents could somehow tell. Maybe they already knew. So, after the requisite forced jubilations freed Colton to roam the crowd, he told the person he wanted to tell the thing he wanted to say. Charlie, I wrote a song for you.

"At funerals we share memories of our loved ones to give us the sense that they live on in us," Charlie begins a memorized speech. "And that's how I started this eulogy, a list of my memories growing up on Fort Mountain. It skinned my shins, broke my bones—my left arm in particular—but still I banded together with the Knights of Dawn to defend it from General Mimruk and his legions of coyote Vikings. Before my mother died, she made me a treasure map, burned the edges and soaked it in tea so it would look super authentic. Together we followed the clues to the base of a tree where I dug until I hit a box that contained this necklace I wear every day even though I kind of hate jewelry. Now, the place where I dug, where I pulled the necklace from the ground…"—she turns and points at the arch—"is somewhere up there in new sky. As I get older and develop my own opinions on things, I feel myself becoming a very different person than my mother. She was a woman fiercely loyal to the things that were killing her. We're wrong when we think this is the tragedy of having children and having parents. It's the privilege. We don't make copies of ourselves. Family forces us to know more, to see more. And some things can never be properly elegized—that my mother and I didn't get to know the women we were becoming.

"Then I thought that sharing these memories would sound too self-centered, as if so many people went to all this work for the sake of one bossy girl's nostalgia. I thought it would be a better use of time to read a dense, scientific article about the dangers of fracking, project on a screen a montage of rural Americans lighting their tap water on fire, conjecture how tonight is the prelude of a more drawn-out global funeral that will increasingly edit our journalism into genre horror unless we counter the powers who make their money by convincing hard-working Americans that everything is okay. But most of you already know this—you too have glass in your lungs. You deserve to hear your names listed, all you who sacrificed a Saturday afternoon or a chunk of financial security in a scary time, all you who were here a month ago when we struck the centring and cheered when the whole thing didn't come crumbling down—but this isn't an awards ceremony, and this isn't the credits of a movie, not the end of some fake spectacle but the beginning of a new earnestness.

"It's a mistake to think that Fort Mountain was just a lump of earth, only valuable through the human experience of it. Why does it sound sappy to point out the plants and other animals that called it home? Where did the den of foxes go, and why did I cross out the foxes five times drafting this eulogy? I get the feeling that every word I'm saying is diminishing the effect of the Gateway, its ability to speak for itself. So forget the St. Louis Arch, that extra-terrestrial monument to manifest destiny—we've built the real Gateway to the Midwest. It's ugly. It's an eyesore. It's a reminder of murder. The world is so choked with memorials we can't remember why we bother building them. We're addicted to memorials. They sprout automatically in the wake of tragedy, like *Let's get this over with*. We don't build them to remember—we build them to forget. As we consign Fort Mountain to fragile human memory, let's not forget to hope that every memorial we build is the last one we require."

Charlie nods at Ben, one of a dozen attendees holding ropes that stretch up toward the arch. The ones in the middle pull first, sheets of black canvas unfurling from high above. They step aside, and their neighbors release their scrolls of fabric, a great erasure of sky. The unveiling is also a veiling, Fort Mountain reclaiming its place on the horizon, blotting out the sunset, one last time. A hundred people or more stop drinking or start drinking as they stare down oblivion for the first time, the hole humanity is leaving.

Colton signals the other members of the quintet, and his hands land heavy on the ivory keys.

Why is it hard to balance on, say, something the generous width of a sidewalk merely because it's spanning a bottomless void? Colton had spent significant hours as a child contemplating such mysteries of the universe. He'd lost interest in this science as he grew older, but now all his old hypotheses come rushing back to him as he's getting to try the experiment out for himself.

It's his own fault. He's the one who pointed out they could walk on the thing, that the hooks holding up the rolls of black canvas could double as climbing pitons. He has to will himself not to hold his arms out to either side, not to pee his harness. His friends don't share his concerns. He gets it—they're not just drunk on youth and art and triumph, but on the recklessness of what they've done. At least the path isn't hard to see in the night, its chalky pigment reflecting the sickle moon and more stars than Colton has seen in a while.

"Why didn't you let me know your mom was planning a craniac flyover?"

"I didn't know!" Zev says. "I was all bummed that she didn't show up, and Dad was all *What can I say?*"

"I would also have liked to know," Colton chimes in, raising his hand. "Did she have to thread the needle during the toughest piano part in the whole quintet? When I saw that white cape and that long beak... I'm lucky I didn't fuck it up."

"You didn't? You mean it was supposed to sound like that?"

"I will push you to your death."

"I hate to point this out, but we're all on the same rope."

At the Gateway's highest point, Ben opens a metal door in the concrete and Zev deposits the time capsule all the attendees had been invited to add to. Colton had contributed the quintet's handwritten sheet music along with his first poetic effort, the untitled fracking poem he'd been too afraid to show Charlie. Zev added a page of the blueprints, Ben his first hat trick puck, Charlie that whole gunmetal notebook of "poems" Colton had salvaged ages ago.

Charlie has walked ten paces down the other side of the Gateway, and now she beckons Colton away from Ben and Zev, who're using an impact driver to seal the time capsule. To reach Charlie, Colton has to unclip from the rope for a few seconds, step around his friends, risk free fall.

"Colton, thank you for writing the quintet. I wish Shane could have been here."

"I'm glad you let me contribute. I know you had a specific vision how you wanted the hill funeral to go."

"Are you kidding me? I went home and immediately deleted the sappy playlist I'd made. And you were worried about getting a piano into a field—after we built *this*."

"Did you like it?"

Looks away. "Of course I did."

"Only…"

"It's just—"

"You don't need to say anything. I know that it gets super sparse at the end. We weren't making mistakes—the quintet is a sort of riddle—but I know it sounded confusing and morbid."

"This is ground zero of confusing and morbid. Thank you for your hard work and your friendship. You're a wonder."

He should say something nice about Charlie's mom. "I don't feel like a wonder. I told you one time that this whole Driftless thing has been rougher on me than it seems…"

"You can trust me."

But what if she doesn't understand? He checks on Ben and Zev, who are having their own conversation, like they know they need to give them space. What if she blames him as much as he blames himself? Sees him as tainted.

"Everywhere I've gone, every story I've entered, I've assumed I was the main character."

"We're teenagers. Lots of people never grow out of it."

"Charlie, Greta's pregnant."

Charlie pauses, but only because that's what a person does after hearing big news. "Of course she is."

"What does that mean?"

"Have you figured out why Ben pretends he's not interested in girls? Why the prom theme is *Written in the Stars*?"

"That doesn't seem so strange."

"It does if you mean it. *Written in Blood* is more like it."

"Are you talking about… arranged marriages?"

"There are lots of different ways to arrange marriages. For Ben, removing himself from eligibility might not have been enough by itself, but he found a way to simultaneously do that and signal that there was something *wrong* with him."

"Plus, he liked you. And you weren't written in any stars."

Charlie turns toward the glow on the horizon. "Driftless." To follow her gaze, Colton has to fend off another dizzy spell. "Gain any distance and it's so little."

"It's not that big of a town."

"It is. Driftless is everywhere. You leave and go to Madison and you take Driftless with you. Madison becomes Driftless over time, at glacial pace. Wisconsin, the country. It's our fault, too, because we kept you in the dark. Zev and Ben and me tried to figure out a way to keep you safe, keep this from happening—but we weren't smart enough."

"To keep what from happening?"

She turns back to him. "Colton, now that Greta's pregnant you can never leave."

"I'll walk out of here by foot. I'll call my parents. I..."

"Every birth creates a hostage situation. Here, even more so."

"I can do whatever I want."

"Let's try to believe that tonight. Tonight is a good night, and I could have loved you if we'd both walked into a different story."

36

Colton walks again that night alone into the Rentschlers' dark house. Again, hopes to survive another sleep knowing that Ben is with Charlie. Again a candle, again an opera. But not just one candle, a whole grotto's worth, the volume of Alban Berg's *Lulu* cranked up proportionally.

He flips on the living room lights but doesn't find Alma imagining herself in her own womb. Approaching the receiver means approaching the speakers, Opera Man and his weapon, Sheer Loudness. Each step closer to Opera Man increases Colton's vulnerability to this deafening weapon. But that's what it takes to fight Opera Man. Luckily, one hit drains all his energy.

"Alma?" Colton calls out.

The Bösendorfer has erupted sheet music. Wires dangle from the ceiling where the smoke detector has been removed. Colton considers blowing out thirty or forty of the candles so the house doesn't burn down, checking to make sure Alma is okay. Instead, he puts on his swimsuit and descends to the man cave.

No light is seeping from underneath Leo's closed door. Colton changes the channel on the PENALTY BOX's TV from Nickelodeon to the NHL Network. The Hawks squeaked into the playoffs without Protein's brother, but they're down three games to none against the Kings in round one. Sinking into the water, Colton forces recent successes to drown out all the cowardice and complicating dilemmas. Tonight is a good night.

He traces his ribs under the water. He weighed in that morning at 148 pounds. Last week at the Steiner gym, working out had turned into passing out. His parents are afraid to talk to him about it.

He knows that his weight loss no longer has anything to do with physical conditioning. Goalies don't need to be, don't *want* to be, too muscly—but they also need to not get knocked over by slapshots. He told himself he'd start eating real meals again after the championship game, but he keeps setting new deadlines. Current deadline is the chamber music competition in Milwaukee three weeks from now—but by then the baby will be three weeks closer to sucking air. Food tastes the same as always, and the skeletal Colton he sees in the mirror does not appear fat through his eyes. It's something else. As Greta's wearing baggier and baggier sweaters, Colton wonders if he's compelling his body down the opposite path for reasons that won't be articulated.

Except becoming an embodied cry for help. Starving himself so true friends will ask the things he can't bring himself to say.

He's gotten addicted to the hot tub and worries about withdrawal symptoms once he heads back to Rockford for the summer. He hasn't much considered the intermediary Illinois months between Driftless and UW. Will it be enough time and distance to drive a wedge between him and Greta? She'll want to come visit, be his date for Nate and Audrey's summer wedding. Will four months back in Rockford with his parents and his old friends be enough to narcotize him, dull his competitive edge and make him forget professional hockey? The real possibility of a fake profession. This bloated recreation. This kids game.

A door opens upstairs. Heavy boots, bottles, crashing terra cotta. Flynn and Alma arguing—"*This has to stop!*"—followed by the basement door creaking open.

Silence.

A hockey bag tumbles down the steps and lands in a heap on the floor of the man cave, scuffing drywall along the way. The hot tub is too hot. Flynn's boots appear. He moves down the staircase more slowly than ever, sideways, bringing both feet to each step before reaching for the next. His right hand uses his two CCMs like hiking sticks, the left clinging to the railing, as if warding off a fall from a great height. He stops halfway down, leans his head against the wall, breathing heavily. In his coat pocket, a fifth of Stoli. Colton's eyes find the bloodstained 88 on the back of teenage Flynn's framed Driftless jersey. The goon lets out a groan between clenched teeth, and Colton debates announcing his presence.

Flynn stops his heavy breathing and looks down at Colton. He has a black eye.

"Are you okay, Mr. Rentschler?"

He starts back down the stairs. "Colton." Clomp. "Have you ever," clomp, "heard the phrase," clomp, "he got his," swig, "bell rung?" Clomp.

"Yeah, sure."

"It's funny, right? Guy got his bell rung." He's reached the bottom and starts dragging his bag across the floor. "He's a cartoon cat seeing Tweety Birds." The bag had been set down in muck and leaves a slug trail on white carpet.

"Not funny if you're the guy."

"No, that's when it's *really* funny. That's when you realize– you realize what it means. You're sitting there on the ice, trying not to throw up, and you get it: your head—your skull—is the bell. Are you with me here, Birdy? Your brain is the *clapper* of the bell. *Bong*"—he swings the vodka bottle like a pendulum—*bong, bong*. Swig. Swig. "Funny how our most tossed-off phrases say lots more than we think."

"How'd you get the black eye?"

"They think it's concussions, the reason why so many enforcers are offing themselves these days. But it's not concussions—that's an additional bonus for some of us lucky goons." Swig. "No. You thought the nerves were bad against Hudson? Now imagine going out there every night for *years* knowing you're probably gonna have to spar with a murder machine. Knowing that's all you're good for, and asking yourself if tonight's the night it all catches up." Flynn stares at the television, which has picked this moment to show a brawl between the Hawks' Jack Phallon and… hard to identify the other guy. "*Fighting is a part of hockey* says those real tough fans who're still mad about not making varsity or cuz their dicks don't work anymore or Mexicans are taking their jobs." Gazing at the television, or through it. "No, hockey is a part of fighting. Sports." He spits the word, turns back to Colton. "What do you think it is, Colton Vogler, that people have against sports?"

"What do you mean? Sports are pretty popular–"

"I mean smart people. Liberals."

"I don't know. It's wasteful? It's our version of gladiator games?"

"People who say 'sportsing' to be funny are the same ones who would've loved saying 'the unwashed masses' a hundred years ago."

"Not here. Not in Driftless."

Flynn abandons his bag, takes heavy steps toward the hot tub. The bottle of Stoli shatters on tiles, one stick clattering to the floor as the other swings up at Colton's face. It stops short, presses against his temple. He can smell the rubbery tape, the vanilla-scented Dr. Zog's stick wax, can feel the scratch of fibrous carbon.

"Under a minute left, our goalie running his mouth like goalies do because they've got guys like me protecting them. One of their guys has had enough, punches our goalie in the head. You know what happens next. I swoop in on autopilot and crosscheck the guy. Their guy swings his stick around. *Bonnngggggggg*. Right here." He presses the point of the blade twice below Colton's eye, too hard. "Earlier in my career, no way it would have rung my bell. But every time it happens, it takes less and less. The clapper gets bigger and bigger. Alma asks if I'm hungry and I shake my head no and almost fall over. I go days without seeing the sun. Cartoon cat, Tweety Birds."

"Can you… your stick…"

"Oh, I'm sorry, is this ruining your hot tub experience?" He presses harder, pushing Colton's head back against the rock wall. "Here's another funny phrase: cock of the walk. You think you can strut into someone else's city, *Birdman*, someone else's family, and just sow those wild oats?"

Call out? He could wake up Leo at least.

"How… how do you know about Greta?"

Flynn's smile is not a smile. "I'm not talking about Greta." His eyes move up to the ceiling, which is again doing a poor job of deadening loud opera.

Colton and Alma Vogler née Rentschler begot Fritz, youngest of?

"Mr. Rentschler, I haven't… with your wife…"

"Of course not. Don't you *think* about my wife. Are you pissing in my hot tub?"

Not yet. "Then what're you saying?"

Loud opera—from above and below.

"There's birds who do that, lay their eggs in other birds'

nests. Brood parasites, they're called. I looked it up on Wikipedia. A country full of brood parasites. Well I'll be goddamned if I'm going to raise some kid's kid as my own."

"Please, Mr. Rentschler, tell me."

"You think you were brought to Driftless to play hockey? Think back. You come from impeccable stock."

In the rink's cold, Colton's hips thrusting against the lubed latex of the contraption, his teammates cheering the race. Three of the five first-years are already done, relieved they'll be the ones getting cleaned off at least, not the one whose mouth will do the cleaning.

"There's teams who play wet cookie." Flynn tilts up his chin, faux-noble. "Here in Driftless, I'm sure you've noticed, we have a greater sense of purpose."

"What happened to Shane?"

"Shane was too trusting he could go to the authorities."

"But why leave him alive?"

The pressure returns. "You know those good gardeners who hang up dead animals to warn their species away? It works even better when they're still squirming."

Flynn winds up, and Colton moves to defend himself from the blade of the stick. But it's the butt-end that slides from Flynn's top hand—*what a pro*—and comes barreling down, so hard that there's nothingness before there's any pain.

37

Imagine a young man. A man living in what we now call the old country. He's a duke, a real duke, his family landowners who made their fortune on industry, glass-blowing let's say. He grew up in a palace—try to envision it. Somewhere in the world there are still people who grow up in palaces. More than you would think. We will call him Duke Wilhelm Kaltenbach. This young man inherited his family's skill for abstract thinking, both the ingenuity upon which they built their fortune but also the sense of whimsy that threatened to ruin it every few generations. Like his father before him, Wilhelm loved chess. He had his own chess tutor, in fact. We'll call him Father Johann, a priest. Every day, Father Johann would summon Wilhelm to that day's chess riddle—the knight's tour, the eight queens puzzle, bone's gambit—with the same words: Wilhelm, lassen wir uns gehen einen König zu töten. *Willy, let's go kill a king.*

Such was his creativity, and such was his love of chess, that young Wilhelm built a chess-playing automaton—what we'd call a robot these days—that toured Europe, drawing large crowds who demanded to know the Turk's secret. That's what the machine was called, the Turk. Yes, it was a little racist. And get this, the machinery—it was controlled by a midget chess master crammed into the cabinet below the board.

*

*On his 30th birthday—the duke had since taken a duchess and pro-
duced a satisfactory heir—Father Johann arrived at his door.* Wilhelm,
he said, lassen wir uns gehen einen König zu töten. *You must
understand, the words for Wilhelm were a bell awakening him from a
trance—or maybe putting him into one. He hadn't heard them in years.
After dining with the silent priest, he was made to change into a white suit,
at which time a carriage arrived at the palace, drawn by six black horses.
Out stepped more royalty, an arrogant young man we'll call Duke Otto
von Kempf. By now you've guessed that Duke Otto was wearing all black,
that he too had a silent escort, a ghastly consumptive, no name necessary
for the purposes of our story. By now you've guessed that the von Kempfs
had made their fortune on mining, that they were social and business rivals
of the Kaltenbachs.*

*There was a door in the Kaltenbach palace that had been locked Wilhelm's
entire life. Many times as a child he'd tried the handle, only to receive a
scolding. A turret, his father claimed, a turret in dangerous disrepair.
Duke Matthias vowed to renovate the turret to his dying day.* Truly—*he
stammered the word on his deathbed, his sad eyes blinking up at his young
son as if seeing through the mist of booze for the first time in years. Of
course it was straight to this mysterious turret door that Father Johann led
the group.*

*But the turret, when the door at long last gave way to Wilhelm's tug, did
not appear to need renovating. The steep, steep spiraling stairs were covered
with a plush red runner threaded with gold, and tongues of flame cast their
glow through polished crystal from new candles. More remarkable still,
there were painted portraits on either side, many of which were copies of
paintings that hung in the palace. Below certain portraits, a smaller painting, a chess piece, black or white. No, he became more and more convinced,*

the portraits in the palace below were the inferior copies.

It wasn't until the quartet was nearly at the top—and Wilhelm recognized his grandfather's birthmark—that he realized the party had been spiraling up through time, touring the Kaltenbach's proud lineage, realized that he could hear his own footsteps approaching from behind. And I don't need to tell you that Wilhelm was both surprised, and not, that the last portrait in the stairway was his own. He could not remember having sat for the portrait. Did he ever show his wife or child such a stern expression? The door at the top of the stairs was carved with the image of a medieval city, one side of it prosperous, a bustling center of trade and culture, and the other dilapidated and plague-stricken, a zero-hour Sodom. Carved above the city: Wisse wenn du winnst. *You better know when you're winning, brother.*

The turret, when Father Johann opened the door, was ringed with windows, which gave it the appearance of a vessel floating in space. All the stars were out above the deep forests of his family estate. But Wilhelm's attention was focused on a table in the middle of the room, on the chessboard and its pieces, a match surely nearing its completion. He studied his white suit and Otto's black, and he knew where to sit. And you're smart enough, Colton Vogler, to guess the rest of the story.

Colton shivers in the dank air of the limestone cave, despite his heavy jacket. It, too, is lit by a number of candles, untroubled by any draft. The speaker is out of sight, tucked into an alcove or around a bend, lending an echoey blur to his voice. The words are archaic—scripted, a role being played—but the voice is young. He'd spent most of story time mentally flipping through his list of contacts since arriving in Driftless. Not Coach Riessen, not Flynn Rentschler, not Dr. Bielenberg, not any of his teammates. A faint familiarity, but Colton can't put a face to the voice.

He'd woken up seated in a simple chair, unrestrained, his bell rung.

"What does this have to do with anything?"

Yes, that is what our young duke was wondering. But he was smart, and you are smart, so surely you have an idea. Or at least questions that are more specific.

"Who'd been playing the chess game? Why was it already started?"

Because we are never there at the beginning of anything, brother. Beginnings are a story we ourselves spin to give our lives structure, a sense of control. And because the Kaltenbachs had been playing this particular chess match against Otto von Kempf's family for many centuries, one move per generation.

Somewhere water drips.

By your silence I can tell you want to know who was winning the chess match. That's how stories work. And because you've been winning your whole life, you will assume it is our story's protagonist, Duke Wilhelm. But this is a new type of story. No, not brand new—one of those stories in which no one is winning, no one except the big faceless system, no one really playing chess at all, a story that is just what you alone make of the words. But new enough. As Wilhelm surveyed the board—surely you've not forgotten he's a chess master—he saw the glaring truth: two moves till checkmate. His only gambit was a desperate one and involved sacrificing his queen. Why, I would ask you in a non-rhetorical fashion, was our young duke suddenly so nervous? It was a game. Being protracted over centuries does not make it inherently more fragile.

"It wasn't just a game."

Elaborate, please.

"I don't know. It was a gamble. There was money on the line."

Bravo, Colton. And more than money. Everything.

How many feet of rock until air in every direction? The dizzying weight of the earth. There are caves like this in the bluffs all along the Mississippi.

And because Wilhelm was the most creative of all the Kaltenbachs, the one who had invented the chess-playing Turk, after all, he was the first one to consider conceding. He placed one finger atop the cross on the white king's crown—Lassen wir uns gehen einen König zu töten—*tipped it back and forth on its green felt base. He considered his son. And then he considered his son.*

One…

Two…

Three…

Four drops of water.

As a kid, did you ever play that game with the genie and the wishes?

"I guess."

This time, brother, you're allowed to wish for infinite wishes. Or don't need to, because you already have them. What is it you want from life? To play Division One hockey? Your wish has already been our command. To go to Hollywood? To enter government? Enough money to run a city. All the girls you could want. Or boys—if the photographs are to be believed.

Despite the threnody to life-as-he-knew-it being sung by every flight-inducing agent in Colton's body, his determination not to show this envoy his panic wins out. "I don't think my girlfriend would go for that."

Laughter that's not laughter. *Do you still think you're playing Greta von Kempf? That she's so stupid she can't tell she means nothing to you? You were awful to Greta, but she's already gotten what she wanted.*

"Why hockey?"

Otto von Kempf's descendants, after they came to the New World, got bored with chess. Nobody gets hurt in chess. It's too much of an abstraction.

"But it's never been about hockey."

Bingo. You might not know this, Colton, but you come from impeccable stock.

As a kid, you must have read those fantasy books where some boy or girl, frustrated with their mundane existence, is rescued by the discovery—out of the blue, on a humdrum day—that they are a key player in some larger drama. Always have been. That their inheritance is awaiting them, if they have the brains and courage to reach out and grab it.

After Duke Wilhelm, inventor of the Kaltenbach automaton, had made his decision, they started down the staircase, spiraling back in time, and Wilhelm saw—impossible!—a small painting of a white queen below his portrait. Don't you see?

One...

Two...

Three...

"So I'm the young man with the big decision to make?"

One...

Two—

No, you've misunderstood. I must have made it sound like a choice. Let me try again. Four young people had a very ambitious idea, a land art project that, as we speak, is directing national attention to our little fortress town...

38

He feels a dizzy giddiness as he swings his left leg out of the driver seat of the Volkswagen. That ski lift feeling. But when he stands upright and shuts the door, a refreshing spring breeze blows back his hair as he surveys a stand of trees in the park across the street, and he feels present in the moment in a way that makes the recent past feel like hibernation. Not since... not since... that drive north to Driftless just over seven months ago. For some reason, this simple trip to the library possesses the same ambivalent capacity of fate and limitless potential.

He's not sure what's inspired his mood, but he's here for answers, here on a hunch—so maybe he'll figure that one out by the time he returns to the car. It's with a sense of deliberateness and purpose that he shoulders his messenger bag, strides toward the building, and locks the car with his key fob as if it's a magical power he possesses. He'd never been to the city library before, but the size of the structure is incongruous with the size of Driftless. Colton approaches the building from the south, across a limestone-paved plaza where a shallow, empty amphitheater watches an elaborate fountain playing more than one tune at the base of a wall of windows five stories in height. To his right, the long, sloping arm of a façade encompasses the plaza, a brutalist aqueduct. The base of the façade comprises a series of storefronts, one of which houses the city's public radio station; a swell of Rachmaninoff from hidden speakers intensifies Colton's cinematic sense of purpose.

The limestone paving continues into the cavernous main room, which resembles an enclosed urban street. To his left loom the five floors of the library, and to the right, above a series of cafes, art galleries, and other merchants, are floor after floor of reading/study areas with comfortable chairs that grant a view of the surrounding city. Above him the ceiling is all skylight—though he knows that somewhere up there is an impressive rooftop garden. Colton also knows that the vagueness of his query, the sense of surveillance, and the building itself would normally overawe him into hesitancy—but today he walks through this place in the manner of someone authorized to be at a secure government facility or a crime scene, straight up to the front desk, where the librarian abets his fantasy by recognizing him immediately.

In her excitement, she is a shame to her profession. "I was so sad I couldn't get tickets to any of the home games."

It occurs to Colton for the first time—that, with a packed stadium, there were people who had wanted to attend the games but were unable to.

"I watched the finals on TV, and I followed the other games closely in the paper."

He couldn't ask for a better segue. "That's actually why I'm here. Is there a way to look at archives of the *Driftless Mirror*?"

"Fourth floor, Special Holdings."

There are three glass elevators that run up through the center of the library, but Colton takes the wide, switchbacking staircase so he can be made queasy by the increasing distance a hypothetical fall would drop his body. The entrance to the fourth floor funnels him immediately to a desk, where there sits a less enthusiastic librarian. His glare would normally make

Colton reconsider his interest in the local news of previous decades, but, almost as a game, just to see what happens, he strides up to the desk and states his demands in a more forceful way than he would normally dream of doing.

"*The Mirror*'s coverage of our first state championship."

This man furrows his brows and folds his hands together in front of his mouth, as if miming the knot of impossibilities between Colton and the answer he wants spoken. But it turns out that the librarian was just thinking, that Colton's confidence was the secret key all along.

"March 12th, 1971. Something very special happened that night."

Colton gives a curt nod, as if to acknowledge the truth of the statement but also to communicate that he's here on business.

"Your phone, your wallet, your keys, anything in your pockets will need to be placed into one of those lockers. You will be given paper and writing utensils inside the Reading Room."

That won't be necessary, Colton's self-assurance almost convinces him to counter. Instead he does as he's told, and it feels strange to enter the room with just the locker key in his pocket, severed absolutely from communication with the outside world, afraid a door might latch behind him that his keys would have been able to unlock. Despite his phone, despite the internet, it's just an intensification of how the last seven months have felt in this island city. At least it will separate him from Charlie's increasingly worried text messages.

Inside the Reading Room, Colton takes a seat in one of the sleek chairs at a desk so unadorned and slablike that the furniture itself is capable of chiding any potential unproductivity. He sits and waits and is fine not having his phone. The studious patrons have assumed the more upright posture that communicates *I'm reading a rare book*. They use as little of their hands as possible. They make use of the primitive transcription materials allowed them. They are grateful for these materials. They will not betray this trust by raking the pencil across fragile pages over and over. They will not meet Colton's eyes for fear of being implicated in whatever chaos that he, in his idleness, might be plotting. The librarian is taking way longer than would seem necessary, and Colton is experiencing the Generation Z terror of having nothing to do. Were the newspapers simply thrown into a giant pit every day, unfolded before thrown so their pages would be sure to fly apart and shuffle together the current events of different pasts—if that was their method of archiving the *Driftless Mirror*, it should not be taking this long.

He hasn't decided whether or not he thinks the story of Kaltenbach and von Kempf has any grounding in history or if it was all allegory, if he'd merely been told the story he needed to hear. That's the phrase that keeps running through his mind: *the story you needed to hear*. Google searches hadn't turned up anything. But just the idea of lineage had given Colton an idea. Google searches had also failed to turn up much history on the dominant high school hockey team in the land, a baffling lacuna. The whole of the internet was as devoid of lineups, statistics, and box scores of those early Driftless teams as the blank rink walls of Steiner were withholding of banners commemorating their victories.

The librarian approaches with a small box in his hands, as if the newspaper had been cremated and these were its remains and the librarian is so sorry for his loss. He sees Colton's obvious confusion and gestures over to a pair of machines against the wall that look like the 1970s' best guess at future spaceship navigation controls.

He shows Colton how to thread the film, how to find his

way around. He gives Colton his very own piece of paper and pencil, then is sent away to fetch subsequent years of championship coverage, in part because Colton is worried he's going to stand there and monitor his research.

Colton adjusts the dials and the news comes into focus like contagious bacteria seen through a microscope. He's so accustomed to his windows into the past being mediated by digitization that there's something that pulls at his heart, seeing humans' attempts long ago to document important moments, turn life into text, convince people to buy shit.

And suddenly he's figured it out, the reason why he's felt since getting out of the car like he's playing a familiar part. This is what they do in the movies. He didn't really need to be shown how to use the microfiche machine—this narrative has become imprinted on an instinctual level. He'd like to do this the rest of his life, maybe: uncover the past badness that's continuing to haunt the present. He should be staying in a motel, conferring with a partner, drinking coffee so he can stay awake to figure out the puzzle before the countdown of its catching-up reaches *here, now.*

In this case, it's not hard to find.

THE BIRTH OF DRIFTLESS HOCKEY

They look like men, not high schoolers. Some of them have mustaches and beards. The jerseys are the same, but the equipment is truly museum pieces. Puffy brown leather gloves that go halfway to their elbows, skates that make Colton's ankles wobble just looking at them, and sticks that are made of wood and nothing else. Like *wood*, from *trees.* And the expressions on their faces are not unfamiliar to Colton, a vying of joy and surprise and exhaustion.

Rentschler is the first name he recognizes. A goalie! Not Flynn, though—he was on the team in the 90s. Maybe Flynn's dad, or an uncle. *Front row, left to right: Konrad Rentschler, Mats von Grimmelhausen, Erik Oberweiser, Linus Biesterveld, Klaus Fricke, Rolf Poehling… Back Row: Ziegelbein… Sielaff… Oldendorf… Gotz… Steiner… Heckendorf…*

Something very special happened that night.

Welcome to Driftless Dynasty Hockey.

Reinhardt…Trautsch… Vogler.

Silas Vogler.

He finds Silas Vogler's face. Not a goalie. Curly blond hair, maybe dead by now. How tall are you? (Tall.) It's not a name that he recalls from those scrapbook showings when his Great Uncle Casey would flaunt his extensive knowledge of the family tree. But, then again, Colton hadn't known there would be a quiz later. Might be time to give Uncle Casey a call. Might be time to give his parents a call.

"We've been waiting for this year," a voice says, and he turns to see the librarian standing behind him with an armful of proof, "the year everything fell into place. For the first time ever. Or the second, I guess. But I bet you already knew that."

Even though Colton wants to find out more, he feels every fiber within him resisting any acknowledgement of his own ignorance to this man. Instead he finds himself standing, maintaining eye contact, and leaving the librarian to clean up after him. He hasn't just been acting out the one role since getting out of his car, that of the research montage participant; he's also, he realizes as he leaves the reading room, been trying on cruelty. In preparation for what lies ahead. In preparation for Charlie.

With that thought his sense of buoyancy is gone.

Still he goes up instead of down when he reaches the staircase, entertaining some vague idea of checking out the rooftop garden, facing the Gateway's direction and seeing if he can make out his last week's self staring back. When he gets to the fifth floor, he's confronted by a barrier even more impregnable than the fourth-floor gatekeeper. Silver letters on a granite façade read GENEOLOGY, and Colton knows he might not need to call Uncle Casey after all.

But a door in the façade opens and propels him back the way he came, having learned enough for one morning.

He needs to get back, anyway. Five o'clock is supposed to find him in Madison, signing papers and practicing with his new teammates for the first time. No better chance to try on his new costume of authority. To look his father in the eyes and ask about Silas Vogler and see what happens.

39

Colton reaches through withered ivy and touches the soil at the base of the *ficus benjamina*. It's totally dry. Somebody's been neglecting their job. He has a water bottle in his bag, and he dumps it at the base of the tree. That's the human equivalent of taking a sip. He picks out a 3 Musketeers wrapper and throws it in the trash. The nearest water fountain is beyond the food court, and it would take him ten trips or more. Would it be quicker to search for a bucket? He looks for leaves that are less dusty than the others, but they've all received comparable neglect. He dusts one of them off, then another.

"Colton!"

He turns, and Charlie wants a hug. He puts his water bottle back in his bag and pretends not to notice.

"What's been keeping you so busy?"

An allegory in a cave.

"I went down to Madison to sign my letter of intent," he says. Some suns are *inside* the cave. Outside is the world of fire and shadows. "I'm what they call a 'commit' now." His father knew nothing about a Silas Vogler from Driftless. Or he knew everything but would say nothing about it. It occurs to Colton that this dual plausibility might furnish a working definition of *father*.

"Congratulations!"

Again movement toward a hug is deflected. Charlie's been

growing her hair out the past couple months, but it's the last three days that have made the difference. Colton is the one who has left and come back, come back a different person, come back a commit, no longer a recruit—but he imagines her the one returning, the hero, not the one about to leave. Seeing her with this laurel crown of curls is another Charlie to love— but why would the perfect theme seek variations?

"Hey, I figured out the riddle!"

"What riddle?"

"The quintet. I listened to Angie and Lucia's recording of it a thousand times, and I figured out what you were doing."

"Did you?"

"You state this big, beautiful theme that's meant to evoke being out in nature, approaching Fort Mountain. Then you repeat it, but with notes erased. Excavated. Mined. You keep removing more and more of the theme until there's nothing left. I'm sorry I seemed lukewarm at first. I love it. Tell me I didn't figure it out."

"You figured it out."

Colton is stalling. It would be so easy to smile, to fall back into their jokes. His hope, her tolerance. To take Charlie's hand and lead her out into the exact middle of the school courtyard, where no surveillance equipment or teammates could eavesdrop, and see if they could figure it out together, untangle history from allegory, unveiling from further veiling. But eventually they would reach the part in the story when the ambiguities suddenly gave way to threats. *Get rid of them—or we will.*

She crosses her arms, giving up on the hug. "What's wrong, Colton?"

"You wouldn't understand."

"That's the line we use on parents—it doesn't work on other teenagers."

"Wasn't that kind of your m.o. for the first few months?"

He can see Charlie's mind going further down the path their conversation is on, setting off in another direction.

"Ben misses you. It's a mystery to him what happened, why you and all your stuff disappeared, but of course we're anxious to talk about it."

"Nothing happened. I'm friends with Protein, so I decided to move in with his family."

It won't be hard, outwardly, delivering the message. Colton thinks if he just said nothing and stared at her the right way, she would know, would walk right out that door and never look back. The same macho warning that bounced off Protein way back when, the spooky night he'd been goaded to Greta, one step and then another all the way to this calamity. The same look but charged poetic—that's all it would take. In one closet of the LaBoda residence, emergency bags ready for immediate flight. Just in case of today. He's seen them. Ben's too.

Just whisper the words to her.

Survive.

No, he's already interrogated himself in front of too many mirrors to waver this late in the game, to ignore what he knows to be true: if she thinks he's still on their side, she'll never leave him behind.

He must be a commit. A recruit no longer.

She tries again. "Did you know today's Shane's birthday? He's eighteen."

"We're all eighteen now."

"Exactly. Are you free after class? I thought–"

Charlie stops talking because Greta is standing beside Colton now. He can tell that Charlie is willing her eyes not to travel down to Greta's stomach.

Greta: "You and Ben thought you could take Shane away

from us, Charlie? Because it's his birthday and as of today he's an adult?"

Now Colton can see Charlie willing her eyes away from him.

"What're you talking about, Greta?"

"You and your boyfriend. I never thought I'd be making fun of a guy for being straight, but I'm not sure I'd want anyone to know I was with you either."

Charlie turns to Colton now, mouth opening to speak but nothing coming out.

"Colton and I've had some good times laughing about it." Greta snaps her fingers, returning Charlie's gaze to her. "Taking Shane away won't fix your guilty conscience."

"Why's my conscience the guilty one, Greta?"

"True or false: if Shane had never met you, he'd be deciding on college right now. He wouldn't have to have nurses wipe his ass for him. He'd be playing the sport he loves."

Charlie looks at Colton again, tears in her eyes. "Colton, I know what's happened. You're my friend. You're still innocent here—"

He holds up his finger to silence her. *Commit.* "You're still a fucking tease."

As they walk away, Colton allows his hand to be taken.

40

There are no tire tracks on the asphalt. No ruts furrowed in roadside sand. But two sections of the fence are newer, the wooden stakes less disintegrated, the metal lattice not so rusted.

The Romans used to line the highways with crucified bodies. This is what happens when you mess with empire. Such barbaric practices have long since been left behind.

Had they debated about whether or not to construct a memorial? Shane isn't dead. Had the crucifix been the stake driven into the ground claiming this plot of land for Shane's memory—or had the photographs and other life detritus started to appear first, the crucifix later legitimizing what it couldn't halt? The sun has filtered all the photographs through a setting called *Choking Transience*. Lots of photos of Shane in his goalie gear, Shane with his parents and brothers, Shane earning merit badges. No Charlie or Zev or Ben. Maybe those photographs disappeared the night his friends left town for good.

Moldering sheet music for the Brahms quintet—an explanation for his chamber group's caginess, why they all had their parts already but the pianist would have to shell out sixty bucks for a new Henle Edition. Colton half expects to separate the wrinkled pages to find the same notations he made on his own copy, to wake up in a broken body blinking hope and caution. Not his handwriting, but still, every scratch: it's so hard, it's so hard, it's so hard, this sport called music. He peels pages apart to find a passage in the second movement where the suggested fingering had struck Colton as awkward, if not impossible. Shane thought so too. He keeps searching, hoping for a poetic burr to catch him out of context, a message from his doppelgänger that impossible coincidence has brought him here today to read. *Leave now,* or *Stand up to them,* or *You see yourself as making a necessary sacrifice, as not having given yourself over wholly to the gods in Olympus, but the result is the same as true belief...*

It's just finger instructions.

The roadside dirt is all glittery here, but it might not be from the accident. Dirt this close to a road has gotten so mixed up with glass and salt and oil that it can't go back to being earth again. He stoops down and pulls a sharp, plastic fin from the weeds. This, on the other hand.

A tree. There's no tree here. Coach Riessen had told him at that first meeting their goalie had wrapped his car around a life. But he's learned in, God, eight months, to let the little stuff slide.

It's one of those spring days it could be dusk from sunup to sundown. A low, immobile cloud ceiling, always about to rain but never raining. A sickly green scrim another barrier from the noumenal realm. Worms would rather drown that emerge to a day like this one.

All the rain's been good for growing things, though. The field's black corduroy rows, a thousand vanishing points to the tangled tree line, is beginning to show its riotous stubble of whatever. Closer to him, though, the tidy rows veer in chaotic evasive whorls, the patch of land just beyond the new fence overgrown with fireweed, velvetleaf, the quickest plants to take advantage of recently disturbed earth. Is the land itself blighted, salt sown with blood and foreign car parts? Or is it some force of repulsion that bends the path of Farmer Sparky's tractor? The same that makes you watch your step in cemeteries. The guilt of owning land that causes pilgrims to pause, fewer and fewer every semester, as if their parade's caution could compensate for past velocity.

A long-gone memory chooses this collision of circumstances to announce that it has never left. The memory has lain dormant for years, waiting. One of a thousand forgotten games in a hundred run-down rinks. On the wall above puck-marked plexiglass, among curling vinyl banners commemorating third-place tournament victories nobody had the heart to take down, black letters on white.

A Kid on Ice
is Seldom in Hot Water

He was a peewee, then, maybe a squirt. He didn't know much about much—but he knew enough to shiver in the cold.

He starts back toward his car, doesn't know what to do with this sharp fin of plastic, looks both ways before returning it to nature.

He gets back into his car and heads west, not thinking about sabotage devices the car might be fitted with, not thinking at all about how it could be now or now or now because he'd prepared for the moment of resigned horror to such an extent that it has become more hope than horror. Nothing habituates us more than sitting in a car, because no other experience has to so radically disguise the terrifying as tedious. Not thinking about tires exploding or an oncoming driver flicking his wrist a miniscule degree or manhole covers stolen for scrap. Not thinking at all about how the whole machine is powered by little explosions. The rules have to be very simple for drivers much dumber than ourselves. People think road rage is so bad because we only see the machine part of the cyborg that is the driving human. Untrue. The number one way to avoid escalating a road rage situation: don't look the other driver in the eyes. See no human there. This is why we're fucked.

A dozen VON KEMPF trucks earthquake by and Colton tries to launch into "Ride of the Valkyries," but he can't trick himself. They sing for thee.

Colton loves approaching the Gateway via this route, from straight south, seeing it rise up like a pillar from the wrecked land. A jog northwest widens the pillar until sky pierces it and grants it an immediate sense of perspective. He continues toward Charlie's house and the arch yawns the sky. It's only when he crosses the train tracks and Charlie's house comes into view that he faces the thing's full breadth. Only from directly east or directly west can an onlooker grieve fully the ghost that's been raised. But east and west are different experiences. Looking from the east, through the arch toward the imagined Mississippi, he feels himself participating in the spirit that's eaten Fort Mountain. Mostly he's looked back east from the west, toward the Great Lakes, surveyed so many mistakes.

Colton pulls into the driveway, defuses his car, and steps out. The house on the edge of the earth has somehow become even more desolate and forsaken. A train passes by and nobody's left to curse it.

He starts back toward the Gateway. Trucks here as well, workers working for money, broadcasting loud sounds and clouds of dust from the peak where they've rigged up a suspended scaffold. They know not to notice Colton as he approaches. One thing they've done is install tall chain link fences strung with razor wire around both bases of the arch, making it far more difficult for a thrill-seeker—very possibly someone

Colton loves—to climb the arch under the cover of darkness, fall from the peak, and set into motion a lawsuit that would doom the Gateway and its builders.

That's the problem with kids. Kids don't think things through. Don't ransack the earth seeking out awful motives.

A piece of paper, a white flag caught on thorny scrub trying to sustain itself on poison. *He strikes twice with his rig—heartland heartburn—and their beasts drank.* He lets the poem scamper off in the wind.

And over there, blueprints with math Colton understands no better than chess. A hockey puck MADE IN SLOVAKIA, made distinctive by one athlete's good game. Colton pockets the puck, wanting to return it to anonymity in a bucket of its peers.

Its elastic band snapped, its pages fluttering like a ruffled bird, Charlie's notebook of "poems." For a few hours it had given Colton power over this girl he was starting to flirt with between classes. The last time he'd opened it he'd been sitting on a toilet in his big hockey jersey, crying. He flips through.

Time is an important component of the time capsule–

The last entry in the notebook is lineated—but not a list.

Narcissus Unlimited

Writing, I know why the free bird
smacks into glass full speed
and, falling to the ground,
lies stunned.

Reading, twenty years later—
did you save yourself,
stop swooping your heart
between a fool and his sport?

I try to choose a man,

but what's bird in me can't flout
the plumage he preens,
the quintet he sings.

The hard-hatted actors on the swing stage climb to the top of the arch, stand there for a second like a couple of stupid, love-sick teenagers before beginning their descent. They've finished their work, finished fixing the Gateway. Wind sweeps away concrete dust like pencil eraser, revealing the memorial's new memory:

$$\text{SAND} = \text{JOBS}$$

41

"Cheers." Protein hoists his Solo cup. "Go Badgers."
"Thanks." Past the pier, the waters of Lake Konigsee mirrorball the moonlight, and Colton worries about returning his tux tomorrow full of sand and smelling of smoke.

"Everyone's jealous, man."

Colton has been trying to avoid talking about college since moving in with the Trautsches—especially given how Protein's been handling his anger as of late. But now it's unavoidable. "Who knows if I'll get to play. Have you decided on a school yet?"

"No, you misunderstood, brother. What I meant was, everyone's jealous of *us*."

"What?"

He pulls up his sleeve and points at his cast.

Colton leans in. "I can't read that."

"Goddam it, you're ruining my big news. It's Coach Salonen's signature. I went down and signed my letter yesterday."

It isn't until this moment of having to will his face excited that Colton realizes how much he'd been looking forward to leaving Protein behind. Cammo picked Denver because of weed and skiing, so it was just going to be him and Boots at UW next year.

"Congratulations! That's awesome."

"Col-teen reunited. You didn't think I was gonna stop

watching out for my goalie, did you?"

A loon's plaintive cry goes unanswered except by its echo. The rest of the group is over by the beach bonfire.

"Too bad that cast is coming off right when you're getting valuable autographs."

"Who cares—they'll be our fucking teammates next year. I've gotta tell you, I know I seem like a pretty calm guy, but I was worried after the injury that I was gonna follow Pettit to the Graveyard. I thought everyone would forget about me."

"We tried."

"I wish I could've been there for the championship. On the ice, I mean."

"Well, you were there for three others."

"But... *senior year*. Don't you feel it? Look out across the lake at the horizon. Am I high, or is it rising up, like a wave?"

"You're probably high, but yeah that's an optical illusion."

"You know what's not an illusion? Another state championship in hockey, another trip to nationals for chess, the perfect girls for the perfect prom... it's a fairy tale ending. Don't you feel it?"

"I only went here for one year. Everyone getting emotional about the last dance, *Written in the Stars*... It all seemed so silly to me. I broke my senior year experience somehow leaving my other high school behind."

"Well thank God you did. Imagine where you'd be."

Boylan's prom is *Wonderful Tonight* tonight. He remembers Paige and Rudy for the first time since Christmas. No envy for that slow dance, no glowing locus on a map, just aggressive indifference.

"I'm more interested in the future."

"Yeah brother, know when you're winning, right?"

Protein stands. Colton doesn't. Still Colton feels like he's the one looking down at the other. Protein doesn't ask what's wrong, doesn't reach a hand down to help him up.

"It was you," Colton stammers. "In the cave. The story of the chess master. No–" He remembers the voice, remembers post-game interviews with NBC and NHL Network. "Your brother."

"That's right." Protein doesn't treat it as a revelation or a secret. "Hugo's a pawn—and trying to stay that way. But let's go ahead and leave behind the chess metaphors. You're terrible at chess, Colton."

I'm learning. "Spencer… why?"

"I think you might have saved my life." He extends his hand. "I'll never be able to pay you back, brother—but I'll never stop trying."

Colton, allowing himself to be helped up, understands what people have against sports. In the heat of a big game, you'll die or you'll kill for people you don't even like very much.

"Now," Protein says, pointing to the fire, which flickers long shadows the length of the beach, "go get some."

Colton's been worried about this part of the night—and not just because of the gross social aspect and hazy logistics. He and Greta haven't been together since he got her pregnant. Or maybe they have. Either way, they haven't had sex since he found out. He hasn't much felt like it. He isn't sure she'll want to either, or if it's safe for the baby.

The smell of the campfire and woods and lake threatens to resuscitate his earlier nature boy phase. At his most enlightened, he'd told his parents he wanted to quit hockey. Human society was too hectic and menacing. He could wander off right now, let the blackness between the trees swallow him, and probably be dead within the month.

Greta stands up when she sees them approach. If anyone

has noticed that she's refusing to drink a sip, or that her prom dress is not so form fitting as her friends', they're not saying anything. She takes Colton by the hand and begins to guide him away from the group. The cheers they receive are the closest Colton has come to an orgy.

No, the closest since October, the players-only practice.

Inside the lake house, there are no pictures on the walls, no real signs of it having been lived in besides what damage the high schoolers have inflicted tonight.

Wisse wenn du winnst.

"It's weird that I still haven't met your parents." Colton's starting to think Greta doesn't have parents. "I'm a little nervous for that one–"

Greta shushes him, puts a finger on his lips, leads him up the stairs to the master bedroom.

One whole wall is windows, angled by the roof into a blade that slowly receives the moon's impalement. Greta lights a candle and puts on music, lies down on the bed. Colton kicks off his shoes, gets in bed next to her, and tries to stroke her cheek with his thumb. She fends him off by reaching for her clutch, opening it, taking out her cellphone.

She swipes through pictures, holds up the ultrasound photo so Colton can see it.

How to arrange his face… Is he supposed to put his hand on her stomach? "Do you know the gender?"

"Girl."

Immense relief—and for a second Colton thinks it's because girls have an easier time in the world than boys. But they don't, and that's not the reason.

"What names have you been thinking about?" she asks.

The first name that springs into Colton's head is Fritz, which is not a girl's name, and which is already taken. A new worry erases his relief. This girl and Fritz will grow up in Driftless together, will be in the same grade at the same schools. Will she even know her own brothers and sisters? And who will warn Fritz that he shouldn't ask this girl to prom when the time comes, should maybe avoid girls by whatever means necessary while living in Driftless? Especially when everyone around them thinks they'd make such a cute couple.

Impeccable stock.

"You haven't been thinking about it." She knows. "You haven't been scrolling through websites. You don't have lists and lists, pros and cons for the names you've narrowed down."

"What are the finalists?"

"You see a little monster is all, ready to devour your life."

"I've heard that mothers fall in love with their babies when they find out they're pregnant, but men don't until they see the baby."

"Are you the man in that scenario? Swipe left."

He does, and there it is. He'd known it existed, ever since that January afternoon Protein tortured Pettit in the weight room with a private viewing of furtive footage. This is a still, the background blurred so that it could be taking place anywhere—an ice rink, a bedroom, a cave. It's unmistakably Colton, unmistakably his freshman teammate, naked, their skin raw from the cold. His face is caught in a moment that could just as easily be ecstasy.

And in an instant it's overturned, half a year of telling himself that he's the victim.

"It's okay if you liked it," Greta says, "if you want to continue liking it. We just wanted you to know."

We? he almost asks. But he knows the answer: the eaters of hills.

"And you're not alone. There's pictures of everyone."

Colton thumbs back to the ultrasound.

"I'll say her name so you'll carry that around with you forever, too: Ilsa."

Ilsa. He wants to say his daughter's whole name to himself, but Greta hasn't decided on a middle name, Colton on a last. The ultrasound—looks like such a warm position. "Safe from the world," he says, curling into a ball on the mattress, clutching the phone to his chest.

The screen goes black. He tries to wake it up, summon back his daughter, but the smartphone doesn't recognize his thumbprint.

42

In the auditorium, the applause is dying down.

"Are you nervous?" The Plague asks.

"No." It's not that they're playing the quintet perfectly, and it's not that the other chamber groups haven't been amazing. Colton's not nervous because a disaster would at least be something. He's decided to let what happens out there on the stage render the judgment he no longer feels capable of making.

The backstage door opens, and five musicians walk through. Relieved, they mostly have grave nods for their competitors, but the one instrumentalist carrying no instrument smiles at Colton like they're best friends, and Colton wonders what he's done to deserve such kindness. Any kindness.

"Go give boners to their ears," is Slava's last encouragement. Everyone except Colton laughs, including the tiny freshman girl who replaced CC.

Marcus Center for the Performing Arts, Milwaukee, Wisconsin.

"*Next up, let's welcome the Shorthanded Quintet from Driftless,*" an amplified voice requests. "*Normally we have a strict list of repertoire that students are permitted to choose from, but our judges were convinced to allow the quintet to perform an original composition. 'Gateway to Industry' is a single-movement work written by the quintet's pianist, Colton Vogler.*"

Colton leads the group onto the stage to scattered applause. It's a big concert hall, and the attendees are spread out. His parents are in the crowd, friends from Driftless, including Greta. A table spans a section of seats where the judges sit a few rows up, poised for the tiniest errors, pens already hovering over the lamp-illuminated staves like the cursors that shuttle across noteheads in Finale's playback. Sharp blades of time. All of them wear glasses, skeptical expressions, hoping to appraise dubiously the progeny of this town that so often takes home the first-place scholarships. Colton is happy to have already secured a full ride for something less competitive than this bloodsport.

Whoa, the piano bench is cranked up to a ridiculous height. Smiley liked to feel himself perched high up, the king of the keys. As the other members of the quintet arrange their music on their music stands, Colton twists the black knobs on either side of the leather seat. He tries it out but his knees don't even fit under the piano. It's a submissive position to assume before judgmental eyes, back arched at a painful angle, butt sticking out, everyone waiting.

Satisfied, he hits the tuning note, and his peers saw away at the A, making corrections with their tuning pegs. Stoner nods at Colton, then The Plague, and then all four of them are ready.

Colton presses the piano key again. They draw back, confused, then try out their fifths to figure out who their pianist isn't satisfied with. Their hands move toward their tailpieces— Zilch pretends to tweak his D—but none of them actually adjust their fine tuners.

Where are they now, Charlie and Ben? He's learned to bear the idea of them being a pair. What's harder: Charlie and Ben staring into each other's eyes, the absolute yes. Their love is intensified, he's sure of it, by their knowledge that it excludes him. No, worse. Much, much worse: he doesn't cross their minds. They're not mad—at most, just glad to be rid of him.

Colton hits the key again, harder. He knows that the musicians want eye contact, a clue as to who's off. But Colton is gazing at his reflection on the empty black void of the Steinway's music stand. He wonders why it hadn't been removed, the music stand, if one of the other pianists had failed to memorize their part. The concert pianist's burden—you play ten times more notes than everyone else, and where you look for instructions, there's nothing. He hits the note again, louder still, and murmurs start to course through the auditorium.

Survive.

These aren't the thoughts to be having during a performance. Nothing gets in the way of passion, joy, darkness than passion, joy, darkness.

Colton turns to his peers, still pretending to tune, and nods.

His hands fall heavy on the opening C major chord, barely giving the others time to ready themselves. The composition might generously be called neo-classical, but the truth is that at best it's a pale imitation of music composed two hundred years ago. The only dissonance that announces itself is in the service of its triumphant resolution, a sense of satisfied progress overcoming minor setbacks like mass extinction. A second unveiling for the Gateway is planned for the summer. An unveiling that's also a veiling, a gateway back in time, memorial to amnesia.

They reach the *da capo al fine*, and somehow it's already half over. Back to the beginning.

This is better than love. Go ahead, wallow in her hatred, her perplexity. These, at least, are powerful feelings. Better than being cast as the pupil, newcomer to neutered virtue. A container for what rages, labeled *Chaste devotee.*

This is what you get for choosing Ben. For the rest of your life, whenever you think of Home, I'll be all wrapped up in it, the one who turned your masterpiece against itself. One day you'll see me on TV doing such beautiful things with my body—I'm quicker than anyone—and you'll understand the enormity of your mistake.

They reach the *da capo* again—but Colton doesn't *al fine*. His hands land back on the big C major chord, and he hears pages fluttering in desperation.

No. That's not how he feels. Zero of that. The opposite, forever.

Then why keep summoning those words, trying them out on your tongue to see if this time they taste right? If you're not careful, someday they will.

Zero would be not allowing the words into your mind. Not flirting with them– No, zero would be the words never occurring to you as a possibility.

The result is the same as true belief.

Coming of age, contamination. A bad joke. Start now, work hard every day, and with a little luck in twenty years you'll be a blank slate again.

He doesn't know if Charlie is the first of many girls who will go to his head—or the only one, the one who will be with him until the end. All maps will glow, unable to pinpoint her location, all cities hum with the possibility of who they might be hiding.

Zev stayed behind to finish school. Zev is an old pro at risking his life, at avoiding hockey players in hallways. But he won't stay out of Colton's dreams. It is Zev who is the friends' emissary at night.

Da capo. Again.

Ben—wherever he is, whenever he steps on the ice, as

much as possible it will just be him and the sport and nothing complicated or extra-extracurricular. Ben, on the lam from his family, a little inbred, but absolutely free.

Is Shane getting the care he needs? Will he ever hear *Gateway to Industry,* translate for his friends Colton's newest poem, the SOS coded into the quintet's rhythms? T-O-R-T-U-R-E.

It was the invisible powers in Driftless that turned the friends' Gateway into propaganda; Colton is repaying the favor by using the platform given to him by those powers to communicate their crimes to the world. Unable to find the timing or the words or the courage to speak the truth, Colton will allow chance to decide for him.

Da capo. T-O-R-T-U-R-E.

Like skating the lines after a bad loss.

Why draw more attention to it—a purloined letter in an audible bottle—with this hijacking of the stage?

Because he wants attention. Because now that he's said it he can't stop. Because he's suspicious that the *Gateway to Industry* might itself be erased before the summer unveiling.

Da capo. T-O-R-T-U-R-E.

How long before someone puts an end to this?

We'll be up here until we get it right.

ABOUT THE AUTHOR

Joe Sacksteder is the author of the short story collection *Make/Shift* (Sarabande Books) and the album *Fugitive Traces* (Punctum Books). His writing has appeared in *Salt Hill, Ninth Letter, Denver Quarterly, The Rumpus,* and elsewhere. He's the Director of Creative Writing at Interlochen Center for the Arts.